DEAD
TO ME

DEAD TO ME

mary mccoy

HYPERION
LOS ANGELES · NEW YORK

First Edition, March 2015
1 3 5 7 9 10 8 6 4 2
G475-5664-5-14349

Printed in the United States of America
This book is set in Baskerville
Designed by Marci Senders

Library of Congress Cataloging-in-Publication Data
McCoy, Mary, 1976–
Dead to me/Mary McCoy.—First edition.
pages cm
Summary: In 1948 Hollywood, a treacherous world of tough-talking
private eyes, psychopathic movie stars, and troubled starlets,
sixteen-year-old Alice tries to find a young runaway who is the
sole witness to a beating that put her sister, Annie, in a coma.
ISBN 978-1-4231-8712-7 (hardback)
[1. Sisters—Fiction.   2. Mystery and detective stories.   3. Hollywood
(Los Angeles, Calif.)—History—20th century—Fiction.]   I. Title.
PZ7.1.M43De 2015
[Fic]—dc23   2014034653

Reinforced binding

Visit www.hyperionteens.com

To Brady, my partner in crime

CHAPTER 1

When I saw my sister in that hospital bed, she was different from how I remembered her. She'd changed her hair. Her cheeks were leaner.

And someone had tried to cave in the side of her head with a baseball bat.

The doctors at County Hospital told me how lucky she was. If the person who'd done this had left her somewhere less public than the boat dock at MacArthur Park, if the blow had come down squarely instead of glancing off her brow, if the maintenance man hadn't found her so soon—the doctors always trailed off before they finished these sentences.

Instead, someone had broken her back, fractured her skull, crushed the bones around her eye, and left her for dead, and because of that, Annie was lucky.

Her purse was gone, but one of the nurses thought to look in the toe of her Mary Janes, and that was where she found me—an old school picture with my name and number scrawled on the back.

I didn't know why Annie would want anyone to call me. I hadn't seen her since I was twelve.

Since then, a world war had ended, I'd started high school, I'd kissed boys, and I didn't know what my sister would think about any of it. In all that time, we'd never exchanged a single letter, not a phone call, not a telegram.

Late at night, when the light in the hospital hallways turned an eerie shade of blue, and the long minutes of quiet were broken up by the sounds of heels clicking on the linoleum, barked orders, and sobbing, it was hard not to think about that. I was alone with a stranger. So why did I stay? Why didn't I leave her the way she'd left me?

In the kinder light of morning, I asked different questions: *Who are you, Annie? Where did you go? And how did you end up here?*

The doctors said she'd wake up, probably. They said it would take time. They said she needed rest. When they asked if I knew how to get in touch with her family, I said I didn't.

Annie had stayed gone for almost four years, and I figured she'd had her reasons. And when she woke up, I intended to be around to hear them.

I'm Alice Gates, California girl, Hollywood High, class of 1950. If you go to the movies, you might think I'm one of those sparkling, impossibly blond youths who go to the beach every day, travel in attractive packs by convertible, and never stop laughing.

If my life were a movie, it wouldn't look like that one.

When my sister disappeared, I kind of lost my taste for movies about young love and girls on horses and silly misunderstandings that ended with confetti and kisses. My favorite movies had titles like *Notorious* and *Nightmare Alley*, and I started reading detective novels by Raymond Chandler and Dashiell Hammett, too. I like them because they don't lose their heads over how great California is. They know it's not all sunshine and oranges and movie stars. In their books, the people who live in the nicest houses have the dirtiest secrets, and those laughing blond California girls get used up and crushed under someone's heel like cigarette butts.

I know it's ugly, but at least it's not a lie.

When you're a kid, people lie to you about a lot of things because they think you're too young to understand the truth. But you're old enough to know a lie when you hear one, and in the end, that's the lesson you learn—not that people are trying to protect you, but that they have something to hide.

I didn't know why my sister left four years ago, and I wasn't any closer to knowing when I found her in the hospital, but I'd always known I'd been lied to. It was only after she turned up again that I realized the lie was a lot bigger than I'd guessed.

CHAPTER 2

"**W**hat are you doing here?"

It was a low voice, deep, and it didn't sound very happy to see me.

I must have dozed off in the straight-backed wooden chair next to Annie's bed sometime during the afternoon. When I opened my eyes, a man in a tan fedora and a rumpled jacket was towering over me.

"She's my friend," I mumbled, feeding him the same line I'd told the doctors and nurses. I didn't want to say too much before I was fully awake.

He walked over to the window, leaned back against the sill, and folded his arms across his chest, glowering at me with eyes so dark they didn't seem to have pupils. He looked about my parents' age, though not as tidily put together. A shadow of whiskers covered his cheeks, and frayed shirtsleeves poked out from the cuffs of his jacket, too short in the arms. Then again, I wasn't surprised he'd have trouble finding a coat to fit him—he was at least six and a half feet tall, and lean except for the beginnings of a potbelly that stretched his shirtfront tight. He stuck a toothpick into his mouth and chewed on it, looking me over, and looking perturbed while he did it. I could see the muscles in his jaw tighten and pop.

"Cut the crap, Alice."

That woke me up. I sat up in my chair and peered out into the hallway, where a stream of nurses in long white dresses and caps made their rounds. Whoever this stranger was, he'd left the door open. Anyone could look in and see us, and that eased my mind a little.

"Who are you?" I asked, massaging the crick out of the back of my neck.

"Jerry Shaffer," he said, handing me a business card. It was printed on cheap cardstock, but it looked official enough and bore his name, the words *Private Investigator*, and an address near downtown.

After I'd had a look, he took the card back and tucked it into the breast pocket of his jacket. "Sorry. Only have so many of these things."

"What are you doing here?"

As I spoke, I got up from the chair and put myself between the private eye and Annie. I knew why I'd stayed then, even through those moments in the middle of the night when my sister seemed like a stranger to me. I was all there was between Annie and whatever came through that door. I was all she had. When was the last time a doctor had come to check on her? The hospital was full of women in labor and car crash victims and old people having heart attacks. No one except me had time for Annie now that she wasn't actively dying.

"Annie's a friend," Jerry said. "We work together every now and then."

"Doing what?" I asked.

"This and that. Missing persons. Stolen goods. That kind of thing."

"She investigates things with you?" I asked, and then a horrible thought crossed my mind. "Did this happen to Annie while she was working for *you*?"

Jerry Shaffer crossed the room and shut the door. I tensed, but then he pulled up another chair and sat down next to the rickety metal bed frame. I'd spent parts of the night picking at the flaking paint and rust while I tried to block out the sounds of a young widow crying in the hall. The detective took in Annie's broken face, then his eyes fell to the floor.

"No," he said, swallowing hard. "Annie was off the clock when this happened."

The Los Angeles County Hospital was a crowded, busy place, no matter what time of day. You didn't have to be there long before most of that noise faded to static. But when Jerry closed the door, the silence washed over me, and the room and Annie and everything that had happened suddenly seemed real to me in a way it hadn't been before. I felt dizzy, and a clammy sweat broke out on my forehead.

"Are you okay, kid?" Jerry asked, lurching to his feet and helping me into a chair.

"What happened to her?" I murmured.

He regarded me with some concern. "How long have you been here, anyway?"

"Since yesterday," I said. "When they called me."

"And you haven't been home?"

I shook my head.

"Have you called your parents?"

"No," I said, my mouth set in a rigid line.

He looked at me with something like respect. "Good. I think that's what she'd want. For now, anyway."

"She told you about our parents?" I asked, a little surprised.

"She told me enough to make me think she wouldn't want them here. Your father especially," he added, shaking his head. "He's a piece of work."

I wondered what he'd meant by that. My mother was the one Annie used to fight with all the time. My father had so little to do with us that I scarcely thought about him at all. The feeling was probably mutual. Sometimes, when we were younger, he'd be in the middle of telling an off-color story at the dinner table, and my mother would touch his elbow and say, "Little ears, Nicky. Little ears," and he'd look at Annie and me as though he'd forgotten we were even there.

"If she wasn't working for you, how did this happen?" I asked. "And how did you know she was here?"

A dark look crossed his face. "Annie and I were supposed to meet yesterday. When she didn't show, I called a buddy of mine at the LAPD to see if she'd turned up anywhere."

In my world, when I'm looking for someone and they're not where they're supposed to be, I call them up. I ask their friends. Maybe I go by their house or the place where they work. Why would Jerry Shaffer contact the police unless he'd expected my sister to be dead, hurt, or under arrest?

I glared at him and started to speak, but he held up his hand to stop me.

"Alice, your sister is a real sweet girl. Real sweet, and a lot smarter than those she chooses to associate with." He looked at me meaningfully. "But she isn't any kind of angel."

Annie had just turned sixteen when she left home, the same age I was now. I thought about that, about how I'd live if I were out on my own in Los Angeles right now, where I'd sleep, the kinds of friends I might have to make to get by. When Annie left, I missed her, I wanted her back, I cried over her, but I never worried about her. She'd seemed like a grown-up to me. Now the idea of her striking out on her own and landing without a scratch seemed a little far-fetched.

"It's okay," I said, swallowing hard.

Jerry continued. "The cop told me a girl was found in MacArthur Park beaten up pretty bad, so I came here to see about it."

He leaned back in his chair and bobbled the toothpick from side to side in his mouth. "Where do your parents think you are right now, anyway?"

"I told them I was spending the night at my friend Cassie's house."

As lies went, it had not been my best effort. Even my oblivious mother had her doubts, since it had been years since I stayed overnight at a friend's house—or, for that matter, had friends.

"I'll take over here for tonight," he said. "You go home, put in an appearance. No telling how long we might have to keep this up."

I snorted. There was no *we* between me and Jerry Shaffer.

"Not likely. I'm not leaving Annie."

He leaned forward, clamping his palms together and fixing his black eyes on mine.

"Do you know what parents do when their daughters aren't where they're supposed to be? They start making phone calls. To the police. To hospitals." He cleared his throat, stalling as he picked over his next words. "You need to do this for your sister. Go home, Alice. Keep them from asking too many questions about where you are, and you might buy me a little time to get to the bottom of this."

I met his stare and held it. Jerry Shaffer could have walked into Annie's room with his mother, his priest, and his first-grade teacher, all attesting to his good citizenship and general trustworthiness, and I still wouldn't have left him alone with my sister.

"You could be anybody," I said. "For all I know, you're the one who did this. Now you're just waiting for me to leave so you can finish the job."

He sighed and slouched down in the chair, stretching out his long legs under the bed. "Would I have told you my name? Shown you my business card? If I wanted to hurt Annie, wouldn't I have knocked you over the head by now and gotten on with it?"

I didn't answer. All I knew was that there was no way for me to be sure about Jerry Shaffer.

Without another word, he took a folded piece of paper from the breast pocket of his coat and smoothed it out on the nightstand by Annie's bed. Then he took out a pencil stub and hunched over the page, scribbling intently for what seemed like ages. When he finished, he tore off a thin strip of the paper and handed it to me along with the pencil. I felt a spark of recognition when I saw the jumble of letters and knew immediately what I had to do to decode them.

"Who taught you how to do this?" I asked.

"Who do you think?" Jerry said, leaning back in his chair. "When I tell you I'm Annie's friend and that I'm here for her, I mean it. Go home and get some sleep, Alice."

I looked at the strip of paper, then at Jerry Shaffer, then back at the paper and what he had written there. There'd been no way for me to be sure about Jerry Shaffer—and then he gave me one I couldn't ignore.

I wrote my phone number down on the slip of paper and handed it to him.

"Will you call me if anything changes?"

"I promise," he said. "I'll see you tomorrow, Alice."

"Okay."

On my way down the hall, I spotted one of the orderlies making his rounds. I recognized him—he'd been to Annie's room twice to change her bandages since I'd been there. I pulled him aside and asked if he'd stop by a little more often. There were five dollar bills in my purse, more money than I usually spent in a week. I gave him all of it.

At first, he wouldn't take the money, but I pressed the bills into his hand.

"Please," I said. My throat started to tighten, and I could barely get the word out.

I swallowed down the tears that threatened to come and folded the orderly's fingers around the money.

"Take it. Make sure nothing happens to her."

This time, the orderly nodded and put the money in his pocket, even though what I was asking of him was impossible, and we both knew it.

CHAPTER 3

My parents couldn't be famous themselves, so they decided to have children to do it for them.

My father was the head of the publicity department at Insignia Pictures. He spent his days telling the world how wonderful movie stars were, and I think he actually believed it himself.

Before she met my father, my mother was a very minor starlet. She started out dressing hair at Warner Bros. Studios, but then her good looks caught somebody's eye and she was brought in for a screen test. The parts she got were never any good—harem girl, bathing beauty, third chorus girl from the left. Getting married gave her a meatier role, one with lines.

If my parents knew anything about being parents, I'm pretty sure they learned it from the movies. They kissed our cheeks and patted our heads, but mostly it seemed as if they were always leaving for drinks, parties, movie premieres—places we weren't welcome.

Annie and I didn't mind, though. We liked being on our own. Annie was the undisputed leader of the neighborhood kids. If she wanted to go to the pool that day, or the park, or the library, Annie decreed it, and everyone went along with her. I never got the feeling that she cared whether anyone came or not. She'd just say, "I'm going to the drugstore for a cream soda," and they followed her.

It was always understood that when she said "I," she meant me, too. She always made a place for me, watched out for me, and I hung on to her for dear life.

There was one situation in which our parents demanded our presence around the house, and that was when they threw a party. About once a month, our mother would come up to the bedroom we shared carrying a set of matching outfits—there was usually a theme: sailor suits or gypsies or something like that. She'd dress us up and send us around with trays of finger sandwiches and olives. If we ever got distracted from our duties, she'd immediately materialize, nudge one of us in the back, and whisper in a perky voice, "Circulate, my dear! Circulate!"

After enough people had remarked on how precious we were, she'd shuttle us off to bed, making a big show of kissing us good night in front of her guests.

It was always movie people, no one you'd have heard of, but people from my father's department, office people, and some of my mother's old friends from her acting days. Occasionally someone important would turn up, if they were in the neighborhood, if they needed a quick drink before moving on to a better party. I always knew who these people were because Annie and I were always dragged over for introductions that were supposed to look spontaneous but were actually quite well rehearsed.

"Now, let me hear you do it again, Alice."

"Hello, Mr. Dietrich. It's a pleasure to meet you," I said, thrusting my right hand forward with plucky enthusiasm. Of course, I knew how to shake hands properly, and I knew that grown-ups didn't stick out their hands like they were directing traffic when greeting one another, but Mother insisted I do it this way. She said it made me look more youthful and endearing.

"And how old are you, little girl?" my mother asked, affecting a gruff, low-pitched voice.

"I'm seven."

"Sir," she said in her normal voice. "Remember to say 'sir,' Alice."

"I'm seven, sir."

Back to the old-man voice. "And how do you like school?"

"I like it very well, sir."

My mother groaned. "Say it with a little more *pep*, Alice."

"I like it very well, sir!"

"That's better. Try to stay bright and sunny, Alice. People will always respond better to you if they think that you're a cheerful person." She sighed. "Now, if only we could do something about those freckles."

She introduced us to anyone important, or anyone she thought was important. Anyone who wasn't one of the threadbare office drones, thwarted artists, or blowsy husband-hunters who showed up anyplace they were lucky enough to be asked.

When we were older, she made me play the piano for them and she made Annie sing. The rehearsals we went through for those parties were ten times worse than practicing introductions and passing olive trays.

Even so, I loved to hear Annie sing. She had a full, throaty alto voice like Judy Garland, and when she sang something she really loved, like "Over the Rainbow" or "My Funny Valentine," I could see her go somewhere else. She wasn't singing to a room of our parents' drunk friends anymore. When she sang, she might as well have been in her own room, singing for nobody but herself.

I would never have gone so far as to say that our parents loved her more than me, but it was clear they considered her more *promising*. Where Annie was "beautiful" and "smart," I was "cute" and "clever." Annie was charming; I was pleasant. Annie danced ballet and tap and took voice lessons, and I backed her up on the piano. And we both went to those awful parties.

Things changed when Annie started high school. Our parents sent her out to talent shows, where Annie sang insipid, perky little songs while I accompanied her. Annie also sang at other parties—Hollywood parties—parties at which I wasn't invited to perform, since I was too young to be beautiful or glamorous, but too old to be cute. My mother zipped Annie into dresses with full chiffon skirts and as low a neckline as a fifteen-year-old could pull off, and pinned her hair into complicated twists on top of her head.

"Mother, it hurts," Annie complained.

"Glamour hurts, dear. Just wait until next week when I take you in to Stella for a rinse," she said, tugging at Annie's scalp. "We'll turn this straw into gold yet."

Other things changed, too. Boys started calling the house, asking for her, sometimes two or three a night. Once or twice, I answered the phone and pretended to be her, but was always found out within a few sentences. Each of Annie's boyfriends annoyed my parents more than the last, until she finally stopped bringing them home at all. She'd say she was going to the library to study or meeting a girlfriend for a soda, and then she'd meet her friends at the beach or go to the drive-in in Van Nuys.

I missed spending all my time with her, but I also liked not being half of a set—the boring, tagalong half. The more Annie fought with our parents, the more I tried to be the perfect daughter, clearing the table while they screamed at each other across it. After she stormed out, I'd sit in the living room and do my homework. I made good grades, friends they more or less approved of—I did whatever they asked me to do. The better I was, the less attention they paid to me.

But I wanted to have it both ways, too. When Annie snuck in through our bedroom window reeking of cigarette smoke and giggly with beer, I'd be waiting under the covers to press her for details. Annie liked telling me these stories. I guess I was a good audience, young enough to be shocked and old enough to be impressed. Besides, she knew I'd never rat her out to a woman who used to dress us in sailor suits for her friends' amusement.

She told me about the time she and her friends snuck into a drag show at a Central Avenue jazz club, and how they raced their cars up and down Highway 1. She told me about the pair of GIs who showed up at their beach party and disappeared with one of the girls before anyone figured out they'd stolen all the beer.

"Sandy says she's moving to San Diego with one of them," Annie told me. "He took her out to this spot real far away from where we were and told her a bunch of goofy stuff, and then Sandy said they wound up exchanging marriage vows right there on the beach."

"That's the silliest thing I've ever heard."

Annie nodded. "It is very silly. Especially since he left town the next day. Without Sandy, I might add."

"Poor Sandy."

"I don't know that she really deserves our pity," Annie sighed. "I've been trying to tell her that he's not coming back for her, but she won't listen. She just moons around the hallways at school, trying to look tortured and wise. Alice, promise me you'll never marry a GI on leave."

"I promise," I said.

Nights like that were fun, but they always made me very aware that I was Annie's kid sister. She had exciting friends who did exciting things, and a whole life that had nothing to do with me. But as always, Annie made room for me. My favorite times with her were Sunday evenings when my parents went out for dinner and drinks with friends and left Annie and me with the house to ourselves. Sometimes we made elaborate desserts like trifle or cherry torte that never came out right, or wrote new endings for the awful movies we'd seen the week before. But most Sunday nights, we did puzzles.

Not jigsaw puzzles, but real ones. Both of us were crazy about any kind of crossword, brain teaser, or jumble, and fought over those pages of the newspaper, eventually reaching an arrangement where Annie got the morning edition and I got the evening edition. It was too good a thing to quarrel about.

Our obsession started during the war after our mother told us about the cryptographers who worked for the government, making up all kinds of codes to transmit secret messages that couldn't be deciphered by the Axis. She wrote out the whole alphabet in Morse code, and Annie and I practiced sending the long and short signals across darkened rooms using flashlights and whistles. I wondered why our mother would ever want to be something as idiotic as a movie star when she could do something like that.

During blackouts and curfews there wasn't much to do, so Annie and I made a game of it: the Gates sisters, cryptographer spies and crusading angels of the Allied forces. Glamorous, elusive, and uncrackable.

We would make up codes and ciphers and hide them around the house. First you had to find the code, and then you had to break it. For a while, Annie preferred the Caesar cipher, a simple letter-substitution code that uses a disk with the alphabet inscribed in a ring. Inside, there's a smaller, movable disk that you align with the letters on the outside ring to tell you which letters to substitute.

So, a code like this:

dtz xrjqq

with a wheel like this:

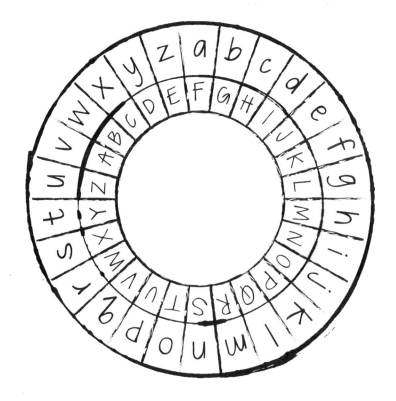

would be broken like this:

dtz xrjqq
you smell

The codes were easy to crack once you had the key, but Annie was very good at hiding them. There were things about our house that only she and I knew. We knew which stairs creaked in which places, where the carpets were loose and could be pulled back, how long you could hide in the laundry chute before your arms gave out and you went tumbling into the basement, and every cubby, crawl space, alcove, and hidey-hole in the place.

Annie and I eventually realized the limitations of the Caesar cipher. Keys can be hidden, but they can also be found by the enemy, so we decided to invent a system that used the Caesar cipher principle without a physical key. Instead of a wheel, the key to the code was located in the greeting or closing of the message, and we must have had a hundred of them. We taught a few of them to our most trusted friends in the neighborhood and used them when we played spies or war or secret mission, but only Annie and I knew them all.

It was fun while it lasted, but it didn't. We grew up. The younger neighborhood kids went back to playing house and school and doctor, and Annie began to spend most of her free time being carefully groomed for teenage stardom by our mother, and I was left somewhere in between.

Of course I didn't like it. You might think I was jealous that Annie was the chosen one, that she'd been whisked away to a glamorous world I wasn't ever going to be a part of, but that wasn't it. We'd both been around movie people our entire lives, enough not to be dazzled by that kind of life. But I missed her. And I didn't like the way she changed when she ventured out into that world.

When we were home on Sunday nights, Annie was full of clever ideas and funny stories, but when she came home from singing at those parties, she looked like all the life had been sucked out of her. She'd ignore me when she came into the room, peel off her dress, and disappear into the bathroom for at least an hour. When she came out, she would sit at her vanity and brush her hair, while practicing coquettish facial expressions in the mirror. After slathering a layer of cold cream on her face, she'd sink into bed without saying a word. It was like watching a mannequin.

In the morning, she'd be herself again, and I'd act like nothing had happened.

Once, I asked her why she wouldn't look at me, why she wouldn't talk to me. All she said was, "Alice, when I get home from those things, I just wish I was invisible, so I pretend that I am."

So, I let her be invisible. It didn't seem like much to ask. If I'd known she would develop a taste for it, that one day she'd disappear altogether, maybe I would have done something else. Maybe I would have tried harder to stop her.

CHAPTER 4

hen I got home from the hospital, I felt like I'd been gone for a year. My head was a hive of hospital sounds and ugly thoughts. My eyes were bloodshot; my hair was greasy. I'd been wearing the same clothes for more than a day, and all I could think about were the bruises and bandages on my sister's face.

"How was Cassie?" my mother asked.

"Fine," I said, too jarred and lost in thought to make up a story about spending the night at my friend's house.

Fortunately, my mother wasn't interested in hearing one.

"I thought we'd have an early supper. Your father and I are meeting friends later on this evening, or at least we are if he ever gets home. I can't imagine where he is right now," she said, chattering as much to herself as to me. "What's the matter, Alice? Better watch out or your face will freeze that way."

My lip had curled into a sneer, listening to her babble on about meeting friends for drinks when across town, her older daughter was lying in a hospital bed. But then I remembered that she didn't know, and that the reason she didn't know was because I hadn't told her. I stopped scowling and helped her set the table.

My father came home later, even more distracted than usual, and we sat down to Sunday dinner. I ate as much as I could on an uneasy stomach, smiling politely and answering their disinterested questions about my sleepover at Cassie's house. After we'd finished eating, they seemed as eager to clear the table as I did.

My head was teeming with questions, and Jerry had raised more of them than he'd answered. When I was at the hospital, by Annie's side, I couldn't imagine doing anything else. Now that I wasn't, I knew I had to do something.

I got into bed exhausted that night, but as much as my body wanted sleep, my brain was having none of it. I thought about what had happened to Annie, played out the ways it might have happened over and over in my mind. What had she been doing out there in the park at that hour? Did she know the person who'd done it? Had she been afraid? Had she even seen it coming?

And then I turned over the things that Jerry Shaffer had told me, how my father was a piece of work and Annie wasn't any kind of angel.

After an hour or so of that, I gave up on trying to get some sleep and decided I could either stay in bed, driving myself crazy, or do something productive.

And that's how I came to be in my father's office, digging through his desk drawers at two in the morning.

Even on the nights they went out, my parents had cocktail hour promptly at five and drinks with dinner, so I wasn't worried that my snooping would interrupt their drunken slumber.

DEAD TO ME

The first drawer I tried was filled with old receipts and folders full of my father's press releases and news clippings. On my father's desk, there's a picture of him and the movie star Betty Grable. Well, sort of. In the picture, Betty's hanging on the arm of a good-looking director in a tuxedo and making her sex-kitten eyes at him, and my father's standing in the background with one of his arms chopped out of the frame. You know those captions in the high school yearbook: "Susie and Joe are crowned Homecoming King and Queen, while Norman looks on." That's how the rest of life is, too. There are the people who look gorgeous and do interesting things, and there are the people who look on. My father is worse because he looks on for a living.

The center drawer was locked. I took the letter opener from his desk blotter and jiggled it into the lock like I'd read about in my detective novels. It must have been a pretty crummy lock because after a minute or so, the drawer popped open.

There were only two things inside, and neither one of them seemed worth locking up.

The first was a matchbook with a maroon cover and gold embossed lettering that read MARTY'S, and a phone number written inside. I didn't know why it was important, but I pocketed it anyway.

The second thing I saw was a postcard, the kind that tourists buy by the handful on Hollywood Boulevard, covered with palm trees and oranges and pretty girls in bathing suits, so they can show their friends that they were there. I turned it over and gasped when I recognized Annie's handwriting. It read:

Dear Occupant:

Right away, I saw that it was one of our old ciphers. As Annie's codes went, this one was pretty easy to crack, a simple null cipher. We employed them only when the message wasn't that secret, or when the perceptiveness of the potential interceptor was beneath contempt. The tip-off was in the salutation. A letter that started with "Greetings" signaled that the message was contained in every third letter, "Hello," in every fifth. "Dear" was the easiest to do, especially if you were in a hurry, and it signaled that the message was in the first letter of every word.

The message read:

Sorry to ruin all the fun, really. Does Alice really miss sis?

That's what my father would have read. To me, though, the message said:

Stratfrd Arms

It was postmarked two months after she'd left home, and she'd meant it as a message for me, even though I'd received it almost four years too late.

Los Angeles is a city where girls get lost all the time. They disappear, change their names, and nobody ever hears from them again. Just one year before, someone found the body of a girl named Elizabeth Short in a vacant lot, cut in half, all the blood drained from her body, knife gashes at the sides of her mouth. The newspapers started calling her the Black Dahlia, and they wrote about her every day for months: her boyfriends, what she was wearing when she disappeared, what was in her handbag.

There was a whole parade of suspects, but the police never found out who did it.

The problem was nobody cared about Elizabeth Short until she was dead. She drifted alone in California for years—no family, no real friends—living in grimy rooming houses. She was a pretty girl with a moon-shaped face and thick black wavy hair, but when they found her, her teeth were so rotten she'd plugged the cavities with candle wax. For some reason, that part made me the saddest. If she'd had someone looking out for her, someone who could see how lonely and neglected she was, maybe she wouldn't have gone off with the wrong person that night. Maybe she wouldn't have turned up dead in a vacant lot.

I'd stayed with Annie for more than a day in the hospital, and no one had come to see her except a private detective. For all I knew, nobody else would. But I knew that if Annie woke up, she was in as much danger as she'd been in before, and that she'd need someone she could trust to help her, the way I couldn't four years before. I wondered what had happened between this postcard and now, what chain of events had led to her being beaten and left for dead in the park. Part of me didn't want to know the people she'd known, the places she'd been, the things she'd done during those years. I didn't want to think of my sister in those dark places.

I was trying to jiggle the lock shut on my father's desk when I realized that the detective novels never talked about that part. When Philip Marlowe or Sam Spade rummaged through a drawer, they didn't care if anybody knew they'd done it. But I did. I lived here.

The plan I came up with was far from perfect, but better than standing there in a panic.

I went to the window of my father's office and pulled up the sash and screen. For a man so meticulous about locking up match-books, he was thankfully less careful about his windows. At least that meant I wouldn't have to break the glass. Next, I went through the other desk drawers again, dumping a few files on the floor and rummaging through the papers on top of his desk. To make it convincing, I lowered myself into the flower bed underneath the window, trampling the bushes before hoisting myself back inside. Now it looked a little like a break-in.

For good measure, I removed several pictures from the wall, even though I knew the safe was behind a particularly large and ugly painting of a mean-eyed rooster. Where my father had acquired it, or why, I had no idea.

More out of curiosity than anything, I tried another trick from my detective novels. A smart person doesn't write down the combination to their safe and leave it lying around their office, and my father was a fairly smart person. However, he was also a person who had trouble remembering his home phone number and his wife's birthday. The combination would be around here somewhere.

I scanned the room, but eventually my eye landed on the rooster. It was ugly, but it did get your attention, I'll give it that. And then something else got my attention. Down in the lower corner, I noticed the painting was signed *B. Grif, 12/4/42*. I didn't care who B. Grif was, but I was interested in the date, which was conveniently combination-like.

And sure enough, a 12 right, 4 left, and 42 right later, I felt the lock catch. Inside, the safe was empty except for a little cash and an envelope with the Insignia Pictures logo in the corner. The words PHOTOS—DO NOT BEND were stamped on the front. My father was always carrying around a stack of these envelopes, all of them stuffed with publicity photos for one movie star or another. When I opened this one, the first picture in the stack was of a woman I didn't recognize wearing a skimpy bathing suit. I wasn't sure what made this envelope worth locking up.

Before I could go through the rest of the envelope's contents, I heard a hacking cough, followed by footsteps in the upstairs hallway. Quietly, I stole over to the door, turned out the light, and stood perfectly still, my heart pounding. I heard water running in the bathroom, and then the footsteps leading back to the bedroom.

It was risky to stay here much longer, and definitely too risky to turn the light on again, but I couldn't stand to leave the envelope behind, even if I didn't know what it was. My father might move it or change the combination on the safe to something less obvious. So I took it, along with the matchbook that said MARTY'S and the postcard from Annie.

Now all I had to do was go to bed and wait for morning. And I realized: maybe it wasn't the worst thing in the world that I'd broken the lock on the desk and faked a burglary. If my father called the police to report it, I'd know he had nothing to hide. And if he didn't, well, then it could mean just about anything, none of it good.

CHAPTER 5

The last fight Annie had with our parents was the worst, even though I was only there for the end of it. My former best friend, Cassie Jurgens, invited me to the beach that day, and we'd spent the afternoon racing barefoot in the sand and dodging the surf at the Santa Monica Pier. We bought ice cream and bottles of soda, and draped webs of kelp over our shoulders, pretending we were movie stars in fur coats. I was Bette Davis and she was Joan Crawford, and we strutted back and forth with our noses up in the air, speaking in trilling, theatrical voices.

"Joanie, dear, why ever did we come to a public beach?"

"Why, Bette, darling, we must study the common people to hone our craft."

We made ourselves laugh until we fell down in the sand, then ran into the surf to rinse the smelly kelp off our shoulders.

Cassie lived next door to us, but we weren't just friends out of convenience. We both loved movies and went to see a matinee together almost every week. After the movie was over, we'd pool our remaining money and go to the drugstore to buy the latest issues of *Screenland* and *Photoplay* and *Motion Picture Magazine*. Cassie cut out the movie star pictures and copied the poses in her bedroom mirror, while I studied the articles themselves, looking for stories about the stars at my father's studio. Back in those days I was like most kids. I was still proud of my father and what he did for a living.

Having Cassie for a best friend didn't do much to discourage me of that idea. She was a little bit in awe of my family— my mother, who told stories about the time she was a chorus girl alongside Myrna Loy, or how John Barrymore once lent her his umbrella; my sister, who floated out the door wrapped in silk and chiffon, on her way to one performance or another. Even though we'd been friends for years, she still got tongue-tied around them.

Sometimes it annoyed me, and yet Cassie had such a good heart it was easy to overlook things like that. Maybe we were too old to be playing movie stars at the beach, but I didn't care. That afternoon, Cassie and I came through the back door together, tracking sand all over the kitchen floor and singing at the tops of our lungs, "Would you like to swing on a star? Carry moonbeams home in a jar? And be better off than you are? Or would you rather be a pig?"

Then we heard the fighting in the living room.

"A man shouldn't have to pick his sixteen-year-old daughter up from the police station," my father bellowed.

I heard my mother sobbing, then Annie's voice, hard and bitter in a way it hadn't been.

"Sure, Daddy, that must have been real rough on you."

Then the sound of a slap.

I stood frozen in the kitchen, the next words of the song still stuck in my throat: *A pig is an animal with dirt on his face. His shoes are a terrible disgrace.*

Cassie covered her mouth with her hands, her eyes wide. I'm sure she was worried, just like I was, but in that moment, all I could think was that my family was just another movie magazine to her, full of spectacle and drama.

"Get out of here," I whispered. Her cheeks flushed red, and a hurt look crossed her face. "I mean it."

Cassie picked up her bag and ran out the back door, while I went crashing down the hall and into the living room. Annie stood rubbing her cheek, and I ran to her, threading my arm through hers. My parents were standing together, my mother's head buried in my father's shoulder.

"Leave her alone," I shouted at them.

My father took a step toward me. "Go to your room, Alice. This doesn't concern you."

Annie shrugged free from my grasp and reached into her pocketbook for a cigarette. With a defiant look on her face, she lit it and blew the smoke into their faces. My father slapped Annie again, this time on the other cheek. The cigarette flew out of her mouth and landed near the red Persian rug. The fringe began to smoke, and I stamped it out with my foot.

"You're lucky I got there when I did, and I want you to admit that much to me." A pained look crossed his face. "I'm your father. I deserve that much."

Annie chortled. "Yup, I'm a real lucky girl."

My mother sniffled and wiped her nose with the back of her hand. Her eyes were bleary and red-rimmed from more than her tears. Sober, she would have used a handkerchief.

"Annie, why couldn't you just let your father take care of this? Why did you have to get involved?"

My mother inhaled sharply, then ran a hand through her blond hair, smoothing the curls that had been pressed against my father's shoulder.

"At least your father still has a job, but, Annie, dear, I think you're going to have to forget about that screen test."

Annie stared at her in disbelief. "Do you really think I care about a screen test now?"

I followed very little of what was going on that day, but I knew about the screen test. Two years of party dresses and singing to strangers had finally landed Annie a chance to read for a supporting role in the new Buddy Pratchett comedy—Polly, the smart-mouthed kid who believes her big sister's fiancé is a gold-digging scoundrel. But of course, it's all a big misunderstanding. Buddy Pratchett winds up being a stand-up guy, and Polly says she's sorry for all the trouble she stirred up and sings a song at her big sister's wedding.

Cassie and I went to see it when it came out, but I walked out of the theater before it was over. It was exactly the kind of movie that my sister would have hated. Besides, the girl they cast as Polly didn't have a singing voice half as good as Annie's, and her eyes were too close together.

"I expect you to care," my father said. "I pulled a lot of strings to get this for you, and you pay me back in hysterics."

"Hysterics?"

For a long time, Annie stood there, staring at the singed spot on the carpet, until finally, she lifted her head and said, "I don't think there's anything else to say about it."

She walked out the front door then, and my parents simply

watched her go. I stood there for a moment, trying to make sense of what had just happened. Then, without thinking, I followed her out the door, running down the sidewalk after her and screaming her name. At the end of the block, I finally caught up with her, and by that time, some of the neighbors had come outside to see what all the screaming was about. Annie narrowed her eyes at me, and I burst into tears.

"Don't make a scene, Alice."

She sounded so unlike herself, so cold and cruel, it only made me cry harder.

"Annie, what's happening?"

Her expression softened, and she dropped to her knees, hugging me around the waist.

"Oh, Alice," she said, leaning her head against my belly. "Ali, I have to go away for a while."

"But why?"

She looked up at me, and I saw there were tears in her eyes, the first she'd shed over any fight with our parents.

"I can't tell you."

I started to explain that we were sisters and she could tell me anything, that she knew I wouldn't rat, but she put a finger to my lips.

"It's not that, and it's not that I don't think you're old enough to understand. Ali, there's no one I trust more in the world, so please believe me when I say it's better if you don't know."

I shook my head, dizzy with all the details. I had so many questions, I didn't know where to begin.

Finally, I asked the most sensible of the questions swimming around in my head. "Where will you go? What about your clothes and things?"

"Don't worry about me. I'll be fine. I have a place."

She let go of me and stood up. Everyone on our block had suddenly decided that their lawns needed tending, and I could feel their eyes pinned to our backs. Annie lowered her voice and put her hands on my shoulders.

"I'll write to you once I get settled in," she said, wiping her eyes. "Will you write back to me?"

I nodded again, speechless.

"Ali, I need you to do one more thing for me."

"Anything," I said.

"Don't believe anything they say. Not about me, not about anything."

She squeezed my shoulders and kissed me on the forehead.

"I'll see you soon, Alice," she said. "I promise."

She brushed her palms off on the hem of her skirt, and walked away. I stood on the sidewalk and watched her go, not caring about the neighbors' stares. I watched until she turned the corner and disappeared from sight. She didn't look back, not even once.

I went back to the house. I had to. I had no place else to go. When I came in through the front door, my parents were seated side by side in the front parlor, holding hands—a united front.

"Sit down, Alice," my mother said. "There are some things we need to talk about."

Within a month, I'd heard several versions of the story.

In the version my parents told me, Annie had made it clear that she no longer wanted to be a part of our family and had gone off to live with her so-called friends. I was told in no uncertain terms that if I ever began to associate with a bad crowd, I'd be sent to boarding school quicker than you could say Jack Robinson, and that Annie's shame should stand as a lesson to me about what happened to girls who turned their backs on their families.

In other words, they didn't tell me a thing.

At school, the stories of Annie's sudden disappearance were more specific and, at times, explicit, though I didn't believe them, either. In one, she'd run off with a gang that ran dope and girls up and down Highway 1. In another, she'd been caught in a compromising position—with whom was a matter of great speculation, and possibilities ranged from the school janitor to the head of Paramount Pictures.

At first, I tried standing up for Annie, but that only made it worse. People intensified their efforts, needling me for information I didn't have. The worst thing was, they didn't even care about her. They just hated not knowing, and when I wouldn't tell them, they hated me, too.

Every morning when I walked to school, I told myself, *You are Philip Marlowe. You are Sam Spade. You are ice, you are stone, and nothing can touch you.*

If you tell yourself something like that enough, you begin to believe it, but that's a problem, too.

Better watch out or your face will freeze that way.

Every day after school I checked the mailbox for a letter from Annie. After a month with no word, I started to worry and to wonder what might have kept her from writing to me. I imagined all kinds of terrible scenarios, many of them as lurid as the stories circulating around school—Annie kidnapped by gangsters or murdered in a ditch.

Eventually I decided to ask around. There *were* people out there, I reminded myself, who cared about Annie, who weren't just chasing after her story. And even if those people didn't know what had become of her, at least they weren't likely to lie to me.

First, I went to the drive-in parking lot where Annie's friends met after school. My parents didn't approve of any of these people—the girls wore tight sweaters and bright red lipstick, while the boys pegged their pants and rolled packs of cigarettes into the sleeves of their T-shirts. Of course, more damning than their appearance was the fact that none of them breathed the rarified air of our neighborhood, and none of their fathers lunched at the Cocoanut Grove or had memberships at the Los Angeles Athletic Club.

When I walked up to them in the parking lot, they recognized me right away, and the girls all hugged me and cried, while the boys bought me more sodas than I could possibly drink. They all asked about Annie, and nobody seemed to know much of anything. She hadn't been coming around lately anyway, they said, and no one knew where she'd been going after school.

Randall Pensler was more or less the leader of their circle, and I knew that for a month or so, he'd almost been Annie's boyfriend. She'd snuck out the window to meet him a few times, but then our parents got wind of it and made her break it off. My coming around seemed to make Randall uneasy, and he found reasons to avoid looking my way, so I was surprised when he offered me a ride home. He was quiet on the drive and smiled a sad, weary smile when I asked if he'd let me out a few blocks from our house.

"Annie used to make me do that," he said, pulling up to the curb. I thanked him and started to get out of his beat-up coupe.

"Alice, wait," he said, grabbing my arm. "I remember there was this guy."

"What guy?"

"I don't think she would have gone with him, but there was a guy named Rex who hung out at this bar I used to take her to. I'd leave her alone for five seconds and when I came back, he'd always be right there chatting her up. Said he was some kind of talent scout, but it seemed shady."

"Annie would never get mixed up with someone like that," I said. "She knows real talent scouts."

"I know, I know. Annie was too smart for that." He shook his head vehemently. "But she was always saying that she was going to be a singer and that she wanted to do it without your dad's help. I wonder if maybe she saw a chance and took it."

I nodded. Annie was impetuous. There was no denying that. Randall studied my face, which was twisted up in thought, and shrugged. "It probably wasn't anything."

"No, probably not," I said.

As I got out of the car, I noticed him staring at me with sad eyes. "You look just like her, you know," he whispered.

I knew it wasn't true, but his words still made me blush, and I hurried to close the car door behind me.

Maybe Annie's friends hadn't forgotten about her, but my parents hadn't even spoken her name in front of me since the day she left home. Night after night we sat at the table, not speaking, eating one solemn roast beef dinner after another until I couldn't take it anymore.

One night, when my father asked me to pass the butter, I said, "You act like she never existed."

His mustache twitched, and he reached over my plate and got the butter himself.

"Annie does not intend to come back," he said. "She made that much clear to your mother and me."

"You're lying," I said. "She wouldn't do that to me."

DEAD TO ME

My mother took my hand in hers.

"Honey," she said, "I know that you and Annie were very close."

"*Are* very close," I said.

She squeezed my fingers and acted like she hadn't heard me. "But your sister isn't well. She's not herself. She's not our Annie anymore. And we can hope with all our hearts that she comes back to us someday, but we can't dwell on what's happened or how we used to be."

"It doesn't mean we're forgetting her," my father added. "It means we have to move forward with our lives."

Even then, I knew the difference between moving forward and running away, and I knew which one this was. They might have moved forward, but I didn't. I didn't forget her. And I didn't forget who took her from me.

Without Annie, everything seemed empty. I still went to the movies with Cassie, but the only ones I wanted to see anymore were the gangster pictures that ended in a hail of bullets. Paging through movie magazines only made me think about my father and how I blamed him for driving Annie away; my mother and how she'd pushed Annie into a life she'd never wanted. Cassie seemed to understand, and she clipped her movie star pictures quietly while I hunched in the corner of her bedroom, reading my crime novels.

Eventually, I started reading in my own bedroom, by myself. Once I got used to that, I found I liked walking to school alone, eating lunch alone, going to the movies alone. Alone, there was nothing to distract me from the only thing I wanted to think about, the only thing in the world that mattered to me.

My sister is gone. My sister is gone. My sister is gone.

One day, my mother knocked on my door holding an envelope

in her hand. Thinking it was the letter Annie had promised to send me all those months before, I grabbed it out of her hands and tore it open, slamming the door in her face.

The letter inside read:

> Dear Alice,
>   I know you don't want to talk about it, but if you ever decide you do, you can talk to me. I miss her, too.
>   Love,
>   Cassie

I threw it in the trash can. *I miss her, too.* It took a lot of nerve for her to write that. She barely knew my sister and couldn't even get a full sentence out around her. What could I possibly have to talk to her about? She hadn't lost her sister. I had.

But then I thought about how badly I'd treated Cassie, how I'd shut her out, and I fished the letter out of the trash.

I turned the paper over and wrote my reply on the back:

> Dear Cassie, Okay, thanks. Love, Alice

Ever since, our friendship had been like that. It wasn't like I'd discarded her for other friends. I didn't want new friends, either. For years, it had been just me and my books and my room. Occasionally, a boy would decide I was mysterious and try to make a project out of me. For a few weeks, I'd allow myself to be pried out of my bedroom and taken to diners and dances and the sad parties people threw in their parents' living rooms. I'd be around people and see what I was missing. The only problem was, nothing ever looked better to me than my bedroom walls. I didn't feel like I'd been missing anything. The boys eventually decided I wasn't mysterious and that there were other strange, damaged girls with thousand-yard stares who made better projects than I did.

Cassie didn't give up on me, though, not completely. She'd occasionally make a nice gesture; I'd respond just enough to keep her from writing me off. She'd invite me to her birthday party; I'd send my regrets and a card. She'd save me a seat next to her at the school assembly; I'd walk homework assignments over to her house when she was out sick. She'd ask me about my sister, and I'd say, *No, I don't know anything. I haven't heard. I'm okay.*

But what I really wished I could say was, *Leave me alone. Stop asking. Stop caring about my life.*

CHAPTER 6

The morning after I burgled my father's office, I woke up early, ate a quick breakfast, and left a note saying that I was going to the beach with Cassie's family. They wouldn't ask too many questions about that.

Then I went to the trolley stop and caught the Red Car across town to the County Hospital. I was relieved to find Annie exactly where I'd left her the afternoon before, but I was heartsick, too. There hadn't been a miracle, and the longer she lay there, the harder it was to imagine she'd ever wake up.

Jerry Shaffer was right where I'd left him, too, asleep in the chair next to Annie's bed, the previous day's *Los Angeles Examiner* folded up on the floor next to him. When I said his name, his eyes flew open and he sat up like a shot. Seeing only me, he relaxed and rubbed his eyes.

"Sorry, kid," he said, clearing his throat. "I must have dozed off there for a minute."

I leaned over my sister and brushed a lock of hair from her forehead. A fresh bandage covered the angry-looking black stitches and most of the ugly purple bruise that had spread across her face. Even after two days, it still felt strange to be this close to her.

"How is she?" I asked.

"One of the orderlies was in here about every ten minutes last night. I was starting to think something was wrong with her, but the doctor just came by. He says she's stable."

"Was there anyone else?" I asked, glad to hear that the money I'd given the orderly had been well spent. "I mean, did anyone else come to see her?"

"Why? Were you expecting someone?"

"She has friends, doesn't she?"

"Of course she does."

"Then where are they?" I asked.

Jerry didn't answer at first. He got up from the chair next to Annie's bed and began to pace the linoleum. It was a simple question. Of course, where Annie was concerned, I was beginning to see there wasn't any such thing.

"I'm still looking for them," Jerry said, then gave me a dark look. "Alice, no visitors is a good thing. A very good thing. There aren't that many hospitals in Los Angeles, and the person who did this wasn't trying to put her in one."

I considered the implications. "You're saying they think she's dead?"

"It would explain a few things."

It was such a strange thing to be relieved about, but I was. I felt a lump in my throat and fought back the urge to cry. It didn't have anything to do with Jerry being there—I didn't care what he thought. Crying would have made me feel better, and I didn't want to feel better. I wanted to do something.

I reached into my purse and handed Jerry the matchbook I'd burgled.

"Marty's?" Jerry drew in a breath through his teeth. "Where'd you find this?"

"In my father's desk," I said. "What do you know about it?"

"I know it's no place you have any business going to," he said, opening up the matchbook. "I don't suppose you tried calling this number?"

I shook my head, and Jerry shrugged. "Something to look into, I guess. There are a few other leads I want to check out this morning. Do you mind holding down the fort for a while?"

"Are you still looking for Annie's friends?"

"Yeah," Jerry said, but he paused before he said it, and I wondered whether that was what he was going out to do at all. "I'll be back in a few hours."

A few minutes after Jerry left, the orderly I'd paid off the night before stuck his head into Annie's room.

"Everything okay in here?" he asked.

I nodded, and the orderly stepped inside. He was nice-looking in an earnest, country way, and there was a little bit of a twang in his voice. I guessed he was probably from somewhere around Bakersfield.

"She's got a lot of people worried about her," he said. "Your friend the detective, he gave me money to keep an eye on her, too."

"Really?"

"He went out for a couple of hours around midnight."

Jerry Shaffer hadn't said anything about that, or about paying off the orderly, for that matter. I wondered where he'd gone at that hour.

"Do you know who did this to her?" he asked.

"No," I said.

"But you think they're going to come back?" asked the orderly, his eyes wide.

"I hope not," I said.

"My name's Eugene, by the way," he said. "I was just stopping by because my shift's about to end, and——"

I opened my purse and started to pull out the dollar bills I'd brought along just in case I needed to pay the orderly again. When I held the money out to him, though, he pushed my hand away.

"It's not that," he said, shaking his head. "I just wanted you to know that I talked to the nurses on the next shift. I told them about you, and they said they'd keep an eye on your friend's room if you want."

It was such a small gesture, but the kindness of it took my breath away. I wasn't alone—Annie wasn't alone. There was a whole floor of nurses watching out for her. When I tried to thank Eugene, no sound came out—I could only mouth the words.

I wish I'd let him know how much it meant to me, what he'd done.

Instead, I cleared my throat and said, "I have to go out for a couple of hours."

It came out more brusquely than I'd meant it to, and Eugene looked surprised.

"You'll be back, though, won't you?" he asked.

I hated leaving Annie again, but there was something I needed to know, and it was something I needed to do without Jerry. If I wanted to find out who tried to kill my sister, I'd have to be smart.

I'd have to imagine what Annie would have done. That was why I'd told Jerry about the matchbook I found in my father's desk, but kept the postcard and the photographs to myself. It was why I'd borrowed a phone book from the nurse on duty in the main lobby. And it was why I was going to leave my sister alone while I went out to investigate the two-word message she'd sent me. If it had been me in that hospital bed, Annie wouldn't have sat around mooning. She would have gone out and gotten some answers.

"Of course I'll be back," I told Eugene.

I took the Red Car from the hospital to Hollywood, got off at Western, and walked south down a side street peppered with courtyard apartments and residential hotels. They were the kind that advertised themselves as respectable rooms for nice young girls. However, with each block, the buildings grew less attractive, less respectable-looking—tree roots pushing the sidewalks up at dangerous angles, fountains half filled with brown murky water, graying whitewash on the stucco.

The battered sign for the Stratford Arms dangled from a pair of chains, though the apartments themselves were hidden from view by a canopy of neglected shrubs and ragged-looking palm trees. I walked through the gate and followed the flagstone path up to a screen door with a sign that read OFFICE. The latch on the door was broken, and the door swung open with a gust of wind before I even touched it. A woman was sitting at the desk, poring over a book of newspaper clippings. At first, I couldn't see her face, just the top of her head, gray roots fighting their way out of a dye job that looked like it had been accomplished with shoe polish.

As the screen door banged against the side of the building, she sat up, her face twisted into a snarl before she'd even had a chance to register the sight of me standing in the doorway.

"Watch the door," she snapped. "You break it, and I'll tack it on to your rent."

Clearly, this was a woman who yelled first and asked questions later. If she thought I was one of her tenants, I didn't have high hopes that she'd remember Annie. But I went into her office anyway, closing the screen door behind me as tightly and gently as I could manage.

"Sorry," I said. "Must have been the wind."

She snorted, then looked at me for the first time. A strange expression crossed her face before it went stony.

"What do you want? I'm not buying any candy bars."

I reached into my purse and took out an old picture of Annie that I had, one where she didn't look like she'd been bleached, painted, and tweezed within an inch of her life. I set it down on the woman's desk.

"I'm looking for my sister, Annie Gates. She lived here a few years ago, I don't know for how long, and I'm looking for a forwarding address."

As she picked up the picture and scanned it with a poker face, I kicked myself for saying Annie was my sister. I should have stuck to the story I'd used at the hospital, that Annie was my friend.

"Yeah, she lived here a few years ago. Doesn't anymore." She gave me a self-satisfied smirk. "I don't forget a face."

"Did she leave an address?"

"I'm not the post office, kid. She was here a few months, then moved on. Why'd you come looking for her now?"

There was something about the way she asked that I didn't like, something a little too much like genuine curiosity. I made my chin wobble and stuck a fingernail into the palm of my hand until my eyes started to water.

"She's my sister," I said, forcing a tremor into my voice. "I haven't seen her in years, and I heard she might have been here. Isn't there anything you can tell me?"

I hoped my performance was convincing enough to make her a little uncomfortable, make her tell me a little something, if only to get me out of her office. But whether she could tell my tears were false or not, she seemed to be enjoying them.

She scrunched up her mouth and looked at the ceiling, tapping her fingers together. At least my act was better than hers.

"You know, I think she left with some handsome young fellow." She nodded, as if that settled it. "I don't know who he was or where they went. That's just what I heard from the other girls."

The other girls, I thought. Now, that was an idea. Maybe one of them would tell me something worth knowing.

"Could I talk to some of them? Maybe one of them can remember his name."

She pursed her lips, and I knew I shouldn't have asked. Now she not only wanted me out of her office, she'd make sure I was off her property in five minutes and not snooping around bothering her tenants.

"Hon, people here tend to stay a few months and move on. I don't have anyone who's been here longer than a year." Then, more firmly and finally, she added, "I'm sorry, but I don't think I can be of any more help to you."

She turned back to her news clippings, which I could see now were from the kind of papers that ran pictures of mangled tricycles and covered bodies on stretchers: FIEND ATTACKS SECRETARY IN LOS FELIZ, CHILD DIES IN FIRE ESCAPE COLLAPSE, that sort of thing. I could tell I was being dismissed.

"Could I have my picture back?" I asked.

She looked up, then gave me the once-over again before handing it back.

"Sure, sorry about that."

I was pretty sure she wasn't sorry at all. I put the picture back in my purse and closed the screen door gently behind me as I left. As I walked down the sidewalk, I peered over the tops of the hedges, trying to get a look at the courtyard bungalows, wondering which one Annie had lived in. Although it was morning, no one seemed to be home, or at least they weren't awake yet. The place was eerily quiet.

Something didn't sit right about the conversation I'd just had, the way the woman had looked at Annie's picture, the way she'd asked *why* I was looking for my sister. Who asks a question like that? *She's my sister. Of course I'd look for her.* As soon as I turned the corner, I doubled back, slipping behind the shrubs and following them up the length of the sidewalk. When I reached the office, I nestled under a leafy cover and listened. She was on the phone.

"Hey, Rex, it's Wanda at the Stratford Arms. Sorry to bother you." Then, after a short pause, "That little blond cupcake who lived over here a few years back, the one with the rich daddy, you still keeping tabs on her?"

There was a twig brushing up against my face that itched like crazy, but I didn't dare move.

"Yeah, I figured. Anyhow, someone came by looking for her. Some kid claimed to be her sister."

Wanda's voice grew more agitated.

"Simmer down, Rex. I didn't tell her anything. I have no idea how she knew to come here. But like I said, she was just a kid. Didn't ask too many questions, nearly broke down crying when I said I'd never seen the girl."

That was interesting. Little as Wanda had told me, she didn't even want this Rex to know about that. The sarcastic bluster disappeared from her voice. Now she sounded meek and eager to please.

"Yeah, I'll call if she comes back. Sorry to bother you, but I thought you'd want to know."

Wanda hung up and her office fell silent. I guessed she'd gone back to her gruesome book of news clippings.

I was about to get up when I heard a small knocking sound behind me. I turned around to see a young woman standing at the front window of the bungalow nearest to Wanda's office, rapping her knuckles on the glass. We made eye contact, and she motioned me to come closer, then disappeared.

The door to her apartment was hidden behind a clothesline hung with sheets and towels drying in the tiny yard. I hesitated until I noticed a fluttery yellow chiffon dress tucked among the linens. A woman with a dress that dainty, I reasoned, was probably not going to knife me in her living room.

I darted from the hedges toward the front door. It opened before I could knock, and the woman pulled me inside, shut the door behind us, and drew the curtains.

She gestured toward a brown horsehair sofa, which was the only place to sit in the entire room. I took a seat. She stood.

My mother was always saying that I could be pretty if I made an effort. Looking at this woman, I finally understood what she meant. She wore a gray shirtwaist dress, and her only makeup, a little dab of plum lipstick, was applied like an afterthought. Her hair was pulled back in a frumpy-looking headband, and she wore black shoes that looked like they belonged on a man or a polio patient. She wasn't trying to be pretty, that was for sure. And yet, she was. She was in her early twenties with a head of auburn waves that shone like freshly polished woodwork, and world-weary eyes that made her look like Lauren Bacall in *The Big Sleep*. If I made an effort, maybe I'd be halfway pretty. If this woman made an effort, she'd be a movie star.

"I'm Ruth," she said. "And you must be Alice."

How was it that everybody seemed to know who I was?

"Are you a friend of my sister's?"

"Friend. That's an interesting way of putting it."

I didn't like the smirk on her face when she said it, and it occurred to me that I should have applied more stringent criteria than "pretty yellow dress" when deciding to sit down in a stranger's living room. Criteria like "lives in the Stratford Arms" and "spies on people out her window." I calculated the distance between Ruth and me and the door, and wondered whether I could get there before she did.

Ruth rolled her eyes. "Oh, relax. I'm not going to hurt you."

Another door lacquered in coat after coat of white paint separated the front parlor from the rest of the apartment. Without another word, Ruth disappeared behind it and left me alone on the couch, watching the door swing back and forth on its hinges.

There wasn't much to keep me entertained in her absence. Aside from the horsehair couch and a scarred-looking coffee table, the room was completely empty. The curtains weren't proper ones. Ruth had just thrown swaths of thick, unhemmed serge over a rod. Even on a sunny Los Angeles day, any scrap of light that found its way through was washed out and gray.

Ruth came back through the door holding two open bottles of Coca-Cola and took a seat next to me on the couch.

"Here," she said, handing me one of the bottles.

"Thanks."

We sat in silence, sizing each other up and drinking our sodas, until we both spoke at the same time.

"What are you doing here?" she asked.

"How do you know my sister?"

Ruth cocked her head to the side. "You answer first. I insist."

I was afraid to open my mouth, worried that I'd say the wrong thing, or say too much to this woman who'd practically come right out and said that she was no friend to my sister. The heavy curtains made it seem stuffy and airless inside the apartment, and the prickly fabric of the couch chafed against the backs of my legs. Ruth regarded me coolly and nursed her soda.

"Annie sent me a message, and all it said was the name of this place. But I don't know why."

"You do know this was the first place Annie stayed when she left home, right?"

I shook my head.

"Before my time, but it was," she said. "Rex put her up."

Rex. There was that name again.

And then I remembered that today wasn't the first time I'd heard it. The night Randall Pensler gave me a ride home, he'd said a talent scout named Rex was always chatting Annie up. It had to have been the same person.

"At least he did until Annie figured out that Rex was tight with your father. That was why she split." She took a delicate sip from her bottle. "That and other reasons."

"Wanda said something about a boyfriend."

Ruth waved me off. "Wanda always says something about a boyfriend when someone comes around looking for one of the girls. It makes them go away."

"Oh," I said. "So, how do you know her, then?"

"Be patient, Alice. It's still my turn," Ruth said, wagging her finger at me. My mouth clapped shut. "So, your sister sends you a message, and you come just like that."

"She's my sister."

"And you came because you thought she'd be here?"

I wondered if this was a trick question, if Ruth already knew good and well where Annie was but was trying to catch me in a lie. Still, better that, I thought, than to tell her too much. I nodded.

"Did you show Annie's message to anyone?"

"No."

"Did you tell anyone you were coming here?"

I didn't answer.

"I'll take that as a 'no.'"

Ruth chuckled to herself. I could feel sweat start to bead and drip on my brow, on the tip of my nose, on the backs of my knees. It had been a mistake to come here. For some reason, I began to think about how angry Jerry Shaffer would be if he knew I was here.

"So what you're telling me," she said, "is you don't know where Annie is right now."

"Yes," I lied.

"And you're sure that's all she said in her message? Stratford Arms?"

"I'm sure of it. I swear."

"Don't ever say 'I swear,'" Ruth said. "It makes you sound like a liar every time."

"I'm not lying."

"I didn't say you were."

We stared at each other, radiating dislike and not bothering to hide the fact.

"Did you have something you wanted to ask me?"

I did, but the problem was, now I didn't know where to begin. Who was this woman? How did she know my sister if she didn't move to Stratford Arms until after Annie left? How did Annie wind up in a seedy place like this? I wanted to know all of it, but at that moment, there was another question that seemed more important.

"Who is Rex?" I asked.

No sooner were the words out of my mouth than an engine revved, sputtered, and stalled so spectacularly that Ruth and I heard it all the way from the street. A panicked look flashed across Ruth's face. She knew that car.

She pulled me up from the couch and said, "Go out the back, through the kitchen. There's a hole in the fence you can slip through."

I started to protest, but then I heard heavy footsteps coming up the sidewalk. Ruth's eyes grew large, and she whispered, "Go."

I went. Or at least I started to. I got as far as opening the screen door, but then let it fall shut. Ruth could have left me eavesdropping outside Wanda's window, but she hadn't. And whoever was coming up the sidewalk right now was trouble. Annie wouldn't have left her alone, and I wouldn't, either.

There was a small closet pantry next to the back door. Quickly, I opened the door and wedged myself in, being careful not to trip over the mop and bucket in the dark. As I closed the door behind me, I heard a gruff man's voice ask, "Where is she?"

He was big—I could tell from the sounds he made hulking around in the living room, and the shuffling sounds Ruth made getting out of his way.

"She just went out the back, Rex. You can still catch her," Ruth said, and I choked back a gasp.

"Why'd you let her get away?" Rex snarled.

"I didn't *let* her do anything," Ruth snarled back. "Now, are you going to stand here and yell at me, or are you going to go after her?"

Footsteps rushed through the kitchen, past the pantry door, and crashed through the screen door.

At first, I couldn't breathe. My chest felt like it had been crushed and my hands shook. I didn't have much time. In a few moments, Rex would figure out I hadn't gone out the back door and he'd come back. And if I tried to run for the front door, Ruth was there. She'd already sold me out. Maybe she'd scream, maybe she'd do something worse. Still, I decided, between the two of them, I'd take my chances with her.

My eyes adjusted to the dark pantry, and I felt around on the shelves for something I could use to defend myself. My hands settled on two interesting items. The first was more immediately practical, a heavy wooden rolling pin. The second puzzled me at first. It felt like a bag of flour, but was too small and the wrapping paper too rough. It was sealed with masking tape, and though I'd never seen anything like it before, I'd read enough crime novels to know what it was. And I realized what a tough cookie like Ruth was doing in a dump like the Stratford Arms, rubbing elbows with a thug like Rex. She'd have a ready stream of potential customers among the desperate, disappointed girls Rex put up here, hungry for a dose or two of oblivion.

I put the package down and brandished the rolling pin over my shoulder like a baseball bat. It felt solid, like I could do some real damage with it if I needed to, which reassured me. Slowly, I opened the pantry door.

There was no sign of Rex, but I caught Ruth rushing out of

one of the bungalow's back rooms. She froze in the center of the kitchen when she saw me.

"Just let me go," I said, choking up on the rolling pin as I advanced toward the front parlor. "Please."

Ruth looked up, her eyes wide with disbelief. I saw something else in them, too. Maybe it was relief, maybe it was shame, but either way, I didn't quite believe it.

"Sorry, Alice," she said. "I didn't have a choice."

Didn't have a choice? I thought. You could have at least given me a head start.

Then I ran out into the parlor, opened the front door, and ran away from the Stratford Arms as fast as my legs would carry me. It was two blocks before I realized I was still carrying the rolling pin.

CHAPTER 7

f I was being followed, I didn't want to risk leading Rex right to Annie's hospital bed, so I went home instead. It seemed like an eternity ago that I'd burglarized my father's office, but to my parents, neither one an early riser, the crime was still fresh.

"Where have you been?" my mother said, grabbing me by the shoulders and shaking me a little harder than she'd probably meant to.

"I was with Cassie," I said. "Didn't you get my note?"

"Note? What note?"

"The one I left in the kitchen."

"In the kitchen?" she screeched, as though only the slightly dim-witted left notes in kitchens. "Well, never mind. You'd better come into the parlor and sit down. We've all had a terrible shock this morning, haven't we, Nick?"

My father's sigh was audible from the next room.

"Don't be melodramatic, Vivian."

Though it was well into the afternoon, my mother still looked fashionably idle in her peignoir, her blond pin curls pulled off her face with a pale blue headband. Only members of our immediate family knew that even this purposely disheveled look would have required at least a full hour of primping.

"Come with me, dear," she said, and pulled me toward the parlor by my arm, a slightly crazed look on her face.

I choked back a gasp as I entered the room. Sitting on the couch with a sweaty glass of iced tea, and looking very ill at ease, was Jerry Shaffer. He met my eyes only for a second, but even from across the room, I could read his message clear as day: *Play dumb, kid.*

There might have been a bit of something else in his look, too. *Why aren't you at the hospital?* I ignored it and shot him back a look of my own: *What are you doing here?*

My father motioned to the chair next to him, and I took it.

"Alice, it seems we had a little break-in last night."

"Really?" I asked, trying my best to look as though I was surprised by this news.

Jerry cleared his throat and looked to my father for permission to speak. He nodded his assent.

"The burglar came in through your father's office window. That's the only room in the house that seems to have been disturbed."

"Did they take anything?" I asked.

"Well, that's just it," Jerry said. "Your father and I have gone over the room from top to bottom, and can't find a thing missing. Nothing valuable, anyway."

My father motioned in Jerry's direction. "Alice, this is Jerry

Shaffer. He's a private investigator. He helps us out at the studio from time to time."

My mother stood at the bar, mixing herself a sidecar. After stirring it with a swizzle stick, she flopped down dramatically on the chaise longue by the window and took an unladylike swig.

"My nerves are just shattered," she said, by way of apology for her afternoon drinking. "Nick, I don't understand why you couldn't just call the police about this."

He scowled at her and said, "Vivian, you know how I feel about those people pawing around through our things. They stir up trouble. Besides, what crime is there to report?"

"What crime?" she hooted. "We could have been butchered in our sleep. And what about your office? Vandalism! Trespassing! Breaking and entering! How are those for crimes?"

"Mrs. Gates," Jerry said, speaking gently to her, "from the condition of your husband's office, it seems that the perpetrator was looking for something in particular."

She gave a grim laugh. "A particular perpetrator. What will they think of next?"

"If that's indeed the case," he continued, "your husband believes that handling this quietly and privately might be the best way to determine what he or she was looking for."

Was it my imagination, or did Jerry look right at me when he said "she"? Apparently, my mother settled on the same detail.

"She?" she asked. "You think a woman did this?"

"It's possible, perhaps even likely," Jerry said. "There's a footprint in the dirt underneath the office window. A rather *small* footprint."

My parents exchanged uneasy, meaningful glances. My father cleared his throat and said, "Alice, would you excuse us, please?

There are a few things your mother and I need to discuss with Mr. Shaffer in private."

"Of course," I said, turning to Jerry as I stood up. "It was very nice to meet you, Mr. Shaffer."

As I went up the stairs, I heard Jerry say, "Well, she's got nice manners," without even bothering to keep the smirk out of his voice.

I went to my room, opened the door, shut it again without going in, and crept back to the top of the stairs so I could hear what was going on.

"I don't know why she'd come poking around here after all these years, Jerry."

My mother chimed in. "She could have come back any time she liked. And through the front door, too."

"Of course, Mrs. Gates," Jerry said.

"I'm afraid she's unstable," my father said. "I'm worried what she might do."

"Do you have any idea where she is now?" he asked.

Jerry wasn't giving up a scrap of information to them, though I wasn't sure why not. If he was really a detective for the studio, he'd know which side his bread was buttered on. There wasn't any money in protecting Annie, and Insignia Studios had deep pockets. I wondered if he was planning to string them along for a day or two of pay, plus expenses, or if he was working some other angle.

"The last time I heard anything, she was living in some flophouse on Main Street." My father sighed deeply. "That was months ago."

"It's someplace to start, sir."

"Just find her, Jerry. And when you do, bring her straight to me."

"It's only that we're worried," my mother added. "If she could do this, who knows what state she's in. I can't imagine what's become of her."

Jerry asked, "During the time that your daughter has been missing, have you ever gone to the police or engaged the services of another detective to look for her?"

I heard a glass, slammed down on the coffee table.

"What do you mean by that?" my mother asked.

"Please, I wasn't implying anything," Jerry said. "It's just helpful to know these things."

"He's right, Vivian. And, yes, we did keep tabs on her for a while. Annie left on a whim, and we always thought she'd come home when she'd had enough of being on her own. Rumors would get back to me from time to time about where she was and what she was doing. Then, a few months ago, we lost track of her completely."

"I see. Did she ever try to contact you?"

"No."

Liar, I thought. I hated my father at that moment. The way he described it all to Jerry was so smooth, so shrugged off, it was like he thought Annie left as a spiteful prank on the rest of us. *We always thought she'd come home when she'd had enough of being on her own.* Like he'd never worried, never missed her, never seen the moment she left as the moment we stopped being a family.

Then again, my father had had someone feeding him information about where my sister was, what she was doing, whether she was safe. He'd known Annie was at the Stratford Arms, under the watchful eye of his dear friend Rex.

Rex put her up . . . at least he did until Annie figured out that he was tight with your father.

I thought my trip to the Stratford Arms had been a mistake, but Ruth had given me a scrap of useful information after all. I still didn't really know who Rex was, but I knew he wasn't the kind of person who came to my parents' cocktail parties. How did my father know him? *Why* did my father know him? I was so absorbed in thought that I almost missed hearing my mother say she thought she had a picture of my sister upstairs. I scuttled on all fours back to my room, as quickly and quietly as I could, turned the doorknob gently, and shut the door behind me without letting the latch catch. I'd had lots of practice at that, having learned from the world's sneakiest big sister.

After I heard her pass the door a second time, I closed it completely and sat down on my bed to think about everything I'd overheard. What I really wanted to do was to crawl out my window and catch Jerry the moment he stepped outside, and make him tell me everything. But, of course, that would have to wait. I was sure that as soon as he left, my parents would be waiting to tell me a ludicrous story about my unstable, burglarizing sister.

It wasn't just that they lied about important things. It was that they didn't even try to make them sound half true. When I asked why Annie left, they told me she didn't want to be part of our family anymore. When I asked my father where he'd been all weekend, he told me he was working, and when I asked my mother why I didn't play piano at her parties anymore, she said I was getting too old for that sort of thing.

If there's one good thing about having your questions tossed off with silly explanations, it's that you get good at noticing when things don't make sense, and good at filling in the blanks for yourself.

I was sure it was only a matter of time before they came to my room, ready to fill my head with well-rehearsed lies. I sat on my bed and waited for it, but when the knock on my door came, they were dressed in their evening clothes and on their way to Ciro's for cocktail hour and dinner. My mother kissed the air near my cheek so as not to smudge her lipstick, and my father told me to be a good girl and not to stay up too late. Neither of them said a word about Jerry Shaffer and the so-called burglary as they breezed out of the house in a cloud of perfume and cognac.

As soon as they were gone, I got out the phone book and paged through the listings for private investigators until I found Jerry Shaffer, and dialed DUnkirk 4-2390. The phone rang about ten times before he answered, sounding out of breath.

"It's me," I said.

"Thought I'd be hearing from you, kid. Now's not a good time."

"What were you doing at my house?"

"Alice, I'm on my way out. I'll explain later."

"No," I said.

"What happened to those nice manners?" he said with a chuckle.

I wasn't in a joking mood. "I thought you said my father was a piece of work. Why are you working for him?"

"I said we'll talk about it later."

"You can help him or you can help Annie. Which is it?"

There was a long pause, then a sigh.

"I came to your father very highly recommended by the head of security at Insignia Pictures, who happens to be a good friend of mine. Let's just say that for five bucks, it was no skin off his nose to tell your father that he was putting his best man on the case."

"He just turned everything over to you like that?" I asked, a little shocked. "You could have been anybody."

"Film people get hysterical over the littlest things, and they're paranoid about police, too. They get a nasty letter, or somebody looks at them funny at the stoplight, and they go to pieces. If a big star like Ava Gardner makes that phone call, you'd better believe they send out the cavalry, but for a small fish like your father? And for a break-in where nothing was actually stolen?"

"They send you."

"That's right. As far as my buddy knew, business was slow and I needed the work. And may I remind you that all of this is your fault anyway?"

"I told you I got the matchbook from my father's desk," I said.

"You didn't tell me you tore the place apart. No more stunts, Alice."

"Okay," I said, realizing that my adventure with Ruth and Rex earlier today probably qualified as exactly the kind of stunt Jerry was talking about.

"I'll meet you at the hospital tomorrow, Alice, and I'll tell you everything then—I promise. But in the meantime, remember I'm on your side. And Annie's."

He hung up on me, and I stood there feeling more confused than ever, and very far away from the truth of things. Jerry hadn't told me the whole story, true, but he'd admitted as much. I certainly hadn't told him how I'd spent my afternoon, and wasn't sure if I was going to. If he really was on Annie's and my side, it would only make him worry. And if he wasn't—well, that possibility was never very far from my thoughts.

Then I thought back to the day before and the strip of paper he'd placed in my hand at the hospital. At first, I hadn't understood. It was just a long vertical row of letters, written in a tiny and cramped hand. But then I remembered something Annie once told me: *It's called a scytale. You can use a pencil or a curtain rod, or whatever you want, so long as you and the person you're sending the message to agree on the key.*

It was one of Annie's codes. I'd wound the strip of paper around the pencil stub, pulling it tight until the letters lined up across the length of the pencil, and I saw what they read:

TRUST ME

Jerry had asked me to put an awful lot of faith in a scrap of paper. Still, I trusted him more than I trusted my parents. I was, at that moment, actually fairly furious with my parents. What kind of people leave their daughter alone in the house the night after a break-in so they can go out for dinner? I'd done the breaking in, of course, but they didn't know that. In a few hours, they'd stumble through the front door laughing or fighting. Either way it would be loud enough to wake me up and remind me exactly how miserable and lonely it was to live in their house.

The idea of staying there for another second was more than I could bear. I packed a bag for the hospital, filling it with toiletries for Annie, a change of clothes, and most important, the envelope I'd taken from my father's safe. I left another note in the kitchen, this one saying that I didn't feel safe in the house and had gone to Cassie's. I hoped they felt terrible when they read it, if they read it.

There was only one more thing to do before I could go, and I dreaded doing it. The last time I asked Cassie to cover for me, I'd been manic and close to tears, and she'd still balked at the idea. If I asked her again, she'd want to know the reason, and I couldn't tell her. Still, there wasn't any way around it. I needed her help.

Cassie's mother answered the front door when I knocked, and

invited me in without looking very happy about it. Even in better times, I'd never gotten the feeling that Mrs. Jurgens was all that fond of me.

"Twice in one week. To what do we owe the honor?" she sniffed, pointing toward the strip of carpet that ran the length of the foyer. "Your shoes, dear. Please."

Mrs. Jurgens was from the Midwest and made everyone take their shoes off when they went inside her house. My mother had gone there for afternoon tea once and came home raving that she'd been treated like a common field hand.

"If she thinks I'm going to track dirt all over her clean floors, then perhaps she shouldn't have invited me into her home," she'd said.

"Maybe it's hygiene," my father had mumbled from behind his newspaper.

"Maybe it's provincial."

I kicked off my shoes and went upstairs to Cassie's room.

Mrs. Jurgens called up after me. "Don't keep her too long, Alice. She has to get up early for field hockey practice tomorrow."

Cassie was sitting on the bed when I got there, brushing her hair and trying to look like she hadn't heard me downstairs a minute before.

"What do you want?" she said. The brush whipped through her hair with such force I was surprised it didn't pull it out by the roots. "I know you wouldn't be here if you didn't want something."

At one time, I would have bounded up the stairs and taken my customary spot on the window seat. Now I stood uneasily in the doorway, waiting to be invited in. When it became clear that wasn't going to happen, I closed the door behind me and took a seat in the straight-backed desk chair.

It had been a mistake to come here. Cassie and I weren't close anymore, not the way we used to be. And yet, in the years since, there'd been an understanding between us that we'd never be the kind of friends who traded in on the history between us. Apparently, that's the kind of friend I was now. The kind who called in favors for old time's sake.

"It's important, Cassie."

"Important how?"

She stretched her legs out across the bed and hugged a pillow in a white eyelet cover to her chest. When we were younger, I used to want a bedroom like Cassie's, with its little-girl ruffles and lace and ballerina music boxes. Now I couldn't imagine someone our age choosing to keep her room that way. Maybe Cassie acted younger than me because I had an older sister to emulate, and she only had a bratty little brother. Or maybe it was because of her ordinary family, and their rules about shoes, and their regular, steady love.

"I can't stay in that house," I said.

"Is it your mother?" Cassie asked. She relaxed her grip on the pillow and her eyes softened a bit.

Cassie knew how much my mother had started drinking after Annie left home, but she didn't know what it was like to live with her. It wasn't like the movies, where the drunks are always yelling and throwing vases at other people's heads. Living with my mother was more like living with a very well-behaved ghost who occasionally woke you up in the middle of the night rattling the doorknobs or crying softly.

I shook my head.

"I don't believe you," Cassie said.

"I'm not lying."

"But you're not telling the truth, either."

"I have to be away for the next couple of days, and they can't know where I am. I need you to cover for me. You probably won't even have to lie to them. I doubt they'll even check."

I tried to meet her eyes so she could see how truthful I was being, but she wouldn't even look at me. There was a brass cup filled with a dozen identical fountain pens on Cassie's desktop. I picked one up and pulled off the cap, then put it back on, then I pulled it off again. When Cassie finally spoke, her words were half muffled by her pillow.

"I'm not going to help you disappear, Alice. I'm not going to lie for you if you're trying to do what Annie did."

"That's not what I'm doing," I said.

"Then why can't you tell me?"

Why couldn't I? My sister was in the hospital. There was nothing shameful about that fact on its own. It was all the other parts I didn't want to tell her. Annie might die, and I hadn't even told my parents where she was. I couldn't decide whether that said more about them or me.

I took a deep breath and said, "If you need to reach me, and I mean if you *really* need to reach me, I'll be at the County Hospital."

"What are you doing there?"

"I can't tell you."

Cassie looked at the clock on her bedside table. "You should probably go. I've got chores."

"Are you going to help me?" I asked.

I'd forgotten that Cassie had a habit of chewing on the inside of her cheek when she was upset about something.

"One day," Cassie said. "If you're not home by this time tomorrow, I'll tell your mom."

Ordinarily, I would have made a crack about tattling, but

Cassie was clearly doing a number on herself with her molars. I was afraid she'd draw blood. I thanked her instead, but she didn't say, "You're welcome."

"Don't make me sorry I helped you, Alice."

I went downstairs, got my shoes, and showed myself out.

CHAPTER 8

When I went back to the hospital, the first thing I did was to beg a pan, a sponge, and soap from the nurse's station. Like most county hospitals, this one was overcrowded and understaffed, and while Annie's condition meant that she at least got her own room, the nurses hadn't been so vigilant about less life-threatening things like grooming. As gently as I could, I gave Annie a bath, washed her face, and brushed her hair.

For the first time since I'd come here, I tried to think of Annie as my sister. Not just the idea of a sister, not just the questions she raised and the dark, vengeful thoughts in my head as I plotted against the people who'd hurt her. But my sister. My sister who knew me, understood me, and loved me like nobody else ever had. I couldn't make her wake up, couldn't find the people who'd done this to her and make them pay, but at least I could do this for her.

Once it was done, I settled in the chair next to her bed for the night. She looked so helpless and fragile lying there, so different from all the ways I remembered her. She didn't look like the girl who worked ciphers on Sunday nights or the girl who sang at cocktail parties or even the girl in the school picture that I'd shown to Wanda.

Picture.

The word knocked something loose in my memory, and I reached for my purse, pulling out the envelope of photographs I'd taken from my father's safe. I hadn't recognized the woman in the first shot, but it wasn't the only glossy print in the envelope. From a different angle, in different clothes, maybe she'd look familiar to me, or maybe there'd be a name written on the back. Or if she'd really been in an Insignia Pictures movie, maybe one of the nurses would recognize her.

I slid the first photograph out of the envelope and studied it more carefully, looking for any clues that might reveal who the woman was. She wore a black bathing suit and satin gloves that reached her elbows. One hand rested on her hip, the other held an apple. Her lips were pursed into a neat little bow of a smile, and she had dark, wavy hair and porcelain skin like Snow White. But when I looked closely at her face, I could tell she wasn't the type to attract singing woodland creatures or charming princes. There was a hard set to her jaw and a defiant yet weary look in her eyes that seemed to say, "Let's just get this over with."

I put the photograph down at the foot of Annie's bed. When I pulled out the next one, though, it wasn't the woman who looked like Snow White. It was a different actress, one I recognized even though I'd never seen a single movie she was in. She was famous for different reasons.

A few years before, Camille Grabo was front-page news after the police caught her snorting cocaine with a married actor in her Hollywood Hills bungalow. Both she and the actor went to jail, but he'd been famous and she hadn't been. He'd made a lot of money for the studio and she hadn't. That didn't stop anyone from splashing her pretty face all over the newspapers, pictures of her cleaning her cell, standing behind bars looking remorseful, or curled up on her prison cot after a bout of food poisoning. After they served their sentences, the actor went right back to work and made more money than ever, but no studio would touch Camille Grabo with a ten-foot pole. Rumors about her filled the pages of the sleazier movie magazines that Cassie read—that Camille Grabo was addicted to heroin and running around with mobsters, or smashing up cars and trying for a comeback as a nightclub singer. That was two years ago, and since then, not a peep, not a headline. It was as if Camille Grabo had disappeared completely. Not Hollywood's most original cautionary tale, but there was certainly nothing halfway about it. I'd give her that.

I wasn't sure what these women had to do with each other, what their pictures were doing in an envelope in my father's office. When I saw the next one, I wasn't sure I wanted to know.

As I pulled it out of the envelope, a wave of nausea passed through my body. How old was the girl in this picture? I wondered. Thirteen? Fourteen? She had been made up to look like Jean Harlow, reclining on a chaise longue in a platinum-blond wig and frilly underwear, but all the makeup in the world couldn't hide the features she hadn't grown into yet, the smile that was a little too eager to please. Worst of all, her eyes looked glassy and unfocused, and I wondered if she'd been drunk or drugged when the photograph was taken.

What if the pictures aren't his? I thought. What if he's holding on to them for someone at the studio?

It didn't help. This girl was younger than me, and her picture was in my father's safe. He hadn't turned it over to the police or ripped it into a hundred pieces. He'd kept it.

I couldn't stand to look at it any longer—I couldn't stand to touch it. But even after I'd stuffed it back in the envelope, I couldn't get the image of the girl out of my head. It made me sick, knowing that a picture like that was lodged in my head, and that I'd have to carry it around with me.

And then there was the girl. I wondered where she was now, if someone was looking out for her, and then a chilling thought crossed my mind. It was bad enough that my father had her picture. What if he knew her? What if he'd stood by and let this happen to her?

I shuddered, and pulled the last photograph out of the envelope, half afraid to look.

In for a penny, in for a pound. What else are you capable of, you rotten-hearted, sorry excuse for a father?

When I saw it, I began to get some ideas.

Because the woman in the picture was Ruth.

CHAPTER 9

The photograph fell from my hands and drifted to the floor.

In place of the tasteful plum lipstick and plain gray shirt-waist, Ruth wore false eyelashes and black garters, but there was no denying she was the woman I'd met that afternoon.

The woman who'd tried to hand me over to Rex.

Rex, who was apparently on friendly terms with my father.

I curled up on the floor next to Annie's bed, gripping the sheets in my fists. I buried my face in them, shutting out the light and noise of the hospital until it was just me alone with the things I knew. Detail by detail, I forced myself through them.

My father had a picture of Ruth in his safe. Ruth knows Rex. Rex set Annie up at the Stratford Arms, but Annie found out Rex knew our father. She ran away, but it didn't matter. Someone tried to kill her. My father had the pictures. My father had the pictures.

The pieces didn't fit, and they didn't make sense.

Who took the pictures, then? Rex? My father? Was that what made Annie run away from home? Was it the reason why she got away from Rex?

I needed a decent night's sleep, a bath, a meal, someone I could trust, a new set of parents, and cab fare. But right at that moment, what I needed most were answers.

That was what finally got me up off the floor sometime around dawn. I let go of the bedclothes, picked up the picture of Ruth, and laid it at the foot of the bed with the others. They weren't pleasant pictures to look at, even for a short time, though I doubted that I was their intended audience. No one who was looking even a little bit closely would have mistaken any of them for professional jobs, much less publicity photos. The costumes and poses were lazy, the lighting was bad, the sets and backgrounds nonexistent. My brain worked to piece together what these people had to do with one another, what their pictures were doing in my father's safe: the woman who looked like Snow White, Camille Grabo, Ruth, and the girl.

Then I noticed something sloppy in the background of Ruth's picture, something any photographer with half a brain would have tried to hide, and suddenly, it didn't matter that I was supposed to be here when Jerry arrived, or that he'd be here at any moment.

I knew exactly where I had to go next.

The receptionist at Fleming's Fine Family Photography told me that Milton Fleming was not in. However, Milton Fleming made an annual appearance at the high schools near Hollywood, hawking his unique photo packages—"perfect for yearbook pictures or head shots"—and while his pitch failed to invigorate my school spirit, his voice, raspy and harsh from a lifetime of cigarette smoking, certainly left an impression. Not even the wad of phlegm lodged in his throat could keep that voice from penetrating the glass door of the back office.

I looked over the receptionist's shoulder, glared in the direction of the door, then back at her.

"He's not here?"

"No, dear, I'm sorry." She gave me a thin smile. "Perhaps I could take a message for him?"

"Yes, please," I said, smiling back at her.

"And what would that message be, dear?"

I cleared my throat and delivered my message loudly enough that it would require no intermediary to reach Mr. Fleming.

"I WOULD LIKE TO DISCUSS A SITUATION INVOLVING PHOTOGRAPHS OF A PORNOGRAPHIC NATURE TAKEN IN THIS STUDIO."

The customers browsing in the showroom froze and turned to stare at me. One woman grabbed her child by the elbow and dragged him out of the shop. The bell hanging above the door trilled on their way out.

"PERHAPS YOU'D LIKE TO SEE SOME OF THEM." I started to reach into my purse, and the receptionist's hands flew to her face.

Before she could speak, though, the office door swung open and Mr. Milton Fleming appeared, in the flesh.

"What the hell is going on out here?" he wheezed.

I nodded politely and extended my hand. "Mr. Fleming. If you have a moment, I'd like a word in your office."

"And who the hell are you?"

"A concerned party."

He snorted. "Concerned party, my foot. Who put you up to

this?" He stepped forward and stuck a finger in my face. I held my ground and pulled the picture of the underage girl in the pinup lingerie out of my purse.

"Who put *her* up to this?" I said, holding it up to make sure he got a good look at it.

The few remaining customers did not even attempt to conceal their eavesdropping.

"I've never seen that girl before in my life, and I don't know what you're talking about. Now, get the hell out of my shop before I call the cops."

Then I took out the picture of Ruth.

"I've never seen her, either," said Milton Fleming.

"Look behind her," I said. "What do you see there? How do you explain that?"

Poring over the photographs in the hospital room, I'd been focused on the girls, looking for the clues in their faces and body language. But that's not where the clues were. The photographs were poorly lit and sloppily composed—the photographers had barely bothered to conceal where they were taken. In Ruth's photograph, they hadn't bothered at all. The stencil on the door was nearly washed out by the spotlight that shone up from below, bathing her face in a sickly light, but I could still make out the letters, reversed in the frosted glass:

FLEMING'S FINE FAMILY PHOTOGRAPHY

It took a moment for Mr. Fleming to see what I was pointing at, caught up as he was in the sight of a winking and scarcely clad Ruth. He gaped for a moment before suddenly remembering that he was a respectable citizen and family man looking at dirty pictures in the presence of a minor. The moment his eyes lit on the stenciled letters, I saw his lips begin to form a protest that died in his throat. All that came out was a long, high-pitched wheeze.

"Girly, I don't know anything about this." His panicked eyes met mine and begged me to believe him. I almost did.

He grabbed me by the shoulders and pulled me in close enough to whisper in my ear, "Please."

Please? I scowled at him.

"Please, not in front of these people, not now," he said. "I could lose my contract with the schools, and I swear I didn't have anything to do with this. There's a back door to the shop off the alley. Come back in an hour, and I promise, I'll give you anything you want."

"One hour," I whispered back. The people in the store froze in place, hanging on the sight of Mr. Fleming muttering in my ear. He nodded, gave my shoulders a shake, and gave me a shove that looked rougher than it really was.

"Get out of here now, girly," he bellowed, chasing me toward the door. "Next time you play a prank like that, I call the police."

We put on a good show for them. At the last minute, I spun around and stuck out my tongue at him, then slammed the door hard behind me.

Since I had an hour to kill in the neighborhood, I found a diner around the corner from Fleming's and helped myself to the first meal I'd had since yesterday's breakfast. I shouldn't have bothered. My toast was cold and the coffee tasted vaguely of dish soap, which at least served to reassure me that the cup had been washed. I was still hungry when I finished, but I needed to save my last few dimes for bus fare.

By the time I finished my meal, it had been close enough to an hour. As I walked down the alley behind Fleming's Fine Family

Photography, it occurred to me that Mr. Fleming might be planning an ambush. The alley was empty, no cars or people in sight. Just to be safe, I pressed my back flat against the wall and inched along until I was standing just outside of Fleming's. When I peeked through the glass door, I saw Mr. Fleming sitting in a leather swivel chair, smoking, and staring daggers at a boy who sat across from him. Mr. Fleming looked too angry to speak, and the boy looked too scared. It didn't look like an ambush in any case, so I knocked on the back door. Mr. Fleming let me in, locked the door behind us, and closed the blinds.

"Meet my son, Alex," he said, offering me a seat. "I believe he's the person you want to talk to."

Up close, I could see that Alex wasn't much older than me. He wore his fine blond hair like a kid's, slicked back with too much pomade, and his stark-white eyebrows made him look perpetually surprised. He had the pale, rheumy eyes of a kitten you didn't expect to live long—not the sort of person I imagined would do well in a criminal underworld. I took the picture of Ruth out of my bag and put it down on the table in front of him.

"Did you take this?" I asked.

He nodded.

"For someone named Rex?" I ventured.

Again, he nodded. He picked it up, and I noticed that his hands shook. "I don't take pictures for Rex anymore."

Mr. Fleming sighed and inhaled deeply on his cigarette. "That's what happens, Alex. You fool with those people, and you pay the piper. You pay and you pay and you keep paying."

With this last sentiment, Mr. Fleming picked up his ashtray and hurled it across the room. It hit the wall near Alex's head and shattered.

"Idiot child," he said more quietly, and went back to his smoking, flicking the ash into a coffee cup.

Alex's hands shook harder as he swallowed and gave me what I'm sure was the steeliest look he could manage at the moment. "What do you want?" he asked. "How much?"

"How much *more*, you mean," Mr. Fleming roared.

For a moment, I was tempted to play along, to continue being whoever it was that Alex and Mr. Fleming seemed to think I was. Because it was someone who terrified them, someone to whom they would have given up anything, information or cash. Maybe they deserved it, but I didn't think there was any joy to be had in terrorizing the school photographer and his son.

"I'm not after your money," I said.

"Then who sent you?" Mr. Fleming asked.

"Nobody sent me," I said, taking the picture back from Alex. "But I need information. I need to know where these came from."

Mr. Fleming looked skeptical, but Alex swallowed and nodded.

He explained that he'd been taking pictures of sunbathers and bodybuilders at Venice Beach for his portfolio when Rex approached him and asked if he'd like to make a little extra money. Rex asked if Alex had his own studio, and being eighteen and proud, Alex passed off his father's business card as his own. Soon they had an arrangement, and Rex started bringing girls by after the studio had closed.

Sometimes Rex would ask the girls if they wanted to take their clothes off, but he never made anyone do it. And even that work seemed mostly on the level, Alex said. It was artistic, tasteful even, and the girls all seemed to enjoy themselves anyway. But then, after about a year, Alex started to notice things that troubled him. Rex started to bring in different girls, and even Alex knew that these girls would never get a screen test. Emaciated girls with dark circles under their eyes and bad wigs and too much makeup. Girls who posed wearing elbow-length gloves to hide the track marks on their arms. Girls who left their children sleeping in the backseat of Rex's car while Alex took their pictures.

"Was it just you, Rex, and the girls?"

"Most of the time. That lady came a few times," Alex said, pointing at Ruth's picture. "She helped out with the makeup and wardrobe. And he had a partner who used to come in the beginning, but by the end, he wasn't coming around anymore. Older guy with a mustache, wore nice suits. He said he was with one of the studios, and chatted up the girls. They all liked him a lot."

Women did like my father a lot. At parties, my mother's friends always swarmed him. He was charming, never said a word about himself, and made them feel like the most beautiful, interesting people in the room. Not that I was certain Alex was talking about my father, but the odds seemed decent.

"Was there ever a girl named Annie here?" I didn't want to know, but I asked anyway.

"I don't know," Alex said. "It doesn't sound familiar, but most of them didn't use their real names."

"When did you stop taking pictures for Rex?" I asked.

"About a month ago."

"And he just let you walk away?"

Mr. Fleming snorted. "Not by a long shot. We pay that piece of garbage twenty dollars a week now. We do that, he stays away, doesn't ruin us."

"So when I showed up in your showroom with those pictures…"

"All Rex's messengers are girls," Alex said. "At first. Then he sends the guys who put cigars out on your arm."

"Was that why you stopped taking the pictures?" I asked. "Because you were scared?"

"No, it wasn't that." Alex's voice was barely above a whisper. "Like I said, some of the girls that Rex started to bring in were in real bad shape. And at first, I figure it's none of my business. I mean, they're all adults and can do what they like, right?"

"But then something happened," I said, trying to help him along with this story he clearly didn't relish telling.

He nodded, his face suddenly stricken. "It was when they brought in that young girl."

I took out the picture of the underage Jean Harlow look-alike and put it down in front of Alex. "You mean her?"

He reached out and took me by the wrist. "I didn't take that one—you have to believe me."

I recoiled from his touch. "If you didn't, who did?"

"Rex shows up with the girl, and she's out of it, like she was drunk or drugged or something. And Rex is barking orders at her, telling her to do what he says or else. I tell Rex I'm calling the police. He says, I do that, and he'll make sure me and my dad take the fall for it. Says he knows the right cops and nothing will ever stick to him."

Alex's face turned red and blotchy as he fought to keep from sobbing.

"I should have called them anyway. I should have at least taken that girl away from them and gotten her to a hospital or something. But I was scared. In the end, I told Rex I wouldn't do it, that we were done, for him to get out."

"So that's how it ended?" I asked, knowing full well it wasn't. Rex didn't seem like a man accustomed to being told no. "He just took the girl and left?"

"No," said Alex. "I didn't throw them out. I tried, but Rex let me have it pretty good. While I was down, he dragged me into the showroom and locked me there. He took the pictures himself, and then he left. Took my camera with him, too."

"Too bad," I said, not very convincingly.

"Lay off," he said. "I don't have to tell you any of this. And I wouldn't, except that little girl is on my conscience."

"What was her name?"

"I'm not sure," he said. "Like I said, nobody around here uses real names anyway."

Alex kept talking, making excuses for the role he'd played, trying to confess this girl off his conscience. Some parts I believed, others I didn't. The longer he went on, the more it became the version of the story that Alex had decided was the truth, just to keep from hating himself.

By that point, I wasn't listening anymore. I was thinking about the girl in the picture. I wished I could find her and take her someplace safe, someplace where none of them could hurt her anymore.

"I'm sorry, I have to go," I said, cutting Alex off midsentence. I stood up and put the pictures back in my purse.

Mr. Fleming walked me to the back door. Holding it open for me, he said, "I'm sorry."

"You didn't do it."

"I'm sorry I raised a son who would do such a thing. I'm sorry you had to come here. I'm sorry you had to see the things you saw."

I wasn't angry with Mr. Fleming, yet I couldn't bring myself to meet his eyes as I stepped out into the alley.

"Yeah, me too," I whispered.

CHAPTER 10

It was afternoon by the time I made it back to the hospital, and Jerry was waiting for me. Judging by the dark look he gave me, he'd been waiting for some time.

"Should I be impressed that you hung around here long enough to brush her hair before sneaking out?" he snapped.

"I'm sorry I'm late, Jerry," I said. "But—"

Jerry raised a hand and cut me off before I could cook up a lie. He spoke softly, slowly considering each word he uttered. "I don't even want to know where you've been this time." He rubbed his temples and winced, then looked back up at me, dark eyes blazing. "First you stage a break-in at your own house. Then you wander over to the Stratford Arms and introduce yourself to Rex and Ruth."

My jaw dropped. "Were you *following* me?"

Jerry ignored my question. "You are keeping me from my

work, and you are putting yourself and your sister in danger. I know you want answers, kid, but what you are doing now is a distraction, and I don't have time for it."

I bristled. "Why didn't you just tell me what you knew from the start?"

Jerry rolled his eyes and enumerated his reasons on his fingers. "Because I have a job to do. Because you're a child. And because, for some reason, I thought that after four years apart, you might actually want to be here with your sister, not out playing detective."

"I just want to find out who did this to her."

"And I might know that by now, if I hadn't been following you all over the city making sure you didn't get killed," Jerry said, giving me a disgusted look.

Annie had been gone almost four years, and I'd never done a thing. I used to think it was because I didn't know what to do, or how to help, or even where to start looking. But as I sat by her bed that first night in the hospital, all I could think of was how none of that mattered. I should have tried. It was a bad feeling, but hearing Jerry's words, I suddenly felt a thousand times worse. Annie was half dead, her body broken. Someone had to keep her safe—someone needed to be here when she woke up, or when she didn't. I was the only one who could do those things for Annie, and I hadn't been doing them.

It was easier to look at it from a distance, to pretend it was a case from one of my detective stories. I wanted to believe I could look for clues, find the patterns, piece them together, and save the day. Even if I could, it wouldn't change things. It wouldn't bring her back, or fix our miserable family, or make up for the years I'd spent without her, but that was beside the point. I wasn't a detective. Jerry was. He was the only other person trying to find out what had happened to Annie, the only other person who seemed to care about her, and all I'd done so far was get in his way.

Maybe it was the soapy coffee I'd had a few hours before, or maybe it was the guilt. I didn't have time to pinpoint the exact cause of the queasy knot in my stomach before I was doubled over the wastebasket heaving.

Jerry cleared his throat, got up, and filled a cup of water from the tap. He handed me a handkerchief and patted me on the shoulder, offering comfort like he had seen it in a movie once but never actually tried it before himself.

"Did I ruin everything?" I asked, wiping my mouth with the handkerchief.

"You didn't ruin everything," Jerry said. "The reason nobody's found Annie is that nobody's looking for her. If you'd said anything they could use, they'd be here right now."

"What are you going to do next?" I asked.

"What I'm going to do next is keep my word," Jerry said, cracking his knuckles and stretching his legs. "On the phone I said I'd tell you everything, and I intend to. Besides, you did manage to get away from Rex. I suppose you deserve a little credit."

"Like I said before, your sister and I worked together, in a manner of speaking. Annie knew all the girls who came through the Stratford Arms. She kept tabs on a bunch of other places like it, too. She knew who was new in town, who was having a rough time, and who worked for Rex and men like him. She helped them all when she could. She'd cover a girl's rent, or give her a place to stay for a week or so if she ran into trouble. Once she even paid for a girl's bus ticket back to Fort Wayne.

"I get a lot of missing-persons cases, a lot of parents from small towns whose daughters run away to the city. Sometimes when I'd hit a wall on a case like that, I'd give Annie a call, and more than half the time she knew exactly where to find the missing girl, even if she'd changed her name, lied about her age, or dyed her hair. What's more, she knew when not to help. There was this one client I had a while back, a salesman from Fresno, who seemed like a real creep. Nothing in particular—I just had a bad feeling about him. I showed Annie the picture of the girl he said was his daughter, and from the look on her face I knew she knew exactly where this girl was, but she wouldn't say a word. And I didn't push her on it, either. She had a good gut instinct for things like that.

"I always paid her for the information. She said she didn't need it, but I worried about her. Didn't know how she was taking care of herself, though she always seemed to have a roof over her head. Never stayed in the same place for long, though. Every couple of months, she'd pick up everything and move to another furnished room in another part of town.

"Then a few days ago, Annie calls *me*, asks for *my* help. She says that one of her girlfriends had gone out the night before and hadn't come back. And that was only the beginning.

"I do a little digging around and find out that Annie's friend was last seen at a bar called Marty's, where she was picked up in a car along with two other girls and taken to a private party hosted by Conrad Donahue."

"*The* Conrad Donahue?" I asked, leaning forward so far I nearly fell out of my chair. I wasn't one to swoon over movie stars, but for Conrad Donahue, I made an exception. He had thick, dark hair, a finely chiseled jaw, and eyebrows that might have seemed unruly, if not for the way they framed his moody, haunted blue eyes.

"I'd wipe off that dreamy look if I was you. Donahue is nobody you'd want in your autograph book."

"What did he do?"

"There were three of them at the party—the actress Camille Grabo, a dancer named Irma Martin, and another girl, a runaway, probably a little younger than you."

Conrad Donahue was the biggest star Insignia Pictures had, and I doubted it was a coincidence that Camille Grabo had turned up in my father's safe and Conrad's party.

"At some point that night, Irma and the younger girl got into a car with Mr. Donahue, and that's the last anybody saw of them," Jerry said.

I swallowed hard. "And my father's involved in that, too?"

"You know how your father got where he is? He used to be a talent scout. His job was tracking down pretty girls, taking their pictures, and trying to make them stars. He had some luck at it, too. You know Delia Montrose? The one who played the nurse who falls in love with the patient at the TB hospital? She was one of your father's finds.

"After he marries your mother, though, he wants more steady work, so he goes into the publicity department at Insignia Pictures. But everybody still knows him as a man who can round up a dozen pretty girls to sing a song, mingle, dance, and generally liven up a party on a moment's notice. Ask any one of these big studio guys if they'd rather go to a party full of aspiring actresses and dancers or one with all the big names, and he'll pick the girls who aren't famous every time. Less trouble and more fun. And that's what your father's good at, so good that soon some of his higher-ups at the studio get wind of it, some of the actors, too, and start asking him to put together private parties for them.

"Your father likes it because he's getting all kinds of face time with the really important people, and he tells himself, well, he's helping the girls, too. They make a few bucks, dance a little, have a few drinks, and on top of that, they get to spend the evening letting famous actors and directors flirt with them. Good, harmless fun, and one or two of them even get a walk-on role out of the deal.

"Some of the men can be a little bit coarse, a little rough, but most of them just like a night out with pretty women who aren't their wives.

"But your father isn't good at saying no, especially not to these people, and word gets around. The parties get wilder, things have to be hushed up, girls have to be paid off. Some won't go to the parties anymore, and a few won't even return your father's phone calls. Then Conrad Donahue comes along. And I'm sure you think he's the most handsome man alive. Everyone does, himself included. But he is not exactly known for playing nicely with others. Especially not women.

"Your father makes arrangements for some girls to show up at a party. Three go in, one comes out. So if he seems a little on edge lately, that's why."

"But what does Annie have to do with it?" I asked, stretching my legs, which had begun to go numb during Jerry's story. "She wasn't even there."

"An operation like this depends on the girls being disposable. Girls nobody cares about. They get hurt, they disappear, and nobody asks many questions about what happened to them. Conrad thought Irma was one of those girls. But Irma and Annie have been friends for years. They look out for each other. They take care of each other. If Conrad did something to Irma, there's no way Annie would let him get away with it."

"Do you think she's dead?" I asked.

"Irma's dead, I'm sure of that. I'm sure she died that night, and I'm just as sure that Conrad killed her, and that no one will ever find her body unless Conrad decides he wants it found."

I thought about the photographs from my father's safe. Two of the women I recognized, but I'd never seen the other girls. Now I was almost certain that the girls in the pictures were Annie's friend Irma Martin and the runaway who'd been at the party with her. The woman in the picture holding the apple, the one who'd reminded me of an exhausted, angry Snow White. She was my sister's friend. Or at least what passed for a friend.

"What about the other girl?" I asked. Even with the wig and makeup, I could still picture her face exactly. "What happened to her?"

Jerry looked over his shoulder, then leaned in so close I could feel his breath in my ear.

"Alice, she's alive," he whispered. "She saw everything, and she's still out there somewhere. Annie was hiding her away somewhere no one could hurt her."

"Where is she now?"

"That's just it. I haven't the faintest idea. I don't know what she looks like; I don't even know her name. I've watched Annie help a lot of girls, but she's never acted like that before."

"Like what?" I asked.

"Like protecting that girl was her own personal mission," Jerry said. "I thought she was being paranoid, but she was right to be. The night Annie was attacked—that was the appointment she didn't show up for. She was supposed to bring the girl to me, and then the three of us were going to go to the police together. But something went bad. Someone else found out what Annie was up to."

"My father?"

"Whatever bad blood was between them, I have a hard time imagining that he'd have his own daughter killed. But if this comes out, there's no way it doesn't touch him. Him and all the people he's supposed to be making look good."

"So what do we do now?"

"We need to find the girl, and fast. As long as she was with Annie, nobody—not Rex or your father or Conrad Donahue—could have found her in a hundred years. But with Annie out of the picture, she's just a scared kid. She doesn't know where to go or who to trust. They'll find her in no time."

"Well, you haven't found her yet. Maybe Annie taught her a thing or two."

"Maybe."

Every Conrad Donahue movie made buckets of money, and I knew firsthand how the studio people fell over themselves keeping him happy. My father wasn't an isolated case. People generally liked making themselves indispensible to famous people. And if that familiar, million-dollar face showed up at your doorstep and asked, "Have you seen this girl?" how could you resist telling him what you knew? It was a testament to Annie's craftiness and knowledge of the city's hard-to-find nooks and crannies that the girl had stayed hidden this long, and I was proud of her for it.

I thought over what Jerry had told me, then asked, "Do you know where Annie was living?"

Jerry shook his head. "She would never have hidden her there."

"That's not what I mean," I said. "What if there's something else there?"

"I've been through everything with a fine-tooth comb already."

"That's just it," I said. "Annie keeps anything important in code. She always has. Or at least she used to. It could be something sitting out in plain sight."

Jerry slapped his newspaper down on his knee so hard that I jumped.

"Don't you get it, Alice? This is not some rinky-dink decoder ring and magnifying glass Kid Sherlock operation. This is no fantasy land, and there are no secret codes leading to runaway girls."

I leaned forward in my chair and narrowed my eyes at Jerry.

"How do you think I found the Stratford Arms in the first place? I know Annie better than anybody, and if there's anything in that apartment that will help find this girl, I'll find it."

Jerry took me by the shoulders and pushed me back in the chair, as though he was correcting my posture.

"You *knew* your sister better than anybody. Get it? Past tense, Alice. I bet you could rummage through every scrap of paper in that apartment and not find a thing you recognized as your sister."

"I can help," I said, wishing I sounded more like I believed it was true.

Jerry took his hands off my shoulders, sat back, and sighed. "Annie told me you were a good kid, that you had a nice, normal life. She was happy for you. Do you think Annie would want you mixed up in any of this?"

I pointed to the comatose body on the bed.

"What if she doesn't know *me* anymore, either?" I asked.

The Annie I knew as a child was just a memory, warped at the edges and faded to dusty golds and blues. The Annie in the bed was a ghost, hollowed out inside with dark pits for eyes. But the Annie who rescued girls and navigated the Hollywood underworld was somewhere in between. The girl who worked with Jerry and taught him secret codes was someone I could try to understand, and maybe someone I could help.

"She wanted to know you," Jerry said.

"What do you mean?" I asked.

Jerry chuckled. I noticed he had a habit of laughing at things he didn't actually find funny.

"It was you, Alice. That's how I met her. She hired me to check up on you, maybe a year or so ago. She wanted to make sure you were doing okay, that you seemed happy."

"You followed me?"

"I didn't peep through your window or anything. I just told her that you went to school, caught a movie now and again. You should know. It's your life."

The way he said it, it didn't sound like much to write home about.

"The funny thing is, I could have been anyone. She picked my name at random out of the phone book. I could have been out sick with the flu that day. Her finger could have landed somewhere else on the page. But it didn't. And now here we are."

"Are you sorry?"

"That's the other funny thing," he said. "I'm not."

It was a strange thing to say, yet somehow I knew what he meant.

"Annie's special."

Jerry nodded. "She is."

We sat there by Annie's bed, neither one of us saying a word. After a long moment, Jerry cleared his throat and met my eyes.

"I'm sorry I said you didn't know your sister anymore," he said. "It wasn't very nice, and it's not true."

"It's okay," I said, and I meant it. I was halfway to believing it myself.

"People change, but the thing is, they don't. Not all the way through."

He looked at her for a moment more, then stood up, put on his hat, and went to the door. I thought he was about to leave without saying good-bye, but then he froze in the doorway and turned around to face me, a strange expression on his face.

"Tell me again how you wound up at the Stratford Arms," he said.

I explained breaking into my father's office, finding the post-card, and how it had led me to Ruth's bungalow.

When I'd finished, he let out a sigh, then motioned for me to follow him.

"Come on," he said. "I'll pull the car around."

I cocked my head to the side, not sure I'd heard him correctly.

"You want me to come with you?"

He nodded, looking like he was already thinking better of it.

"There might be something I could use your help with after all, Alice."

CHAPTER 11

Jerry's car was a two-seater Plymouth, the kind traveling sales-men favored because it had a big trunk for hauling vacuum cleaners and sets of encyclopedias. In any case, it was a good car for people who traveled alone and carried a lot of baggage with them.

"Get in," he said.

We crossed the river, and downtown Los Angeles rose up from the horizon like some mountain kingdom blanketed in clouds and mist. As we got closer, it wasn't half so magical. The buildings that peeked through the smog were squat and derelict with fire escapes bolted on the front, and ads for chewing tobacco painted on the sides. When we turned onto Main Street, the first thing I saw was a man in a stained undershirt holding up his pants with one hand and making violent gestures with the other. On the opposite cor-ner, I spotted the target of his abuse, a white-haired man who was trying to sweep the sidewalk in front of a small grocery. He looked so frail and hunched that it would have been a long job, even if the gutters had not been overflowing with cigarette butts, bottles, and other, much worse things.

Jerry parked the Plymouth in front of the store and nodded to him.

"Hi, Otto." He pointed to the man in the stained undershirt, now reeling across the street with malevolent but unsteady purpose. "This guy giving you a hard time?"

Otto shrugged. "He knows I don't sell bottles on credit. Never keeps him from asking, though."

"Somebody should tell him to ask nicer," Jerry said.

We positioned ourselves on either side of the old man and stared down the man in the stained undershirt. He sized us up and decided we didn't look like much of a threat.

"Sell me a drink, or I'll break your face."

Jerry put a nickel in the drunk's hand and folded his fingers around it. "Get yourself a cup of coffee, fella. Later, if you still feel like it, you can come back and break this old man's face."

His voice was gentler than I'd ever heard it before, but there was a coil of steel running through it.

The man started to make a nasty remark, thought better of it, lurched forward a step or two, regained his balance, and then stumbled off down the street.

Otto shrugged his thanks. "No need for you to get involved. I had him."

Jerry winked at him. "I don't doubt it."

Otto grunted, and went back to his sweeping. "You're here to see her, I suppose."

Jerry nodded. "You seen her lately?"

Was it my imagination, or did Otto's face seem to droop as he shook his head?

"Not for ages. If you see her, you tell her Otto is trying not to have hurt feelings that she doesn't pay rent in person anymore. You tell her not to be a stranger next time, okay?"

Suddenly, Otto noticed me and grinned broadly. "And who is your lovely assistant?"

"Nobody you ever saw," Jerry said, touching a finger to the side of his nose.

Otto returned the gesture as Jerry slipped a five-dollar bill into his palm. "Never saw her in my life."

We walked into the alley next to the shop, and Jerry led me up a rickety wooden flight of stairs that seemed to have been tacked onto the wall as an afterthought. The stairs creaked under our weight, and I held my breath as we ascended to the second, third, and fourth floors. Finally, Jerry opened the landing door and we stepped into a comparably sturdy hallway. Jerry stopped in front of the next-to-last doorway and opened it with a key he pulled out of his pocket.

"She'd kill me if she knew I let you see this place," he said.

It wasn't much of a place.

Most of the floor space was taken up by a twin cot piled high with blankets, and a fiberboard chest of drawers. There was a small, rust-stained sink crammed into a corner beneath a window that let in an anemic ray of sunlight. The cheeriest things about the room were the two coat hooks on the wall, as though years before some glass-half-full kind of tenant had installed them thinking that if he had no place for his guests to sit, well, at least he'd have somewhere for them to hang their coats.

Jerry sat down on the cot and gestured to the room in all its shabby glory.

"Go ahead," he said. "Have a look around. See if you can find anything I missed."

I pulled open the top dresser drawer and inhaled sharply. It was filled with blouses and sweaters and camisoles, all stacked in neatly folded piles. Annie's things. I reached out to touch them, carefully, as though they held some kind of magic, having been chosen by her, touched by her. A lump rose in my throat.

But then the breath I'd taken registered in my brain, and I knew something wasn't right. The clothes all smelled of mothballs. My eyes fell on a peach-colored sweater—Annie loathed the color and never would have worn it. As I burrowed through the clothes, I saw that the nicest pieces were stacked on top. Beneath them were cotton shifts in indiscriminate sizes and styles, stained slips, blouses with torn sleeves. Clothes that could have been bought cheaply and by the sackful for a quarter or two.

I got on my hands and knees and peered under the bed. There, I saw a hot plate with a frayed cord, and a stack of paperback novels with the same mothball smell as the clothing in the dressers. I paged through some of them, but found nothing except mildew in the bindings.

Jerry was right. There was nothing here, and certainly nothing that had ever belonged to my sister.

"Annie never lived here," I said.

"You're a quicker study than me," he said. "But this is the only address she ever gave me. Like I said, she moved around a lot. As far as I can figure, this was the address she used when she had to give one out. She and Otto had some kind of arrangement—she paid rent on time, and he didn't ask any questions, like why she never seemed to be here."

"So, there's just enough here to make someone who didn't know Annie very well think that they'd found her place."

"Bingo." Jerry nodded. "She even planted a couple of false leads here and there, just so a nosy snoop didn't have to walk away empty-handed. I spent an hour or so running down a fake locker combination she'd written inside one of those books before I realized what she was up to."

"Really?" My eyes lit up. "Can I see it?"

He handed me a particularly unloved and waterlogged-looking dime novel, and indicated the address and numbers penciled in the margin. It read:

FIGUEROA YWCA
86 64 50 77

"I had to get a lady friend of mine to test out the combination on every lock on every locker at the YWCA on Figueroa, and believe me, she wasn't happy about it."

For a moment, her handwriting had the same magical quality as the clothing in her dresser when I'd first opened it. But again, I knew immediately that something was off. Unlike my father, Annie would never in a million years write a combination where it could be found by any snoop. I studied the page for a moment longer, then erupted in a giggle that almost made Jerry swallow his toothpick.

"That's not a locker combination," I said, digging in my purse for a paper and pen. "It's a word."

If you ever want them to be read, ciphers need keys. The

problem with keys and code words is that they can be intercepted, guessed, and found out. People are rather predictable about things like that. They pick their dog's name, their birthday, their phone number. But if your key is too obscure, the person you want to decrypt it can't—unless you find another way to give them the key.

The beauty of Annie's key was that it hid in plain sight. Jerry saw a locker room at the Young Women's Christian Association on Figueroa Street. I saw everything I needed to crack the code.

The most basic, simple way of making a cipher that turns letters into numbers is to start with a Polybius square:

	1	2	3	4	5
1	A	B	C	D	E
2	F	G	H	I/J	K
3	L	M	N	O	P
4	Q	R	S	T	U
5	V	W	X	Y	Z

This creates a chart that gives every letter of the alphabet a two-digit number to stand in for it. A is 11; Z is 55. ALICE becomes 11 31 24 13 15.

The problem with a Polybius square by itself is that it's too easy to figure out. A is *always* 11; Z is *always* 55. You don't have to see many of these before you're fluent in them. So you have to make things a little bit more interesting.

The first part of the key was the FIGUEROA. Annie used that to throw off the predictable A-to-Z progression of the Polybius square.

	1	2	3	4	5
1	F	I	G	U	E
2	R	O	A	B	C
3	D	H	K	L	P
4	N	P	Q	S	T
5	V	W	X	Y	Z

Now A wasn't 11 anymore; F was.

But there was another step, too. I knew because there were numbers in Annie's cipher bigger than fifty-five.

YWCA was the key; YWCA, otherwise known as 54 52 25 23.

So, to decode the cipher, I needed to subtract the numbers in the key from the numbers Annie had written down:

$$\begin{array}{r} 86 \ \ 64 \ \ 50 \ \ 77 \\ -54 \ \ 52 \ \ 25 \ \ 23 \\ \hline 32 \ \ 12 \ \ 25 \ \ 54 \end{array}$$

Jerry looked over my shoulder while I worked, his eyebrows scrunched together.

"Now I see why she never showed me anything more complicated than the trick with the pencil," he said.

"This is a Nihilist cipher," I explained. "Russian revolutionaries used them to pass messages to one another. They're one of Annie's favorites."

Jerry rolled his eyes. "Well, whatever it is, don't let HUAC get wind of it, my little Bolshevik. You and your whole family will be blacklisted before you can say 'Joe Stalin.'"

Once I'd used the key, the only thing left to do was to plug the sum back into the Polybius square.

```
32  12  25  54
H    I   C   Y
```

Or at least that should have done it. Instead, when I'd finished, I was left with a row of letters that didn't mean anything. I wondered if I'd made a mistake somewhere along the way or if Annie had invented an extra layer of encryption.

Even though she'd never lived here, it was impossible not to see Annie's hand in the cleverly disguised front, to feel her presence here. It had been a long time since we played our games, and yet here she was playing them with me, still a cryptographer spy and crusading angel of the Allied forces. Still glamorous, elusive, and uncrackable. I loved her for it.

While I was puzzling over the code, Jerry shook his head and laughed in disbelief.

"What's so funny?" I asked.

"Only that you've been working on that thing for half an hour," he said.

"I have remarkable powers of concentration when I want to."

"Apparently," Jerry said. "Also, I'd like you to know that while I may not be able to crack a Nihilist cipher, I have not utterly wasted my time here."

"You were just sitting there," I said.

"I was *thinking*," Jerry said. "And I was wondering whether the people who got here before us allowed themselves to get quite so engrossed in your sister's secret codes. I suspect they may have lacked your powers of concentration."

I sat up straight and set down the book.

"Someone besides us has already been here?"

"They were careful to cover their tracks, but yes. This room's already been searched."

"How can you tell?" I scanned the room, admiring Jerry's eagle eyes. There was hardly a thing here to be out of place, and nothing was.

"Well, it might have been that piece of cigarette ash in the corner, or that the mirror above the sink is just slightly crooked."

I gasped. "Really?"

"No. Otto saw them sneak up here two nights ago." Jerry slapped his knee and gave a little bark of laughter. "And they neglected to slip him a fin or two when they did it."

"Who was it?"

Jerry's face turned serious now. "It was dark. He didn't get a good look at them, but it might have been Conrad Donahue's people. Or Rex's. Or your father's."

Jerry walked over to the window and peeked out at the street below. He had to stand on his tiptoes to do it.

"Aren't those all the same people?" I asked.

Jerry came away from the window and removed the toothpick he'd been gnawing on from the corner of his mouth.

"It's beginning to look that way," he said.

"Then what do we do next?"

Jerry sank down onto the cot again. It creaked under his weight.

"I don't know," he whispered.

"Beg your pardon?"

He cleared his throat. "I said I don't know. I've checked out all our old meeting spots, a few old apartments, friends she's mentioned, enemies too. Nothing's shaken loose, and I don't know where to look next."

He stared at his hands, folded uselessly in his lap, his face as bleak as the room itself. "I'm letting her down," he said.

"You're not letting her down."

I sat down next to him on the cot and put my hand on his shoulder.

"Was there anyone Annie really trusted?" I asked. "You said you talked to her friends. If anyone knows where that girl is, wouldn't it be one of them?"

Jerry let out another laugh that wasn't really a laugh.

"If they knew anything, they weren't saying a word about it to me."

I thought about that for a minute, then asked, "Do you think any of them would talk to me?"

"Why? You're a kid."

Jerry scratched at the stubble on his cheeks, and little bits of dead skin snowed down onto his pant leg.

"I'm Annie's sister," I said, wrinkling my nose in mild disgust. "And a girl. And not a detective."

"You might have a point there." A pink flush spread up Jerry's neck as he brushed the flakes onto the floor. "There is one friend of Annie's who might be worth talking to again. Maybe he'll have more to say to you than he did to me."

"He?" I asked.

DEAD TO ME

I tried to imagine Annie with friends. Friends she could go out with at any hour of the night, friends who didn't have to drop her off a block away from her parents' house. *Boy* friends.

"His name's Cyrus. Annie and her friends found him and more or less adopted him. He was like a little brother to them. Or a pet. I never could tell which."

"What's he like?"

"He wants to be an actor," Jerry said, his voice dripping with scorn, "though not a bad kid despite that. He works hard, that's for sure. Last I heard, he was holding down two jobs, and that's not counting the work he does for me."

"What kind of work?" I asked, hungry for details. This was Annie's inner circle, the people she'd chosen over my parents and me. I wanted to know what she saw in them.

"He works at a bar not too far from here. It's the kind of place where a person overhears interesting things from time to time."

"Marty's?"

"You catch on quick, kid," Jerry said. "He buses tables at the Musso and Frank Grill, too. It doesn't pay as much as the bartending job, but you get a lot of producers and directors and writers in a place like that. Not a bad place to be if you're an actor trying to get discovered. He's good with a camera, too. I've taken him along with me on stakeouts before."

Up until now, my sister's closest known associates included a thuggish pornographer and a dope peddler who posed for scandalous pictures. Compared with them, Cyrus sounded downright wholesome.

"I'd love to meet him," I said.

CHAPTER 12

When Jerry pulled his car into the parking lot behind Musso & Frank, the smell of steak filled the car before we even opened the doors. In the seat next to me, Jerry's stomach gurgled, and I realized I hadn't actually seen him eat since I met him. I wondered *how* he ate if he was spending all his time working a case where there wasn't a paying client, especially since he'd shelled out more than a week's worth of grocery money to Otto. If I'd had more than a dime in my purse, I would have gotten him a sandwich, but a dime wouldn't even get you a cup of coffee in that place. As for myself, I wasn't hungry. I'd been to Musso & Frank exactly once in my life and that had been enough.

Probably I was the only person in Los Angeles who felt that way, but it was haunted for me. I don't know why *that* place, *that* night stood out. It's not like it was the worst dinner I ever had with my family. Maybe it was because of how fast everything went downhill afterward. All I knew was, I looked at the place and a shudder went through me, and it was my twelfth birthday all over again.

When that day started, I'd thought it was going to be a good day. There'd been a wrapped package on my chair at the dining room table and a fresh-cut daisy in a vase next to my glass of milk. My mother kissed my cheek as I sat down at the table, and then said, "Open it."

It was a pair of black patent-leather shoes with low but unmistakable heels and a little strap that buttoned over the ankle.

"Just the thing for a young lady," she said.

I wore the shoes that night along with a dress that was more grown-up than the ones I usually wore. The skirt was longer and not so full, the sleeves not so puffed. Instead of white socks with lace at the cuffs, my mother let me borrow one of her treasured pairs of nylon stockings. During the war, you couldn't find them anywhere, and most women went without or drew fake seams in eyebrow pencil on the backs of their legs. Not my mother, though. She took such good care of the few pairs she had that people in our neighborhood gossiped that she must have been buying them on the black market.

Once I was dressed, my mother set my hair in curlers and pinned the waves into ornate-looking rolls that framed my face, and she finished the whole thing off with a spritz of her Shalimar perfume.

There was a knock at the door promptly at five thirty: Cassie dressed in her Sunday best—a salmon-colored sailor dress and white cotton gloves that made my mother suck in an appalled breath when she saw them. Still, she smiled broadly and said, "You girls look lovely."

My father drove us all to the restaurant, Cassie and me jostling along together in the backseat. Annie wasn't there. She had plans that afternoon with her friends, so she said, and had begged our parents to let her come to the restaurant late. At first I was upset, but with my elegant hair and new shoes, I found I didn't mind so much. For once, I was the pretty, doted-upon Gates sister.

Musso & Frank had paneled walls and soft leather booths and crisp-jacketed waiters. It wasn't glamorous, exactly, but it made me feel like I might be, sitting next to Cassie with cloth napkins unfolded on our laps and champagne flutes of seltzer water and maraschino cherries bubbling in our hands.

People my parents knew came over to our table to say hello. They were all writers, set designers, directors, and other unrecognizable but important people. Their smiles weren't the indulgent "cute kid" smiles I was used to. These smiles said "pretty girl" and "lovely daughter." Everyone was still charming and happy and on their first drink, and I felt the way a twelve-year-old girl is supposed to feel on her birthday.

But then it turned into any other day. Annie was late, and we didn't order any food because my parents were waiting for her. They drank too many cocktails on empty stomachs and got crabby with each other. Cassie and I got tired of looking glamorous and began trying to tie cherry stems with our tongues, which made my mother smack the back of my hand and hiss, "Stop that this instant." Then the waiter came to the table for the fifth time and asked if we were ready to order, and my father snapped at him, saying that when we were ready to order, he'd be the first to know about it.

All the magic was off the evening by then. Cassie's gloves were stained pink with cherries, and two wet circles darkened the armpits of her dress. I wasn't much better—I could smell my sweat stinking through the Shalimar. I'd picked out half the bobby pins in my hairdo and stacked them on the table next to my fork. My scalp had begun to ache from them, my feet felt pinched in the shoes, and I'd had too many glasses of seltzer water.

"May I be excused?" I asked, already sliding out of the booth.

They hadn't yet answered when I felt the back of my stockings catch on a splinter of wood, and a telltale rip sounded so loud that my father stopped yelling at the waiter and turned to see what it was.

My mother looked up from her martini, and the blood drained from her face as she registered exactly how unkempt and disappointing I looked, and she said, "Sit down this instant."

My father cleared his throat and said, "Vivian, leave the girl be. It's her birthday."

The waiter, who was still standing there, brightened and clapped his hands together. "Ah! Then let me bring a little something for the birthday girl. Compliments of the kitchen, of course."

"I told you," my father said, throwing his napkin onto the table and sloshing his Manhattan, "that we were not ready to order yet."

At the same time, my mother lifted her martini glass and said, "Another round of these, please."

"Are you sure, madam?" the waiter asked, shooting a pointed look at my father.

"She asked for a drink, now bring her a drink."

"May I *please* be excused?" I asked.

"Me too?" asked Cassie.

"I don't care what you do," my father said with a sigh.

It was another hour before my parents finally got tired of waiting and ordered Welsh rarebit for Cassie and me. It was a baby's meal—toast and cheese—and Cassie and I picked at it like babies while my father paid the check and stared at his watch without speaking until we cleaned our plates.

Annie never even showed up. She didn't come home until the next morning, raccoon-eyed and defiant. When I woke up to the sounds of our mother screaming at her in the hallway, I found a silver bracelet lying next to my head on the pillowcase. It wasn't what I wanted, and even then, I'd known there was a decent chance she'd shoplifted it from Woolworth's, but at least my sister hadn't forgotten about me.

As we got out of the car, the memory sat there like an undigested dinner roll wadded in my stomach.

"Are you okay, kid?" he asked.

"Fine," I said. I closed my eyes, took a deep breath, and followed Jerry to the parking attendant's stand.

"Is Cyrus working tonight?" he asked.

The parking attendant was a stern-looking man with slicked-back black hair and a scar on his upper lip. In Hollywood, you had to be nice to everyone just in case they were someone important, but the attendant seemed to know right away that we weren't the kind of people you had to be nice to.

"I'm afraid I couldn't say," he said, slouching against the stand.

Jerry reached into his wallet and handed the man a couple of singles.

"You can say."

That made the parking attendant stand up straight. "I'd have to check," he said, pocketing the money.

"Tell him it's important. It's about Annie."

"That his girl?"

"How about you just see if he's in and don't worry about that."

DEAD TO ME

The parking attendant glared as he went inside the restaurant, but a few minutes later, he reemerged and escorted us toward the kitchen, scooting us out of view of the paying customers.

"Five minutes," he said, holding the swinging door open for us. "No more."

The air in the kitchen was boggy and filled with the sounds of loud men in a hurry. All around, people yelled out orders, dodged one another, and darted back and forth bearing heavy trays of meat through the swinging kitchen doors.

Half hidden behind a rack of bowls and chafing dishes stood a boy who looked like he'd collapse under the weight of one of those trays. And yet, he held one piled high with plates and bones balanced on one shoulder. Even before he pulled us out of the kitchen traffic and into the only quiet corner of the kitchen, I knew it was Cyrus.

As I turned the name over in my head, it occurred to me that I'd decoded Annie's cipher perfectly:

H I C Y

It just didn't have anything to do with the missing girl. It wasn't a decoy to throw her enemies off track. It was a game, just like the ones she used to play with me to pass the time during blackouts. I could almost imagine Annie sitting on the floor of her Main Street apartment with this boy, teaching him how to make a Polybius square.

"You shouldn't be here," he said, by way of a greeting.

Jerry acted like he hadn't heard him. Instead he kicked me in the back of the heel until I stumbled half a step forward, and Cyrus really looked at me for the first time. Something about his gaze made me self-conscious about the film of grease and steam that was already settling on my face. I looked away and fiddled with the clasp of my necklace.

"You're the sister," he said, setting down his tray.

"Alice," Jerry said.

"I know what her name is."

He was too tall, too thin. His neck was too long. His ears stuck out a little bit. His nose was crooked like it had been broken once, and his chin was pointed. Taken in individual parts, his face was all wrong, but taken together, there was something about it that made you want to keep looking. He didn't look like an athlete or a brain or a member of the thespian society. If he went to my school, I couldn't imagine a single table in the cafeteria where he would have looked at home.

Which meant that he probably would have ended up sitting with me.

"Jerry, why'd you bring her here?" he asked.

"I thought you'd want to meet her."

Cyrus gave me a look, then sighed and shook his head. It was a look I recognized, having received some version of it from my mother at least once a week for the past four years. There was pity in it, a pinch of disappointment. *You're not her*, it said. *You're not Annie.*

"You think I don't know what you're doing? I already told you everything I know, Jerry."

"It's been two days, Cyrus. You sure you haven't heard anything since then? Anything at all?"

Cyrus looked over his shoulder, where a mustachioed man in chef's whites stood at a chopping block, fingering the blade of his knife and glaring at us.

"I've been working," he said, clutching the kitchen towel that was tucked into his apron ties. "Right now I'm just trying to stay out of sight, which is what you'd be doing if you were smart. This is bad business, Jerry. People are going to get hurt, and if Annie knew you'd roped Alice into this, she'd kill you."

"What about Irma's people?" Jerry asked. "Has anyone called them yet to let them know?"

Cyrus shook his head. "Millie would be the one to do that. Not that Irma really had any people. There might have been a sister in San Antonio—I'm not sure."

"Who's Millie?" I asked.

"It's complicated," Jerry said, trying to change the subject.

"It isn't. Millie's a friend," Cyrus said. "She and Irma live in the same building. Or at least they used to. They were tight, like me and Annie were."

He stood up a little straighter when he said it, like somebody was about to pin a medal on his shirtfront. I wasn't surprised that he felt that way about Annie, but there was one question that nagged at me.

"If you and Annie are so tight, why haven't you been to the hospital?" I asked.

"The hospital?"

Cyrus cocked his head to the side and squinted like he was trying to see me through a dense fog. Jerry swore under his breath.

"She's—she's still alive?" he whispered.

He turned to Jerry, his eyes searching the detective's face for a sign that it was true.

Jerry put up his hands and took a step back. "I was going to—"
Cyrus didn't let him finish.

"I don't care what you were going to do," he said.

His hands clenched into fists at his side, and for a moment, I thought he might take a swing at Jerry.

"Calm down, Cy."

"You didn't tell me," he said through gritted teeth.

Cyrus looked like a wire about to snap even though he hadn't touched Jerry, hadn't even raised his voice.

"The last time I saw you, I didn't know where she was—I swear," Jerry said.

Cyrus unclenched his fists as he considered Jerry's words.

"If I'd known, I would have told you, Cyrus," Jerry said.

He stepped forward now and placed a hand on the boy's arm. Cyrus's shoulders slumped, and he let out a long, weary breath.

"I just wish I'd found out sooner," he whispered.

"I'm sorry, kid," Jerry said. "She's in pretty bad shape. She hasn't woken up yet, but the important thing is, she's alive."

Cyrus turned to me, a sad half smile on his lips.

"So I guess that's why I haven't been to see her," he said. "I don't know anything I didn't know two days ago, and I'm not sure I want to know. Annie was the strongest person I ever met, and they got her anyway. If you think you and Jerry can do any better than she did, you're either very brave or you don't understand what you're up against."

I knew he was scared, and as I listened to him talk, I began to wonder if I'd been scared enough.

"What are you still doing in town, then?" I asked. "Why don't you just leave?"

From his station, the chef with the knife bellowed Cyrus's name while carving slabs of meat from a standing rib roast with great speed and violence. Cyrus nodded to him and carried the tray of dirty plates back to the industrial-steel sinks that lined the back walls of the kitchen. Once he'd unloaded this, he passed through the swinging kitchen doors and disappeared into the sea of diners. A few minutes later, he returned laden down with a teetering pile of dishes and highball glasses and joined us back in our corner of the kitchen.

Breathing heavily under the weight of the tray, he said, "I can't leave Millie here by herself. And besides, I need the money. I couldn't leave if I wanted to."

I saw then that Cyrus wasn't so much thin as underfed. I wouldn't have believed it was possible, working in a place where you were surrounded by steaks and lobster all day, but then, I guessed that probably wasn't what Cyrus got to eat.

"You have to go now. Both of you. I don't want to get fired."

We'd had our five minutes, and I didn't want to get Cyrus fired, either. I started for the door, but Jerry wasn't so easily dismissed.

"Where's the girl?"

Cyrus was already halfway to the sink when Jerry asked. The stack of dishes swayed dangerously before he caught them and eased them back into place. Slowly, he turned around, a weary, hounded look in his eyes.

"I told you I don't know," he said, shifting the heavy tray to his other shoulder. "I can't help you. I don't know anything. I didn't see anything. I don't know who hurt Annie. I don't know where the girl is, and I don't want to know. Do you want me to wind up like them?"

I could tell he wasn't telling the truth, not all of it. But then I wondered, why should he? Jerry had plenty of chances to tell Cyrus that my sister was still alive. He could have done it this morning.

He could have done it the night he'd sent me home from the hospital, but he hadn't.

On top of that, Cyrus was afraid. One of his friends was dead, one was in the hospital, and what was in it for him if he talked to us? As far as he was concerned, I was a spoiled rich girl and Jerry might as well be a cop. He wouldn't talk to us unless he was desperate.

"Besides, we both know the person you should be asking is Millie," Cyrus added.

Jerry made a face at the suggestion.

"I know," Cyrus added, "but that's not my problem. You know I'm right."

Jerry stood there for a moment, waiting for more, but Cyrus was done talking. Eventually, Jerry took the hint and started toward the kitchen door, but I hung back.

"I'm sorry," I said. "I didn't know Jerry hadn't told you. I didn't even know you existed."

"It's not your fault, Alice," Cyrus said.

He watched the door until it swung shut after Jerry, and we were alone. Then he grabbed me by the arms and leaned in close to me. I jerked back, startled by his touch and the urgent look in his eyes.

"Why are you doing this, Alice? I know you're smart. I know you think you can handle this, but you can't. You don't have to get yourself killed trying to prove how much you love her."

Anger flared up inside me. I didn't like the way this boy talked to me like he knew better than I did, or the protective tone in his voice. I didn't like the way he assumed things about me even though we'd only just met. I had nothing to prove, and this had nothing to do with love.

I pulled free from his grasp.

"You don't know anything about me," I said.

By the time Jerry and I left Musso & Frank, the parking attendant, the bartender, and the maître d' were all giving us dirty looks. We didn't linger in the parking lot to discuss what had just happened. No sense in being more memorable than we already were.

We drove east on Hollywood, then south. In the rearview mirror, I could see the HOLLYWOODLAND sign nestled in the hills. Big as it was, it was easy to forget about the sign sometimes. You could go weeks in the city—you could go weeks in *Hollywood*—and not see it once, and then suddenly, you turned a corner and there it was, neglected, ugly, and embarrassing. The H had fallen down the previous year, and no one had even bothered to put it back up. Missing panels dotted the remaining letters like knocked-out teeth.

"Where are we going?" I asked as Jerry turned onto a side street just south of Fountain Avenue.

He pulled the car over and pointed out a rooming house halfway up the block, a three-story stucco covered in flaking whitewash.

"Millie's place," he said. "Cyrus was right about one thing. If anyone knows something, it's her. She and Irma live right across the hall from each other. Or they used to."

"They were friends?" I asked.

"Best friends, and that's a rare thing between actresses. Especially the kind with careers that haven't quite worked out."

"Were they ever in anything I'd have seen?"

"Maybe. People thought Millie was the pretty one, but Irma was the one with the real talent," Jerry explained. "She started out in the burlesque houses and worked her way up. That girl danced alongside Cyd Charisse, Fred Astaire, and Judy Garland, and she held her own. It should have been the beginning of something for her."

"What happened?"

Jerry shrugged. "Oh, the usual. A bottle, a needle in the arm, money troubles, and a lot of bad boyfriends. She had a good head on her shoulders despite everything. She kept working, kept her problems as much a secret as she could, never wound up in a flophouse or a jail cell. In certain circles, she was still considered a working actress."

"In Conrad's, though..." I trailed off.

"Just a thing to be used up and thrown away," said Jerry, finishing the unpleasant thought for me. "His sense of things, not mine. Annie always had a very high opinion of Irma. So did I."

"Then what's your opinion of Millie?" I asked.

"Not so high. She can't tell the difference between good attention and bad attention," Jerry said, opening the car door. "Also, she happens to be Camille Grabo."

"You're kidding," I said. I guess she *had* been in a few things I'd seen before—the front page of the tabloids and the picture in my father's safe.

"Her real last name is Grabowski. She changed it when she hit the big time, or when she was at least headed that way."

"But you said Camille Grabo was at the party."

"A Hollywood party," Jerry said. "She was Camille Grabo to everyone in that room, and will be until the day she dies. She's a laughingstock to them."

"Then why did she go in the first place?" I asked.

Jerry shrugged. "Millie still loves a party, and I guarantee you, she didn't care what anyone in that room thought of her. Come on, let's walk."

Soon we were standing in front of the apartment house, and I saw that despite its shabbiness, it was a cheerfully landscaped little place. Lemon and pepper trees hugged the building walls, and a sloppy jacaranda shaded the front stoop, dropping lavender blossoms all over the sidewalk and lawn.

Jerry stopped beneath the tree and took off his hat, holding it to his chest. "So, are you very brave, or just a girl who doesn't understand what she's up against yet?"

I wasn't sure what he was getting at, but I didn't like the way he pulled Cyrus's words out of his hat like a magician's silk, like there was another question hidden behind them.

"What's the difference?" I asked, frowning at him.

He cleared his throat. "What I'm trying to say is, I can't go up there with you. You asked before if there was anybody who might talk to you a little more freely than to me. Well, if there's anyone who fits the bill, it's Millie."

"So, the not-having-a-high-opinion thing, that goes both ways?"

"She hates my guts," he said. "But I don't care about that. What I really want to do is take a look around Irma's apartment."

"Where do I come in?"

"Millie, for all of her faults, was rather devoted to Irma. I've poked my nose around here twice already, and both times she's caught me and told me to get the hell out. What I need you to do is go up there, knock on her door, see if you can get her talking. I'll be right here at the foot of the stairs. If I see you get in, I might have a chance."

"What am I supposed to ask her? What if she's being watched? What if she doesn't answer?" I asked.

"There's no way Millie would pass up an opportunity to put on one of her performances for you. Trust me, she'll answer."

Ducking under the bough of a lemon tree, I stepped into the arched stairwell. It was poorly lit and claustrophobic, but I took a deep breath, balled my hands into fists at my sides, and climbed. My heels clicked on the tiled stairs, too loudly for my liking, and I realized that Jerry had only answered the least important of my three questions.

The hallway I stepped into was almost as dim as the stairwell, but at least it was carpeted, silencing my approach. I knocked at the apartment door, three firm raps. There was no answer, so I knocked again and put my ear to the door. I heard the sound of running water, but couldn't decide whether it sounded like a faucet or a broken toilet. Otherwise, it was perfectly quiet in Millie's apartment.

If there was anyone who had a reason not to open her door to strangers, a reason to be deeply, truly afraid, it was Millie. She'd been at the party the night Irma was murdered. She must have seen something.

I wondered what Jerry had been thinking sending me up here alone. I'd agreed because he'd said it was okay, because he'd said he'd be standing at the foot of the stairs if anything went wrong. But how could he promise something like that? A trace of panic fluttered in my guts. He'd said "Trust me," and I had, and all he'd had to do was agree to let me tag along.

So deeply was I contemplating this that I didn't realize that the sound behind me was a doorknob turning.

DEAD TO ME

By the time I'd realized it, the door was already open. And by the time I began to run, the arm was already wrapped around my throat, and by the time I started to fight, I was already inside the dead girl's apartment.

CHAPTER 13

"Didn't your mother teach you not to lurk in corridors?"

Then she giggled. She actually giggled, as I stood there struggling to catch my breath and will my heart back to a regular tempo.

"Oh, don't be mad," she said, flashing a dazzling, dimpled smile at me. "I was just having a little bit of fun. Cy called the minute you left the restaurant. He said you might be coming over."

This was all Millie offered in the way of explanation or introduction or apology for scaring me half out of my wits. I was too preoccupied to be angry about it, though, because sure enough, Millie was Camille Grabo. Gone were the penciled-on eyebrows, tight sweaters, and platinum cotton candy hair that made up her signature look, but even if I hadn't known who she was, I would have known she was trying not to be recognized. Of course, she was overdoing it in typical movie star fashion. She'd dyed her hair black and cropped it into a severe bob, then tried to hide her face behind a pair of round dark glasses and a black hat with a veil attached to the front. It was like she'd forgotten the whole point of a disguise was *not* to call attention to yourself.

"You're Camille Grabo," I said stupidly, stammering a little bit. I'd been around lots of famous people before, but never a notorious one.

She pulled off the glasses and looked at me as though she didn't have the faintest idea what I was talking about. "Oh, darling, I get that all the time."

She could say whatever she liked, but she was Camille Grabo. I knew it, and she knew that I knew it. She gave me a cool, level gaze and a smile that didn't come anywhere close to reaching her eyes.

"In any case, please call me Millie."

We shook on it, and I realized that it didn't matter if I wasn't sure what to ask her. Millie wasn't the kind of person who needed any prompting to talk.

"You'll have to forgive me," she said. "I'm a little on edge these days. I haven't been sleeping much, and there's so much to do."

Without further explanation, she turned on her heel and walked out of the room. I trotted along after her toward the back of Irma's apartment. It was a pretty place, several rooms connected by arched doorways, hardwood floors that gleamed with a fresh, dark varnish. The furniture was old but good-quality stuff. But little things here and there seemed wrong. There was a shelf of records, but no record player. Strangely empty spots in the front room, gaps on the floor and walls where it seemed likely that there'd once been a lamp, an end table, a clock, a painting. I took in as much as I could without lagging behind.

In Irma's bedroom, I found more of the same. An empty

jewelry box, a picked-over wardrobe, and on the dresser a worn leather kit containing a strap, a syringe, and a spoon. I turned away from that bit of grimness, and something else caught my eye. Irma's bedside table was covered in framed photographs, dusted, immaculately arranged, cherished. Several were of movie sets, one of the columns of palm trees that extended for blocks up Highland Avenue. There was one of her and Millie in matching black bathing suits, wearing enormous headdresses made of fake fruit on their heads and laughing like goons. And there was one of her and Annie, glamorous and smiling in their sunglasses and red lipstick as they rode the merry-go-round at the Santa Monica Pier.

"I thought someone should go through her things and make sure there was nothing here that would look wrong, if you know what I mean." Millie ignored the drug paraphernalia on the dresser as she crossed the room and plucked the photograph of her and Irma off the table. "I was looking for that," she said, dropping it into the canvas bag she carried with her. She sat down at Irma's vanity and opened one of the drawers, pulling out a stack of letters. She handed them to me. "Go through these, won't you? Pull out anything that looks, you know, *wrong*."

"You mean anything from you," I said.

If Millie heard the contempt in my voice, she ignored it. "Now you're getting it."

I flipped through the stack of letters. Most were postmarked from San Antonio, but a few were local, a few had return addresses I recognized, and one bore a chilling inscription that made my eyes go wide: *Open If I Am Dead or Missing*.

In the whole pile, there were only a handful of notes from Millie.

"Here," I said, handing them to her. She took them, then went back to flipping through Irma's address book, tearing out whole chunks of pages as she went. She stuffed these into the bag with the photograph.

The rest of the letters I stacked to the side for myself. If Millie asked what I was doing, I planned to tell her I was only tidying up. But she was too busy rooting through Irma's makeup to notice.

"So, where's Jerry Shaffer?" she asked, testing out a half-used tube of lipstick she'd found in one drawer. "I'm surprised you didn't bring him along. Or vice versa. You can't possibly be old enough to drive."

"I'm old enough," I said, even though I didn't actually know how to drive.

Once she'd finished sifting through the vanity, Millie moved on to the nightstand, which seemed to contain nothing but pill bottles, all murky brown and green glass with tan paper labels and names like secobarbital and Nembutal. I'd seen similar ones in my mother's bedside table. Millie tossed these on the bed, too, but I noticed that she slipped one or two into her bag.

"He said it might be better if I came alone," I said. "And that you hated his guts."

She snorted. "I'm surprised he'd send you up here by yourself. Or maybe I'm not all that surprised. What is it they say about bullies? That they're really just cowards themselves?"

"You think Jerry's a bully?"

"A bully and a creep. Always following us around in that beat-up Plymouth. Every time I see it, I think he's probably got a body in the trunk."

That seemed a little melodramatic to me. "He knows you're in danger. Maybe he's watching because he doesn't want you to get hurt."

"Well, isn't that nice of him," Millie said with a sneer. "I've caught him more than once, hunched down in the front seat with his hat pulled down, watching us like some kind of pervert. And that was *before* I was in danger."

Up until today, I realized, everything I knew about Jerry had pretty much come from Jerry. What if he'd been lying to me all along? What if he wasn't my sister's friend and employer, but her stalker? That would explain why he knew so much about her. And why he seemed to know so many girls who were young enough to be his daughters. I felt nauseated by the thought.

"Were he and Annie friends?" I asked.

Millie sat down on the bed. She extended a finger and started to push the row of pill bottles across the mattress. They clinked together as she rolled them almost to the edge of the bed, then back toward her again.

"Jerry doesn't have friends. He has a cabinet full of broken dolls like your sister. And he acts like he wants to fix them, but the truth of it is, Alice, I think he likes them broken."

I felt a hitch in my breath, and reached for the sealed envelope, the one inscribed *Open If I Am Dead or Missing*. The paper was a luxurious cream-colored cardstock, the curious inscription in ink so glossy it still looked wet. I ran my fingers over the soft paper and wondered who had written it. I wondered what Jerry was looking for, why he wanted to get into this apartment so badly. He was supposed to be here right now, not me. If he were the one rummaging through Irma's vanity and bedside table, what would he take?

"I've decided I'm done with Los Angeles," Millie said, lifting up the mattress and peeking under the box spring. "I'm buying a ticket to Las Vegas and getting out of this place. No more flirting with directors twice your age for a part that has two lines. No more slugging it out against a hundred girls who all think they're the next Lana Turner. I'm sick of fighting for scraps."

Irma's sleigh bed was a heavy oaken thing that looked like it had come out of the last century, and Millie was trying to move it. Between each word of her rant, she gritted her teeth and gave the frame a shove until spots of red appeared on her cheeks beneath the veil. I went around to the other side of the bed to help her push.

"It doesn't matter how young and pretty you are, because everybody's young and pretty. It doesn't matter how much talent you have, because the job doesn't require any. And what's it all for? Nothing. I've been working my ass off in this business since I was sixteen, and I don't have a thing to show for it. It's a job only an idiot could want."

When we'd moved the bed about two feet, Millie got down on her hands and knees and ran her fingers over the floorboards. Finally, she found the one she was looking for and popped it loose. Her hands disappeared beneath the floor, then came up a moment later holding a lock box. She produced a key from around her neck, opened the box, and leafed through its contents, careful to hold the lid so I couldn't see what was inside.

"And besides, it's just getting too dangerous around here." She produced a thick wad of cash from the lock box and grinned. "Never mind Las Vegas. I'm going to Paris."

She slammed the box shut and put it back under Irma's bed.

"Help me move this," she said, and together, we tugged at the bed frame until the headboard was flush with the wall.

The only piece of furniture in the bedroom that remained untouched was the wardrobe. Millie flung it open and began to sort through the items that hung there. She was selective—a few dresses, a good wool coat, a pretty silk scarf. She tossed these things onto the bed and left the rest.

"Millie," I said. She half looked over her shoulder without stopping what she was doing. "Do you know anything about a girl Annie was protecting? She might have been there the night Irma was murdered."

Millie shook her head. "I never heard of any girl."

She didn't even bother trying to sound like she wasn't lying. It annoyed me, especially since I'd just helped her drag a hundred-year-old bed across the floor.

"But you know Rex, don't you?" I asked. When she didn't answer, I added, "I know you do. I saw the picture."

Millie spun around, and in two steps had crossed the room and pinned me against the wall with a sharp elbow. A cruel smile played across her lips, and when she spoke, it was scarcely louder than a whisper.

"Have you ever kissed a boy, Alice?"

When I didn't answer, stunned as I was, she dug her elbow into my collarbone.

"I *said*, have you ever kissed a boy?"

This time I nodded.

Flecks of spit hit my cheek as she spoke. "Did you kiss him or did he kiss you?"

There had been several boys, several kisses, but when Millie asked me, it seemed as though there had only been one, that the kisses and the boys all melted together, and I could no longer tell them apart.

"He kissed me," I said.

"Did you like it?"

DEAD TO ME

At a movie theater, behind the changing room at the country club pool, in basements at parties, but always in the dark, always in a corner, always secret.

"I don't know. I guess I didn't really mind."

"But that's not the same as liking it, now, is it?" There was that smile again, like a slice of bitter melon.

"No," I said.

"And did he try anything else after that?"

Sometimes they did. And then it was always a matter of weighing out which you wanted less—to make a scene or to let him touch you. At least, that was always the way it was with the boys I'd known.

I nodded.

"And what did you do then, Alice?"

"I pushed him away."

Or at least, sometimes I did.

"Maybe you and I aren't so different," Millie hissed into my ear. "You'll let a boy you don't like kiss you. Maybe you don't want to, but you'll say you didn't really mind. Maybe that's what I do, too. So don't stand there asking questions like you think you're better than me."

She pinched my cheek between her fingers, hard enough to leave a mark.

And then she let go, as though nothing had happened, smiled brightly, and went back to emptying out Irma's wardrobe. I clutched my smarting cheek.

When she was through, she closed the wardrobe doors and gathered up the bundle of clothes and the canvas bag that held the money, the photograph, and the letters.

She strode out of the room without even looking at me. Quickly, I gathered up my own pile of stolen goods, stuffing the letters into my purse before following her. She was taking another pass through the apartment, poking through kitchen cabinets and underneath cushions.

Satisfied at last, she went to the door, took a final look back, and said, "That about does it, I think."

"Millie," I said.

She stood in the doorway, her back to me. Slowly, she turned around, a wry, icy look on her face. "Is there something else you wanted?"

"You haven't told me anything."

She arched an eyebrow. "I think I've told you enough to make you think twice about showing those letters in your purse to Jerry Shaffer."

"What do you mean?"

"Her name is Gabrielle," Millie said. "That's who your sister was protecting, who she was willing to go to the *police* for. That's who saw Conrad Donahue murder a woman in cold blood. That's who everyone's looking for now. So, how much do you think Annie trusted Jerry Shaffer if she wouldn't even tell him *her name?*"

Millie reached into her purse and pulled out a matchbook. Inside, she scrawled a number and pressed it into my hand.

"I want to help you, Alice. Really, I do. Call me at this number tonight at ten. We can talk more freely then. Right now, I'd prefer to put a bit more distance between myself and your friend Jerry before I tell you anything else in confidence. What you do with the information after that is up to you. I just don't want any part of it."

"What am I supposed to do?" I asked.

"That's up to you, gumdrop. But if I was you, I'd be careful."

She stepped into the dark hallway and turned the key to her own apartment door.

I went back inside Irma's and cleaned up as best as I could. I put the letters from home back in the vanity, folded the clothes in the drawers Millie had rummaged through, and returned them to the bureau. I went to the nightstand and took the picture of Irma and Annie. Maybe it wasn't the smartest thing in the world to take, but I understood Millie's impulse to clean any sign of herself out of that place. Besides, I wanted it.

I took all the pill bottles and syringes and put them into a bag by themselves, planning to throw all of it into the first trash can I found. I told myself that what I was doing was a kindness to Irma's memory, even if it was too late to save her. But the truth was, I wasn't ready to leave the apartment.

To hear Jerry tell it, he cared about Annie and her friends. He wanted to protect them and help them in any way he could. But then I thought about the things that Millie had said. Cyrus, too—I was almost sure he'd been lying back at the restaurant. Annie's friends didn't trust Jerry, and it was beginning to look like maybe Annie didn't, either.

Jerry told me that Annie was supposed to meet him the night she was attacked, that she was supposed to bring Gabrielle with her so the three of them could all go to the police together. With what I knew now, though, that story didn't add up. Annie wouldn't have let Jerry near Gabrielle if she didn't trust him completely.

Maybe that was why Annie hadn't shown up for her meeting with Jerry—she'd never intended to. Or maybe there never had been any meeting in the first place.

Either way, it didn't explain what my sister had been doing in MacArthur Park the night she was attacked, and it didn't make me feel any better about facing Jerry Shaffer.

When the apartment was clean and I couldn't stall any longer, I made my way down the stairwell and into the sunny courtyard, where I found Jerry slouched against the trunk of the jacaranda tree. My head spun with uncertainty, and suddenly I wanted nothing so much as to put a few dozen blocks between myself and the private detective.

"I'm going home," I said, thrusting the bag of narcotics into his arms.

"Wait," he said, shuffling to his feet. "What happened up there, Alice? What's wrong? Did Millie give you a rough time?"

I shook my head, but when I opened my mouth to explain, no words came out, and a sick feeling passed through me. *Why does everyone you try to help end up getting hurt?*

I turned my back to him and started walking down the sidewalk.

"Alice, I'm sorry," he said, following after me. "Let me give you a ride home. Let's get you out of here, get you a bite to eat, and you can tell me all about it."

I shook my head again, and this time, I managed to squeak out a few syllables.

"I'd rather walk," I said.

CHAPTER 14

When I saw my mother through the kitchen window, I almost turned around and went back to Millie's place. She was sitting at the table, a martini glass folded into her hands, her face a perfect, inscrutable mask. I sighed and opened the back door.

"Alice, honey." My mother looked up from her drink, startled. She floated over to the door without a sound, without so much as scuffing the feet of the chair on the kitchen tile. Even half-lit, my mother was always a graceful woman. She smoothed my hair back from my forehead and tucked it behind my ears, a gesture so warm, so familiar, I longed to believe in it.

"I was starting to worry," she said. "Where have you been all day? Where were you yesterday?"

"With Cassie," I said.

She eyed me suspiciously. "Is everything all right?"

"I'm tired, I guess."

"Well, you look terrible. Go upstairs and draw yourself a bath. I'll bring you something to eat."

While I could have lived without the dig at my looks, it still sounded like the best idea I had ever heard. I dragged myself up the stairs to my room, where I stripped off my now-rumpled skirt and blouse and hung the strap of my purse over the bedpost. It was tempting to skip the bath and the food and climb straight into bed, where I could burrow underneath the sheets, cover my head with a pillow, and sleep through the night. But it had been more than a day since I'd last been home, longer since I'd bathed, and truth be told, I was starting to get a little ripe.

Sliding into the warm, soapy water was almost as good as bed, though. I closed my eyes for what seemed like seconds but must have been longer, because when I jerked awake, my mother was standing in the doorway with a plate.

She set it down on the rim of the tub—bacon, lettuce, and tomato on toast.

"You shouldn't fall asleep in the tub, Alice," she scolded. "It's dangerous."

But I was too busy devouring the sandwich and licking mayonnaise off my fingers to pay much attention. If you've never eaten a bacon sandwich in a hot bath before, believe me, you're missing out.

"This is the best thing I've ever eaten in my life," I said.

"Well, you're welcome, then."

She laid some fresh towels out on the hamper for me and left, shutting the door behind her.

"Thank you, Mother," I called out after her.

After I finished my sandwich, I set the plate down on the tile next to the tub and ducked under the warm water. As I held my breath, closed my eyes, and let the waves of underwater noises pulse in my eardrums, I thought it might be nice to stay here forever. Jerry could find Gabrielle and hunt down Irma's killer by himself. Annie could wake up when she was good and ready. The letters in my purse could gather dust or read themselves for all I cared.

Suddenly I sat straight up in the tub, rubbing the water from my eyes and reaching for a towel. I shouldn't have let the letters out of my sight, not even for a second, not even in my own room.

I dried off and threw on my bathrobe, and without even combing my hair, I ran down the hall to my bedroom. The purse was gone.

When I came crashing down the stairs, leaving a trail of bathwater footprints behind me, Mother had once again taken her spot at the kitchen table, a fresh martini in one hand, one of Irma's letters in the other. I snatched the page from her fingers.

"What are you doing, going through my things?" I shouted, my hair flinging droplets of water onto the table and the letters as I spoke.

My mother picked up the thick cream envelope and read the inscription aloud. "'Open If I Am Dead or Missing.'"

"Mother—" I started to speak, but she held up her hand.

"What are you fooling around with, Alice? Where did you get these? And don't you dare lie to me."

Her neck strained forward as she spoke, her eyes so wide they bulged. The broken capillaries in her cheeks flushed red, and her voice sounded hysterical, halfway between a scream and a sob.

"They aren't hers, if that's what you're thinking."

"Then why is her handwriting all over them? Why is her *picture* here?" She dropped the letter to the tabletop and picked up the framed photograph I'd taken from Irma's apartment.

I knew I'd been an idiot to take it. Any other picture might have been all right, might have been explained away somehow, but not the one with the dead girl and my sister in it.

"Do you know where she is?" my mother asked.

I tightened the belt on my bathrobe and folded my arms across my chest, trying to ignore the slippery, cold puddle of bathwater gathering at my feet. I felt defensive, on edge. I'd let down my guard for a lousy bacon sandwich, and my mother had pounced on the opportunity to steal my purse and dig through my things.

Still, I wished what I'd said to her next had been less cruel.

"You haven't cared where she was for the past four years. Why would you care now?"

She shot back a reply like it had been sitting on the tip of her tongue, waiting for a chance to get out.

"I care every day. It tears my heart out every goddamn day, Alice."

Her jaw tightened and her chin began to tremble. With her thumb, she traced the outline of Annie's face, smudging the glass. All the while, I heard her murmuring in a choked, small voice, "My pretty girl, my pretty, pretty little girl."

"Mom, please."

It just slipped out.

I never called her that. In fact, I don't think I ever had. "Mother" was formally, clinically, legally accurate, and I'd always felt it served our purposes well enough.

"Mom, please," I whispered again. "I'm sorry."

"Your father hasn't been home since the detective was here. I've been alone since then, Alice." She put the picture down and put her head in her hands. "Alice, I've been thinking such terrible thoughts."

She let out a fresh sob. Not quite sure what to do, I sat with her, squeezing her hands and saying nothing while the tears cascaded down her cheeks and pooled on the table. Eventually, the jag slowed, and she inhaled deeply and reached for a tissue.

"Please make me some coffee, Alice," she said, blowing her nose, then frowning at the sight of me sitting at the kitchen table in my bathrobe. "And put some clothes on. This isn't a spa."

She got up and disappeared down the hall into the powder room. By the time she came out, I'd changed into a clean skirt and blouse, and the coffee had finished brewing. Her skin was scrubbed clean of makeup, and though her eyes were still red-rimmed, they were clear and alert. She poured herself a cup of coffee and one for me, too, then sat down at the table.

"Did I ever tell you about my first day in Los Angeles, Alice? I marched right up to the gates of Warner Brothers and didn't leave until they gave me a job."

It was a story I'd heard a hundred times. She told it to everyone and never failed to brighten when she did. Even now, she smiled at the mention of those stupid Warner Bros. gates.

Like a thousand other girls, my mother had gotten on a bus for Hollywood the day she turned eighteen, the prettiest girl in some godforsaken southern town she'd never once suggested we visit. But once she got to Los Angeles, she quickly realized that the city was full of pretty girls just like her, and that she didn't know the first thing about how to be a movie star.

But my mother had something those other girls didn't: a skilled trade.

All through high school, she'd worked at the local beauty parlor, setting the curls and rinsing away the gray of rich women who acted like a sharecropper's daughter should be so lucky as to lay her hands on their heads. If she could handle women like that, she thought, she could handle anyone.

The next day, my mother marched up to the gates of Warner Bros. Studios and asked directions to hair and makeup, and the guard had waved her on through. And luckily, there were fifty chorus girls in need of identical chignons, and one of the regular girls had called in with the flu. Not one of the hairstyles she arranged shook loose during the dance numbers that day, and she was asked to come back.

She started with chorus girls, then worked her way up to styling the hair of leading ladies. After a few months of that, my mother felt like she finally knew how to be a movie star. She took modeling jobs and went on cattle calls until she landed her first chorus girl role.

"And the rest," she always said, "is history."

I'd heard her tell the story so often I swear I knew every beat. She loved the way it made her look—scrappy, bold, full of pluck and gumption. The exact opposite of anything I'd ever known her to be.

"I hate that story," I said.

"I know you do, but Annie loved it," my mother said, a faraway look in her eyes. "I thought it was what she wanted. It was so hard for me when I was trying to break in, and all I could see was how easy it was going to be for her with her looks, her talent, your father's connections. If I'd known, I never would have pushed her."

"Known what?"

My mother poured another cup of coffee for herself and acted like she hadn't heard me.

"I want you to be happy, too," she said when she sat down again. "I guess I haven't done a very good job at that, either."

I started to say that I was fine, that I *was* happy, but decided I'd already told my mother enough lies for one night.

DEAD TO ME

"If you'd known *what* you wouldn't have pushed her?" I asked again.

My mother had never spoken so freely with me about my sister. I wondered if seeing my sister's handwriting, her picture after all these years, had cracked something open inside her. Yes, I wanted information. Yes, I wanted to know the truth, but even more than that, I wanted her to keep talking about Annie like she was a person we knew and loved and hadn't tried to erase from our lives.

My mother pressed her lips together, and she shook her head.

"If I'd known she could get hurt," she said.

She stared at the table, twisting her rings and kneading her fingers, first one hand, then the other, faster and faster until finally I reached out and covered them with the palm of my hand.

She stopped fidgeting and looked up at me.

"Alice, if I'd been there, if I'd been the one who picked her up at the police station, things would have been different. I wouldn't have said she made the whole thing up. I wouldn't have cared how it made the studio look."

It was the thing I'd always wanted to know, but as I realized what my mother was telling me, I felt myself pulling away from her.

I wanted to talk about Annie, but not like this.

"I never thought she was lying," my mother said. "I always believed her, but she hated me anyway, right along with your father. You hate me, too, don't you? You think I let her go. You think I took her away from you."

There was a time when I would have told her that was exactly what she'd done. But sitting across from her at the kitchen table, I saw the suffering in her eyes, and I wondered if I'd been wrong.

"I would have given anything in the world to be able to fix it," she said.

My mother folded her arms across the table and buried her head in them. Stark, animal sobs wracked her body. I put one of my hands on her shoulder until they slowed, then gave her a tissue. She took it without lifting her head from the table.

"I don't hate you," I said.

I wanted her to tell me exactly what had happened to Annie, to confirm the big, ugly thoughts that bubbled in my head like hot tar: Annie had gone to the police. She'd told them a story. Someone had hurt her. My father said she'd made the whole thing up, so he could protect the people at his studio.

This wasn't the kind of thing that happened to people in my world. Or maybe it was the kind of thing that happened all the time—how would I know? No one ever talked about it. No one ever called it what it was. No one said its name.

We agreed to talk around it and fill in the blanks with whatever thoughts let us sleep at night.

I would have stopped it.

It would have been different if I'd been there.

I knew why, too. It was the same reason that I couldn't ask my mother the question I already knew the answer to.

At last, my mother lifted her head and looked me in the eye.

"I don't know what you're doing, Alice, but promise me you'll be careful. Promise me you'll come back."

I didn't know whether she was talking about tonight, or always, but either way, the promise stuck in my throat. In a few hours, I'd be sneaking out of the house to call Millie. After that, I'd be back at the hospital with Annie. I already had so many promises to keep.

And I was so tired. It had been three nights since my life was turned upside down. Three nights since I'd slept properly. Even though I was sitting up, my eyes began to droop shut.

My mother sighed and said, "Never mind," before I'd managed to promise her anything. She pinched her eyes shut and then brushed her hair out of her eyes with her fingertips and straightened her blouse, and she was herself again. It was almost as if our conversation had never happened.

"You should go to bed, Alice," she said. "I'm going to sit up a bit longer."

I took Irma's letters with me when I went up to my room, and my mother didn't try to stop me. I left her there at the table, cradling the photograph of Annie in her hands.

To Whom It May Concern:

I'm writing this because a woman has been murdered, and I believe my own life is now in danger.

On July 3, 1948, Conrad Donahue murdered Irma Martin. I saw this with my own eyes, and would swear to it in a court of law.

Should my word fail to convince you, go to Irma's apartment at 6326 Lexington and lift up the floorboards under her bed. I believe what you find there will be of interest.

If my life is forfeit, it is my last wish to see that justice is done.

Signed,
Millicent Grabowski, a.k.a. Camille Grabo

Up in my room, I had to read Millie's letter twice before it could sink in. She'd seen me take it, so she must have meant for me to have it. Unfortunately, I had no idea what she expected me to do with it. Take it to the police? She could have done that herself, and it would have meant a lot more coming from her lips than mine. Give it to Jerry? I knew what Millie would have to say about that.

And I had other questions now, too. For somebody who'd witnessed a murder, Millie was awfully bold to be lingering around her own apartment. Annie hadn't even been there the night that Irma was murdered, and look what had happened to her. There was something more to it, but whatever it was, I couldn't make it out.

I put the letter down and picked up the one that had been calling out to me since the moment I first saw it. There was something indecent about reading a dead girl's letters, but the moment I saw that tense, angular penmanship, I couldn't help myself. It was the postcard that led me to the Stratford Arms; it was the Nihilist cipher at the flophouse all over again. It was another piece of my sister, only this time, she wasn't hiding anything.'

Dear Irma,

Is this heaven? I keep pinching myself to make sure I'm not dreaming. And when I'm not pinching myself, I'm slapping myself in the face for not thinking of this sooner. And when I'm not busy pinching and slapping myself, I'm having the best time I've ever had in my life.

You never feel crowded in Los Angeles, so I didn't quite appreciate the difference before. It's not more space I want. It's land. Wide-open stretches of land, and pastures with honest-to-god cows and horses grazing on them. And it gets so hot here. Unbelievably hot, so that all you want to do at night is sit on the porch and drink cold beer and listen to cicadas. I met a boy with a guitar last night, and we sat and sipped and sang all night, and he wouldn't call me anything but "Miss."

The only good thing about leaving is knowing that I'll come back, and that next time, I'll bring you with me. Even if I have to drag you out here by your hair.

Send my love to the girls. I miss you. Be good.

Love,

Annie

It was Annie there on the page, the charming, chatty Annie who'd gossiped with me under the covers long past our bedtime. Only she'd changed. No more dreams of being a movie star or singing to a crowd of thousands from the middle of a giant stage. All she wanted now was a little breathing room and a little quiet, and maybe a few friends to share it with. The way she wrote about it, it sounded so nice that I started from the beginning and read it again. By the time I finished, I was crying.

I cried for what Annie had been through to survive. I cried because now I knew that at least once, at least for a little while, she had been truly happy and free. And I cried because it didn't last.

I didn't have it in me to read the rest of Irma's letters then and there. Instead, I wiped my eyes and blew my nose and hid the letters in my sock drawer. It was another one of Annie's old tricks. Everybody thinks to look inside a sock drawer, but nobody ever thinks to look inside the socks. I folded each letter in half long ways, stuffed it inside a kneesock, then folded the sock with its mate, making sure that no telltale envelope was sticking out. I did this with every letter except one.

Until I figured out what to do with Millie's letter, I wanted it on my person at all times. I pinned it to the inside of my skirt waistband, checking my profile in the mirror to make sure it didn't show. It didn't. I should have tried moving in it, too, to make sure that the paper didn't crinkle when I walked, but I only made it as far as the bed, and honestly, by that point, I really didn't care. I didn't bother to turn back the covers.

Falling asleep was like falling down a well. When I hit the bottom, everything went black for a while.

It was still black when I opened my eyes, but even then, I could tell there was something strange about my room. Still half asleep, I propped myself up on my elbows and squinted into the darkness until I made out the silhouette by the window. I knew that person.

What are you doing here? I whispered even though we were alone.

You tell me, she said, stepping into the swath of light that fell across the floor. It bathed her face in a soft, ghostly glow. She wore the same gray shirtwaist dress I'd seen her in that day at the Stratford Arms, the frumpy headband and the little dab of plum lipstick.

You don't make sense. You're not like Annie's friends.

Of course I'm not. She stepped away from the window and approached my bed, still ringed in that strange silver light.

I was sitting straight up now, alert, my backbone pressed against the headboard, and yet I couldn't bring myself to move. It wasn't exactly because I was afraid. It was that feeling you have when you're little, when you know that the horrible thing in your closet, under your bed, can't touch you as long as you stay tucked under your covers. In bed, nothing could get me. Ruth couldn't get any closer. I was safe there.

But the second I got out, it would all start again. The moment my feet touched the floor, they would have to fly.

DEAD TO ME

I don't understand what you have to do with my sister, I said.

She sighed, then shook her head and turned away. *Well, then, you'd better wake up.*

I gasped and bolted upright, immediately reaching for the clock on my nightstand. It read eleven o'clock. I'd overslept, and now I was late for my phone call to Millie. The dream left me feeling rattled and off-kilter, but I shoved it aside. I needed to be clearheaded, and I needed to find a pay phone. Wherever Millie was hiding out, I didn't want to risk giving her away with a long-distance phone charge.

I flung my legs over the side of the bed and smoothed my skirt. A little rumpled, but I was presentable enough for the hour and my destination. The closest phone booth I could think of was a few blocks from my house, near a gas station on Santa Monica. Traffic would be light this late in the evening, but at least I'd be out in the open at a big intersection.

Leaving the window unlatched, I stepped out onto the small balcony outside my bedroom window. It was too narrow to be a real balcony, and when Annie and I were younger, our mother had covered it with flowerpots and hanging plants. Annie had trampled every one of them, sneaking in and out of our bedroom window, and after she was gone, Mother had never thought to replace them. Once I was out the window, I climbed over the balcony railing and pitched myself off, reaching out in the darkness for the palm tree that grew next to our house. I wrapped my arms and legs around its trunk, then shinnied down.

When I was on the ground, I saw that the light was on in Cassie's bedroom. It seemed odd that she'd be up at this hour. The Jurgenses were early risers, all out the door with full stomachs at the crack of dawn. I was sure Cassie had field hockey or marching band or diving practice, or possibly all three, in the morning. Two weeks into summer, she already had a deep tan and brassy blond streaks in her hair, while I still had the pallor of a larval worm.

I was still looking up at Cassie's bedroom window when I heard someone clear a throat, someone standing only a few feet away from me there in the dark. I jumped, and the house keys fell from my hands.

"Who's there?" I whispered.

I was relieved when Cassie stepped out of the shadows, but only until I got a good look at her face.

"One day. That's what you said. You promised."

She must have been spying on me all night, waiting to see if I'd sneak out and prove once and for all that it had been a mistake to trust me.

"It's not what it looks like," I said. "I'm only going to the pay phone."

"You have a phone."

She had a glint in her eye that said, *You think you can lie to me, Alice Gates?*

It said, *You push me around, you shut me out, you take every kindness I've ever shown you for granted.*

It said, *I am done feeling sorry for you, and really, isn't that all our friendship has been since we were twelve? Me feeling sorry for you and your sad, rotten life.*

For a second, it felt like there was a fist wrapped around my heart. My life floated up before me, and I saw what it would look like without even the illusion of a friend, a sister, a family. Cassie was my safety wire. As long as she was there, I didn't notice how completely alone I really was.

"What?" Cassie said in a tone that sounded more like an accusation than a question. "What is it?"

I whispered, "It's Annie. Someone tried to kill her."

I told her about MacArthur Park and the days I'd spent in the hospital with her and how I'd met Jerry there.

"Do you have any idea who did it?" she asked.

I shook my head. "I'm not sure, but I think it might have been Conrad Donahue."

Cassie's eyes had been wide with amazement as she took in my story. Now they narrowed.

"Is this a joke to you?"

I took a step back and held up one hand to her, a truce. A promise.

"Annie knew something about him, Cassie. Something bad. He was afraid it was all going to come out."

Biting her lower lip, she asked, "If that's true, then aren't you in danger, too?"

I didn't answer her. Was I in danger? Sure, I'd had a close shave with Rex, but it was nothing like the kind of danger Annie had faced. I was like Cyrus. I wasn't part of this. I still had the option to stay out of sight.

"I'm fine," I said at last.

"Then why are you sneaking off in the middle of the night to use a pay phone?"

I was beginning to be worried that I'd told her too much, that the more I told her, the more she'd want to know. Nothing good could come of that.

"I'm going to call a friend of Annie's. Someone who doesn't want to be found."

"Is it someone we know?"

"It's Camille Grabo," I said.

I regretted the words the instant they were out of my mouth.

Cassie gasped, then drew back her hand and slapped my cheek. "You're unbelievable, Alice. Camille Grabo? Conrad Donahue? Do you think I'm stupid?"

Before I could stop her, before I could convince her I was telling the truth, she stormed onto her porch steps and through the front door. A few seconds later, she appeared in her bedroom window. Looking down at me, she pulled the curtains shut and turned out her light.

And then I was alone, just like I'd always wanted.

I used to dream about disappearing and leaving a mark on someone like the one Annie had left on me.

But Annie left her marks in different ways. She loved people; she took care of them. The only marks I ever left on people were the kind they regretted.

I took one last look at Cassie's darkened window, then pulled myself away and set off toward the gas station.

I didn't pass a single car on the road as I crept through the quiet residential streets of my neighborhood. Not even a porch light was on. Santa Monica was better lit but almost as desolate. I threw back my shoulders and crossed the street to the gas station, trying to look like a perfectly respectable person with a very good reason for making a phone call in the middle of the night. Which, I reminded myself, I was.

Picking up the receiver, I inserted some change and dialed the phone number Millie had given me. I wondered if it was in Las Vegas and whether she'd made it there or not.

DEAD TO ME

The phone rang at least ten times. I was about to hang up when I heard a click, a flare of static, and then a voice that sounded like it was coming from the bottom of the ocean.

"I was beginning to think you weren't going to call, Alice."

"Where are you?" I asked.

"About as far away from Los Angeles as you can get in six hours," she said. "My life might be forfeit and all, but I'm not going to make it that easy for them."

A husky laugh filled my ear, then suddenly there was nothing on the line but the static and the sound of Millie's shallow breaths. A snarl entered her voice. "No one's listening in, are they?"

"I'm on a pay phone," I said. "There's no one listening."

"So, what did you think of my letter? Colorful reading, wasn't it?" And just like that, the cheery, easy manner was back in her voice. "Pity it isn't true."

I gasped. "What do you mean, it isn't true?"

"Oh, don't get me wrong. Irma's dead and Conrad did it, sure as sunshine. I just didn't actually see it happen."

I processed this for a moment, and then it dawned on me what Millie was saying and why she'd been in such a hurry to skip town once her letter was in my hands.

"You're protecting Gabrielle," I said.

She heaved a sigh. "An ill-considered promise I made to your sister. Annie has handled some pretty desperate cases in her day, but I've never seen her this *fixated* on rescuing anyone before. I swear, her backup plans had backup plans."

"And you're one of them."

"A dozen people saw me leave the party with them," Millie said. "But Conrad and Gabrielle are the only ones alive who saw what happened next. I'd had a bit too much to drink that night, and Conrad feared I was going to upchuck on his leather interior. He told me to get lost. Not that I mind in hindsight."

Suddenly I felt like I had a stick of dynamite pinned into the front of my skirt. Millie could have been a hundred miles away by then or across the border, where no one could touch her. Yet it was hard to fault her—she could have done that the night Irma was murdered. Instead, she stuck around, wrote that letter, and made sure it got into my hands because that was how Annie and her friends operated. They were loners, except when it came to protecting one another. Then they were like a pack.

It was then that I noticed the black Rolls-Royce idling in the gas station parking lot. Had it just pulled in, or had it been sitting there the whole time? I tried not to stare, instead taking in as much detail as I could from the corner of my eye, memorizing the plates, the face of the man at the wheel.

"Alice, knock the wax out of your ears. I asked you a question."

"Sorry," I said. "It's just that . . ."

She ignored me. "Did you show it to Jerry or not?"

"No," I said. "What am I supposed to do with it, anyway?"

"Know any honest cops?"

I didn't answer. Even I knew how the police department worked in Los Angeles. If you were white enough, rich enough, famous enough, powerful enough, there were few charges you couldn't shake. If I showed that letter to the wrong cop, it might as well have never been written.

"Yeah, me neither," Millie said.

"I don't know what to do, Millie," I said. "Is there anything else you can tell me?"

There was a burst of static on the line.

"Like what?"

DEAD TO ME

"Like any of it. Who I'm supposed to trust, where Gabrielle is now, who tried to kill my sister."

"Listen, gumdrop," Millie said. "The thing about what happened to your sister is, I think you already—"

I didn't hear the rest of what Millie was trying to tell me, because at that moment, a thick, gloved thumb pressed down on the telephone hook. My body went stiff with fear as I felt a coarse cotton shirtsleeve brush my shoulder, and hot, wet breath that stunk of tobacco on my neck.

"Get in the car," a man's voice whispered in my ear.

The black Rolls-Royce roared to life, its tires squealing as it completed a hairpin turn in the parking lot and pulled up alongside us. Shaking, I turned around to see the face that went with the voice. As I did, he caught my arm and twisted it behind my back. The pay phone receiver dropped from my hand and dangled by its cord inches from the pavement.

He had a meaty red face and the bulk of a prizefighter beginning to go to seed, but he was still plenty strong and plenty dangerous. We hadn't formally met, but I would have known Rex anywhere.

CHAPTER 15

I struggled frantically, but the time to run had passed. Even if I could have slipped out of Rex's grip, at that moment the back door of the Rolls-Royce swung open and another man leaned forward, arms outstretched to catch me if I broke free.

I fought anyway. I flung my weight against Rex's grip and opened my mouth to scream in the hopes that I might attract a neighbor or a passing car. I barely got out a squeak before he clapped his free hand across my mouth. One hand there, one pinning my wrist between my shoulder blades, he marched me to the car and stuffed me into the arms of the other man waiting in the backseat. Rex climbed in after me and slammed the door, so I was sandwiched tightly between them.

"Drive," he said.

I froze in my seat between the two men, folding my arms and

shoulders in close so I didn't have to touch them. My whole body shook.

Wordlessly, the driver put the car into gear and hit the gas. We turned out of the parking lot and ran a red light through an empty intersection. It hadn't taken more than a few seconds, and with a sick surge of fear, I realized that no one had seen a thing.

From the front seat, a familiar voice asked, "Was all that really necessary, gentlemen?"

Rex and the other man were muttering their apologies before Conrad Donahue could even turn around, but Conrad didn't seem to hear them. His stormy eyes were fixed right on me. I stared back.

"I'm so sorry if we frightened you, Alice, but I had to speak with you right away. It's about your father."

The movie magazines called Conrad Donahue "the man with the golden throat." I'd heard that voice in at least a dozen movies, but there was something about it that the microphones couldn't capture.

When I was nine, I came down with pneumonia. The coughing kept me awake all night and nearly tore my lungs to ribbons. In the middle of one of my crying and coughing jags, my mother came up to my room with a small glass of hot whiskey with honey and lemon mixed into it. When I drank it, it settled my chest and soothed my crying, and the last thing I remember before I drifted off to sleep was my mother's voice murmuring, "Hush now. Be still. All will be well."`

Even after I'd been tossed into the backseat of his car, Conrad's voice filled me with that same sense of calm. His voice reached out to me, and I felt myself bend toward it. This man was the man I'd seen on the big screen, composing love songs for Joan Blondell on a ukulele or running through a rainstorm into Olivia de Havilland's arms.

"Normally, I wouldn't track you down in the middle of the night like this, but I'm worried about your father. I'm afraid he might do something rash."

The pain on his face, the tenderness in his voice, seemed so real, it was impossible to reconcile them with what I knew about Conrad Donahue, and what I knew he was capable of.

Almost as if he'd guessed at my thoughts, Conrad said, "You've heard things about me, is that right? Unkind things?"

I couldn't speak. I couldn't move. Fear turned me into a rag doll, and all I could do was sit there and hope that if I hushed and was still, all would be well.

"Your father has gotten himself mixed up in some very dangerous business, Alice. I want to help him, and I need you to help me. Have you ever heard him mention anyone named Gabrielle?"

I shook my head.

"Have you heard that name anywhere else? Maybe from one of Annie's friends?"

Hearing my sister's name on his lips, hearing him talk about my family like he knew us, made my skin crawl.

"I don't know anything," I said, my voice trembling as I spoke. "Let me go."

A sneer flickered across his upper lip and he laughed, then muttered something to the driver. A few minutes later we were idling in front of the County Hospital.

Dread settled over my thoughts like a thin layer of frost.

He doesn't know she's here. He can't *know she's here.*

"Speaking of your sister," Conrad said, "I'd like to show you something."

He reached over the backseat and caught me under the chin, drawing my face close to his. His lips brushed my ear as he whispered, "A little birdie told me that Annie Gates is here at County Hospital, and far less dead than we'd all supposed."

A wave of dizziness passed over me as Conrad's thumb pressed into my throat.

"I want you to know exactly how easy it would be for me to walk into her room and put a pillow over her face."

My head spun and Conrad's laughter buzzed like static in my ears, and when the whimper passed my lips, it sounded like it was coming from somewhere else. He let go of my chin and pushed me so I fell back against the seat.

Then he turned to Rex and said, "Tie her up."

Rex leaped to attention. "Should I gag her, too?

"What's the point?" Conrad asked, then murmured some directions to the driver.

We crossed the river and drove north until we reached the winding, narrow roads and switchbacks of Griffith Park. The farther up we went, the darker and more remote it became. All I could do was stare straight ahead, and all I could think about was that eventually, they were going to stop the car. I didn't dare think any further than that. Conrad had been right—there was no reason to bother with a gag. No matter how loudly I screamed up here, it wouldn't matter.

As Rex taped my hands behind my back, I studied the other man in the backseat, desperately trying to find something in his face that seemed human, something that would not allow Conrad to hurt me. I saw nothing promising in Rex, but I held out hope for the other man. He was plain-looking, neither handsome nor brutish, and wore jaunty blue polka-dot suspenders. I tried to meet his eyes, but the man stared intently out the window of the Rolls-Royce.

The driver turned onto a shell road and slowed down as the car jostled and rocked over the bumps. Dense masses of coastal sage scrub encroached on the road, and oak trees created a canopy that seemed to close in on us. Finally, the driver pulled off to the side of the road and parked.

"Get out," said Conrad.

My legs turned to water as the man in the polka-dot suspenders dragged me out of the backseat by the elbow. Conrad stood at the rear of the car and snapped his fingers for the driver. As the old man stumbled around to the back, Conrad slipped an arm around my shoulder and pulled me to his side. He stood behind me, his chest pressed to my back and a hand on either shoulder. I tensed at his touch, and he chuckled softly in my ear.

"Open it," Conrad said, bouncing on the balls of his feet like he was about to open a Christmas present.

As the driver turned the key, I thought, He's enjoying himself. The more I flinched from him, the more scared I was, the more he seemed to like it. And he couldn't wait for me to see whatever was inside the trunk. I squeezed my eyes shut and prepared myself for the worst. Maybe they'd found Gabrielle. Please, I thought, not another dead girl.

I guess I got my wish. It wasn't a girl Conrad wanted to show me.

It was my father.

He was bound with tape at the wrists and ankles and gagged with a dirty kitchen towel. His hair was greasy and mussed, his eyes blackened, his normally impeccable suit stained with mud, oil, and blood, but he was alive and struggling furiously against his bonds.

Conrad nodded to Rex, who untied the towel from around my father's mouth. He gasped and retched and panted for breath, red-faced and wide-eyed. When he saw me looking down at him, his eyes went from wide to wild.

"Conrad," he wheezed. There were bruises around his neck, too, and his vocal cords sounded like they'd been shredded. "You said you wouldn't hurt her."

"And I haven't," Conrad said. His fingertips slid down my arms, lingering along the sides of my breasts before coming to rest on my hips.

I tried not to move, but there was the tiniest hitch in my breath, the smallest shudder in my arms, and I knew that he'd felt it. I knew because he chuckled again and pulled me closer to him until my bound hands rested between his legs.

When I met my father's eyes, I tried to look like I wasn't afraid.

"I'm just out for a midnight drive with the youngest Gates daughter. She must be the smart one, because she sure ain't the pretty one, right?" Conrad said with a nasty bark of laughter. "But maybe she's not so smart after all," he continued. "Because when I ask her a simple question, all of a sudden she doesn't know *anything*. What do you make of that, Nicky?"

Conrad jostled me by the shoulders as he spoke. "She doesn't know a single thing, just like her dear old dad. So, I'm struck with an idea. Maybe if I get the two of you in the same place, give you a chance to put your heads together, maybe you'll think of something you know after all."

"I didn't know about the detective," my father said, struggling to sit up. "I didn't know he knew Annie."

Conrad regarded him scornfully. "Clearly."

"I just need another day or two," my father said, pleading. "I can find the girl, Conrad. It'll be like nothing ever happened. Believe me, it's better if we do this my way. Nobody else has to get hurt."

"Nicky, you've had plenty of time. You've had so much time that it's given me the opportunity to do a little thinking myself, and from where I'm standing, you're starting to look like an awfully convenient solution to my problem."

I tried to stop myself from shaking, but it only made it worse. The harder I shook, the closer Conrad pulled me. My heart fluttered like a hummingbird's wings.

"Let's say you were overwhelmed with guilt by what you did to that poor dancer, and you decided to end it all. Let's say you left behind a very detailed note confessing what you'd done and asking your family to forgive you. You couldn't find the girl, Nicky, but that doesn't mean it's too late to make yourself useful."

As Conrad's words sank in, my father began to scream and cry and thrash his feet against the inside of the trunk, pulling at the tape. Rex took a step toward the car, and for the first time, I noticed the gleaming barrel of a revolver holstered at his waist.

When I saw the gun, I screamed, too. Conrad hadn't brought us here to talk, I realized, and this wasn't some plan he was cooking up for another day. It was all about to happen.

I shook Conrad's hands off me and leaped toward the car. I don't know what I was planning to do. Throw myself between Rex and my father? Wrest the gun out of his hands with my hands tied behind my back? There was nowhere I could run, and Conrad recaptured me immediately, tightening his grip around my waist. The moment I felt his hands on me, I realized my mistake. Conrad realized it, too.

"What's this?"

He spun me around to face him and patted at the front of my skirt.

As Conrad stuck his hands down the front of my skirt, I turned my head and tried to make eye contact with the man in the polka-dot suspenders and the driver. Neither one would look at me; they just stared at the tops of their shoes. Rex looked, though. I could hear him laughing. But I didn't scream or flinch while Conrad's hands went everywhere, not even when he stuck me in the hip with the pin I'd used to hold the letter in place. Instead, I stared at the men with tears in my eyes and imagined how much I'd enjoy watching them rot in prison.

Conrad had the letter in his hands now, and I watched the expression on his face change as his eyes flicked back and forth across the page. No one spoke or even moved. When he was finished, a slow smile spread across his face. He gripped the letter in his fist and shook it at me.

"You stupid little bitch."

His fist swung down and cracked me across the face. The blow stung, but not as much as the crisp edge of Millie's letter, which filleted the skin under my eye. My head spun and I fell to my knees. Towering over me, Conrad drew back his hand and struck me again, this time catching me under the chin.

Splinters of light exploded in my eyes as my teeth clashed together, and I thought I could hear my father screaming something strangled and hoarse and very far away. My cheek felt slick with blood, and when I spat, that was blood, too.

"If you thought that was going to work, you're even dumber than your sister."

He pulled a lighter out of his pocket, lit the corner of the envelope, and waved it under my nose. "So much for your letter."

He dropped it to the ground and let it burn.

"Get up."

I was about to pull myself up off the ground when I realized that listening to Conrad would probably get me another fist in the face. I spat another mouthful of blood, then hunched over on my knees, pretending to retch into the dirt.

"I said get up." Conrad's voice was more agitated this time.

I stayed where I was on the ground but looked up to see Conrad circling me and jeering. I saw Rex and the man in the polka-dot suspenders watching, waiting to be told what to do next. And behind them, I saw my father, who had taken advantage of the distraction to free his hands.

The driver was at least ten yards away, relieving himself in the dense scrub brush, and he must have taken the keys with him to do it because they weren't in the ignition. In the midst of it all, my father was hunched over, clawing furiously at the tape around his ankles.

If he managed to free himself and run back the way we came, they'd have to turn the car around to follow him. On a road this narrow, that would buy him at least a few seconds. It wasn't much time, but it might be enough for him to disappear into the woods, enough to have a fighting chance. Of course, it would give me one, too. If they wanted to follow both of us, they'd have to split up. It was as good a plan as I could think up, and I suspected it was the best chance either of us was going to have.

Dad, I thought, this is more than you deserve.

DEAD TO ME

The moment he broke through the last of the tape, I leaped to my feet and ran, my hands slapping uselessly against my back as I plunged toward the dark, empty road.

Conrad let out a bellow, and the other men sprang to attention. The driver scrambled back toward the car, zipping up as he ran. Then my father climbed out of the trunk, but he didn't run away like I'd expected.

Instead, he went for Rex's gun.

I couldn't be sure of what I saw out of the corner of my eye as I ran, it happened so fast. Behind me, I heard a shout and the sound of a struggle, then a gunshot.

I ran faster and didn't look back.

I was a half a mile down the road when I heard the car, its tires crunching the shells and pebbles as it rolled slowly up the road. For an instant, I froze in the middle of the road, then dove into the scrub brush that grew in thickets along the berm, wading in until I found a small clearing big enough to crouch in. I hoped there were no rattlesnakes here—the hills were full of them. My whole face throbbed, and the cut under my eye burned, the blood on my cheek turning thick and sticky. I closed my eyes and waited for the car to pass.

The car slowed not ten yards from my hiding place, and a flashlight beam swung from one side of the road to the other. I burrowed down and hid my face in the scrub. It was too close, and I'd missed my chance to crawl farther away from the road. Now I didn't dare move, for fear I'd rustle the brush.

"Girl," a voice whispered. "Come out if you're back there. I'm not going to hurt you."

Whoever it was, I didn't believe him for a second. I didn't even know if my father was still alive. For all I knew, Rex had gotten to the gun first. In fact, that seemed likelier. I guessed that Rex had a lot more practice taking guns away from people than my father did.

The car door swung open, and I heard footsteps pacing up and down the side of the road. The flashlight beam shone down, illuminating patches perilously close to my hiding place.

Don't move, don't breathe, I thought.

The footsteps grew fainter, and I heard the squeak of the car door. A few seconds more and I would have been free to make my escape, to spend the rest of the night crawling down the snake- and mountain lion–infested hills in the pitch dark. But instead, I sneezed. When I felt it coming, I smothered my mouth and nose in my lap. It hardly made a sound at all, but it was enough. The flashlight beam froze, then swung back around, pointing right at the spot where I was. I lurched out of the brush and started to run, but the scrub was too thick, my legs half asleep, and I'd barely taken two steps before a hand came down and caught me by the collar.

I twisted against his grasp and he let go, but not before he'd wrapped a thick arm around my waist the way that Conrad had. My body went rigid. I opened my mouth to scream, but nothing came out.

He spoke again, still in a whisper. "I'm here to help you. It's okay."

The man held me still, his arm wrapped around my waist, and he whispered it over and over again until I stopped shaking and my muscles went slack, and I finally found the courage to look back over my shoulder to see that it was Conrad's driver. He'd been quiet as we drove up the hill; he hadn't spoken to any of the men in the car, hadn't even looked at me. I'd barely gotten a glimpse of his face, but saw now that it was heavily lined, with swollen purple bags under his eyes. His steel-gray hair was freshly barbered and parted to the side with oil, but his mustache was full and bushy. He smelled faintly of peppermint.

Once I'd calmed down, he let go of me and cut the electrical tape around my wrists with a pocketknife. I shook them and gritted my teeth as the blood rushed painfully back into my fingertips.

"Hurry," he said. "There isn't much time."

I got into the backseat of the car, selecting the passenger side, out of arm's reach. If anything happened, I could always open the back door and bail out. If the driver took offense at my precautionary measures, he didn't show it.

We drove through the hills in silence, tires kicking up gravel as we hurtled around the hairpin turns. Once we neared the edge of the park, he pulled over to the side of the road.

"Can you make it home from here?"

I nodded, hardly daring to believe what had just happened. I was only a few blocks away from Hollywood Boulevard now, and it felt like a million miles from that desolate road in Griffith Park.

"I've got daughters of my own," the driver said, meeting my eyes in the rearview mirror. "I'll tell Conrad I lost you in the woods."

"There was a gunshot...." I said, trailing off.

The driver knew what I wanted to ask, even if I couldn't bring myself to ask it.

"He went into the woods," the driver said. "I don't know if he was hit, but when I saw your father last, he was running."

"Thank you."

I wished I had better words for this man who'd risked so much for me.

"Go," the driver said. "Get out of here, as fast as you can."

The moment I was out of the backseat, the car made a U-turn and shot back up the road, kicking up a fog of dust and gravel, and then it was gone.

CHAPTER 16

For a moment, the darkness and the nighttime noises closed in around me. I heard rustling in the brush, tree branches creaking in the wind, a coyote's howl. First I froze, and then I ran, my arms pumping, my feet slapping against the dirt road. The only human sounds I could hear were my own gasping breaths. I ran to the edge of the park and didn't stop until I saw the lights from Hollywood Boulevard shining in the distance.

It was late and the streets were quiet as I turned the corner and headed toward the Red Car stop. The only person I passed on my way was a bum wearing three-day stubble and pants that were shiny with grease. He took one look at me and crossed to the other side of the street.

All I'd been able to think about was getting to safety. My face hurt—I knew that much—but I hadn't even thought about how it must have looked. I found a store window and inspected my reflection under the streetlight.

My left eye was almost swollen shut, and beneath it, an angry-looking cut oozed blood. My jaw was sore, the skin on my wrists raw. I tried to blot at the cut under my eye with the collar of my shirt, but the blood was too sticky to wipe off without water. Now I had a gory eye *and* a blood-smeared shirt.

Sitting on the bench next to the streetcar stop, I saw a discarded section of the previous day's *Los Angeles Times*. I sat down on the bench and unfolded it, trying to look like I was deeply engrossed while I waited for the Red Car. The westbound cars went to my neighborhood, while the eastbound traveled to downtown, toward the County Hospital. I decided to get on whichever one came first. Out in the open like that, every minute I waited passed like an eternity. I was sure that every passing car I heard was the Rolls-Royce, terrified that if I looked over the top of my newspaper, I'd find Rex standing there.

When the westbound Red Car finally pulled up, I used the paper to shield my face, and took a seat in the back of the car. My breathing eased once I was on the move, and I willed my heart to stop racing. I was going home. I needed to think about what I was going to do once I got there.

Conrad knew Annie was alive, he knew where she was, and he'd be coming for her. It wouldn't matter how much I paid Eugene the orderly or how many night nurses were looking in on her, or even if I was standing by her bed myself. Conrad had dropped me to the ground in a few seconds. I squeezed my eyes shut to hold back tears, and my swollen face throbbed with fresh pain.

DEAD to ME

My sister was in more danger than ever, and there was nothing I could do to protect her. Worst of all, I couldn't think of anyone who could. Not the police, not Jerry Shaffer, not Annie's friends or our parents. Conrad was right. If he wanted to send someone through the doors of County Hospital to put a pillow over my sister's face, it would be easy.

The Red Car made its way down Hollywood Boulevard, rattling my teeth together as it jiggled along the track. I felt empty. I was out of time, out of hope, and out of solutions.

Then a thought kindled and flickered in my brain.

It wouldn't be easy, I thought. Not anymore.

Conrad Donahue was running out of time, too. He'd read Millie's letter. Soon he'd be rushing over to Irma's apartment to pry up the floorboards, looking for whatever evidence was hidden there. But before he could do that, he and his cronies had to get out of Griffith Park, and before they could do that, they'd have to look for my father. And me. They'd kidnapped and assaulted us, and we'd escaped. We were loose ends. Liabilities. The driver said my father had run into the woods after the gun went off. I hoped he'd gotten a good head start before the other men set off after him. And Conrad didn't know his driver had helped me. As far as he and his friends knew, I was still staggering around the woods with my hands tied behind my back. Hopefully, they'd waste a little more of Conrad's precious time looking for me there.

For the past few minutes, I'd been staring at the same two pages in the newspaper without seeing them. It was the entertainment section, I noticed now. Hedda Hopper's Hollywood gossip column, movie previews, and interviews with starlets. No matter where I went, I couldn't seem to escape any of it.

And then, Conrad Donahue's face jumped out at me halfway down the page. He was wearing a tuxedo in the picture, his arm wrapped around a pretty woman I recognized from a gangster movie that had come out a few months before. Even in newsprint, his smile looked golden.

My eyes slid to a slight figure partly out of the frame, and I gasped. It was *her*, the girl from the picture in my father's safe.

She had big, loopy curls and a china doll face, and she wore an airy, soft-hued dress that bared her shoulders. I'd guessed at it before, but now I was certain. This was Gabrielle.

She stood just past Conrad's shoulder, smiling and holding a drink in her hand, just another pretty young face at a Hollywood party. I might have missed her had my eye not fallen first on the man she was talking to—crisp, impeccably dressed, and as always, looking on while the famous people occupied the foreground.

My father.

The newspaper dropped from my hands, its pages scattering across my lap. I couldn't stand to look at it anymore. The whole way from La Brea to Fairfax, I stared straight ahead, not caring who saw my battered face.

When that picture was taken, Irma was alive, and a few hours later, she would be dead, and Gabrielle would be on the run, and my father would be home, sleeping soundly in his bed.

He'd been there. He'd talked to her, and either he hadn't noticed she was just a kid, or he hadn't cared. Couldn't he tell she had no business being there? Couldn't he for once forget about all the celebrities he had to charm and put her in a cab home?

Of course, I had no reason to expect better from a man who'd wrapped his older daughter in low-cut evening dresses and sent her out to sing at wild parties when she was fifteen.

Careful—he's the only father you have, I thought. And now, he might be dead.

I wondered if it had crossed his mind, as he lay tied up in the trunk of Conrad's Rolls-Royce, that his predicament might have been avoided if he'd only had the decency to walk the underage girl out of the party. I hoped it had.

It wasn't his fault, not all of it, I thought.

He didn't kill Irma. He didn't take the disgusting pictures of Gabrielle. And I couldn't believe he would ever hurt Annie. Maybe he was being set up. Maybe he hadn't known about any of it until it was already too late.

He was my father. He was a monster. He made unforgivable choices, but he didn't deserve to be murdered and framed for things he hadn't done.

Whatever it was I felt for him at that moment, I hoped the driver had been right.

"Please don't be dead," I whispered.

Two fat teardrops landed on my knee, stinging the cut under my eye as they fell, and I wiped my face with the back of my hand. At the front of the car, I caught a middle-aged woman in heavy makeup staring at me. I shot her a dirty look, and she went back to looking out the window.

I took the paper, got off the Red Car at Fairfax, and crossed the street. With every block, the light grew dimmer, the sounds of traffic fainter, until I came to my street. It seemed wrong some-how that it was just the way I'd left it.

I stayed off the sidewalks and kept to the shadows as I walked down my street, stopping occasionally to duck behind a hedge and scan the cars parked along the curb. There was no sign of the

Rolls-Royce, but that didn't mean it wouldn't be coming. I wasn't sure what I'd tell my mother when I saw her, but I knew I needed to warn her, needed to get her out of there before the sun came up.

Carefully, I picked my way down the street, through the front yards of my neighbors: the banker whose forehead always seemed to be sweating; the widow who used to pay Annie and me a dime each to pull weeds out of her flower bed; the magazine editor whose wife brought everybody on the block a basket of oranges at Christmas.

And then I was in front of my house, the least-welcoming home on the block.

It looked half lived-in, like my family spent part of the year on long vacations and never really settled in when we came back. All the lights in the house were off, and the porch was dark.

But it wasn't empty. Sitting on the front steps, his busboy apron folded across his knees, was Cyrus. It was lucky for him it was so late at night. Even though he wasn't doing anything but sitting, he looked so out of place I was sure my neighbors would have called the police if they'd spotted him.

"What are you doing here?" I asked.

At the sound of my voice, he looked up. When he saw my face, he leaped to his feet and ran down the sidewalk toward me.

"Oh my god, Alice, what happened to you?"

My jaw throbbed. I didn't want Cyrus—or anyone else—to see me like this. I remembered what he'd said to me at the restaurant, that I didn't have to get myself killed trying to prove I loved Annie. I didn't need his worry or sympathy, and I didn't want him thinking he'd been right about me. All I wanted was to go inside and put a bag of ice on my face.

"I don't want to talk about it," I said, walking past him toward the front steps.

With a few strides of his long legs he beat me to the door. "Alice, please. You shouldn't be alone right now."

I tried to go around him, but he sidestepped between me and the door.

"Excuse me," I said, glaring at him.

"Let me help you bandage that cut," he said, pleading. "At least let me stay with you for a while."

"You can't come in," I said, fishing my house key out of my skirt pocket. "My mother would kill me."

"Your mother isn't here," Cyrus said, pointing to the driveway.

Sure enough, her car was gone. I curled my fingers into a fist around the house key and swore under my breath.

Couldn't you drink at home, Mom? I thought.

"Fine. Have it your way," I said, too tired to argue. Cyrus stepped aside, and I unlocked the front door.

He could come in long enough to say whatever it was he'd come to tell me and long enough to make sure Conrad and Rex weren't hiding in the linen closet, but that was it.

Cyrus followed me inside, and I locked the door behind us.

"Alice, the reason I came over is because I didn't tell you everything before."

I snorted. "Obviously."

As I led Cyrus through the foyer, I saw him craning his neck to look up at the crystal chandelier, the gold gilt mirror, the Persian carpets that lined the hardwood floors.

"You don't have to take your shoes off," I said. He wedged his heel back into his loafer and followed me down the hallway to the kitchen.

I remembered what Jerry had told me about how Cyrus worked two jobs to support himself. I always thought of my house as normal, but compared with Irma's apartment and Annie's flophouse on Main Street, it must have looked like a mansion to Cyrus.

"Iodine?"

He said it like it was a question, and I realized he was asking me where it was, and that he intended to bandage that cut after all. I wasn't sure I wanted a boy I'd known less than a day dabbing iodine under my eye, but I pointed him in the direction of the powder room anyway.

"Go sit down," Cyrus said. "I'll be there in two minutes."

It was half that long before he came into the kitchen holding a bottle of iodine, a wad of cotton gauze, tape, and a towel ratty enough that it wouldn't be missed. He opened the freezer and fished around until he found a bag of frozen peas.

"Put that on your jaw," he said, handing it to me.

Cyrus ran the towel under the faucet and wrung it out. Then he sat down next to me and began to blot away the blood on my cheek. The water was just the right temperature, warm and heavenly.

"How'd you know where everything was?" I asked.

He shrugged. "That's my job. Knowing what people need. Getting it for them. Usually it's booze and saltshakers, so this is a nice change of pace."

I couldn't help smiling, though with my sore jaw it came out more like a wince. "How'd you know that's what I was going to ask for next?"

He smiled back at me and poured iodine onto a square of the cotton gauze.

"Crack wise while you can," he said, "but this next part is going to sting."

Once he'd finished cleaning up my bloody face, Cyrus dabbed the gauze under my eye. I flinched, and he quickly pulled his hand away.

"Does it hurt?"

"A little," I said.

He blew a cool, gentle breath over the cut. Without meaning to, I shivered.

"Sorry," I said, looking down at the tabletop. "It tickled."

I could feel my cheeks flush with embarrassment, but if Cyrus noticed, he was polite enough to act like he hadn't. He applied salve to the raw skin on my wrists and knees and cleaned the cuts I'd gotten in Griffith Park. While I switched the frozen peas from my jaw to my blackening eye, he got me a cup of water and shook two aspirin tablets out of a bottle for me.

As I swallowed them down, I realized how normal it felt to be sitting in my kitchen, drinking out of a juice glass, despite everything that had happened that evening. For the first time since my bacon sandwich in the bathtub, I felt safe.

"Thank you, Cyrus," I said when he'd finished.

"It's nothing," he said. "And please, call me Cy."

He leaned back in his chair and took a deep breath.

"Alice, I'm sorry I didn't tell you everything sooner."

We'd passed the first aid and small talk portion of the evening. He'd come here to tell me something, and I could see him working up the nerve to do it.

"Was it because Jerry was there?"

He shook his head.

"It didn't have anything to do with that. I didn't tell you because I didn't see what good it would do. I can't prove anything. I can't do anything about it."

In the kitchen at Musso & Frank, I'd known Cy was holding something back. When Jerry asked him if he knew where Gabrielle was, he said he didn't know. But he also said that he didn't know who tried to kill my sister, and that was a question Jerry hadn't asked.

It had to be more than that, though. Back at the restaurant, Cy had told Jerry he was trying to stay out of sight, that he was afraid of ending up like Annie and Irma. He'd acted like he was being hunted.

"You know something about the night Annie was attacked, don't you?" I asked.

"How much do you already know?" he asked, looking at me warily.

I didn't have evidence, and like Cy, I couldn't prove anything, but there was only one direction everything I knew pointed.

"Was it Conrad?"

Cy nodded. "I was working at Marty's that night. Conrad and a guy named Rex came in, and they offered me some extra money to give them a table in the back and make sure no one bothered them. Nobody would have anyway—all the men who go to Marty's are sailors and traveling businessmen trying to get laid."

Cy turned a deep shade of scarlet when he said this.

"I'm sorry. That's just the most polite term I can think of to describe their intentions."

"It's fine, Cy. Go on."

"So, the usual customers buy a lot of drinks, flirt, try to look like big spenders. But the thing is, all the women in Marty's work for Marty. I pour them ginger ale all night, they pretend it's champagne, and they just keep ordering more. Before the guys know it, their wallets are empty and they're too drunk to argue when we toss them out. That's Marty's business model, anyway. No one in that room gives two shits about Conrad Donahue—sorry, Alice. No one cares about—"

"Just say what you want to," I said.

I couldn't stand to hear him be careful around me, like I was some sheltered little priss who would pass out cold if I heard bad language.

"I just didn't want to offend—"

I cut him off before he could finish.

"Like the patrons of Marty's, I also do not give two shits."

"So I took the money and let them sit wherever they wanted," Cy said.

He seemed a little bit more at ease with me now, but I could tell he was still trying to figure me out. I wondered if he'd watched his language around Annie.

"They left Marty's around midnight, and an hour later they were back. Conrad's not much of a drinker, but he put away three whiskeys in a row. I heard him say to Rex, 'The girl wasn't with her,' and he was pretty upset about it, but Rex told him not to worry because she wouldn't get far without her friend.

"I didn't put together what they were talking about until the next morning, when Jerry came around looking for Annie. Conrad didn't pay much attention to me when he came to Marty's, but I don't think he knows Annie's my friend, either. That's why I've been lying low."

Cy sank back in his chair, exhausted.

"So, that's what happened. That's what I didn't tell you before."

And now I knew.

It wasn't exactly a shock, but knowing for sure that they'd done it made everything seem more real. I could see what had happened that night in the park like it was a movie playing in my head. Cy told me what he knew, Jerry told me what he knew, and the rest I could fill in for myself.

Annie went to the park that night to meet a police officer, only instead, it was Conrad and Rex waiting for her. They got a surprise, too, because Gabrielle was supposed to be there with her and she wasn't. They didn't care about my sister. It was Gabrielle they were after, and when Annie wouldn't tell them where she was, they tried to beat the answer out of her.

There was still something I didn't understand, though.

"How did Conrad know she was going to be there?" I asked.

Cy put his elbows on the table and rested his chin in his hand as he thought.

"Annie was nervous about the plan from the beginning—too many people knew about it. That's probably why she didn't bring Gabrielle with her," he said. "My guess is Jerry's contact at the LAPD let the word slip. Maybe on purpose, maybe not."

I thought about how brave Annie was to walk into the park that night knowing the whole thing might be a setup. She'd done it anyway, and she'd done everything in her power to make sure that Gabrielle was safe. I wondered what she thought when she found Conrad and Rex waiting for her there, knowing that the people she'd trusted to help had failed her.

"Are you okay?" Cy asked, and I realized that I wasn't sure how long I'd been staring at the same spot on the kitchen table and that my hands were shaking.

"I'm—I'm not," I said. I didn't recognize my own voice, it sounded so cracked and wrung out.

DEAD TO ME

When I lifted my head, Cy was craning his neck, trying to get a better look at my face. He looked unsure of himself, and a little like he'd rather be somewhere else. Maybe he could patch up a scrape, I thought, but a girl who turned strange, dead-eyed, and quiet for minutes at a time was beyond his skill or patience.

Or maybe I was wrong.

"Come here," he said, and held out his arms to me.

I'd never liked being touched—it came with too many strings attached. If one of the boys I'd dated had opened his arms to me like that, a minute later, he'd be trying to snake a hand up my shirt. My mother only fussed over me when she was putting on a show for her friends, or when she was feeling drunk and maudlin. And the last time Annie had given me a hug, she left.

But Cy didn't know me. He didn't owe me anything, and I didn't have anything he wanted. Maybe that was why I leaned into his arms.

I rested my head on his shoulder and let him pull me close to his chest and stroke my hair. Every time I thought he was about to let go, he held me tighter, and every time, I felt relieved because I wasn't ready to let go yet.

No one had ever held me like that before, hard and close and as long as I needed.

I don't know how long we stayed like that, but when I finally let go, I felt like I could breathe again. I looked at him. He looked at me, and neither one of us said anything until I saw Cy's eyes flicker up to the clock that hung over the sink. It was four in the morning.

"Oh, shit," he said, and this time he didn't correct himself. "Alice, I'm so sorry, but I have to go to work."

"You just came from work."

"I know, and now I have to go to my other job."

"I'm sorry I kept you up all night," I said. "How many jobs do you have, anyway?"

Cy thought about this for a minute.

"Is that a hard question?" I asked.

"No, I just realized that I must be an extremely lazy person, because I work one less job than your sister does," he said. "There's Marty's, where I'm going now to clean bathrooms and take out the trash, and Musso and Frank. I work for Jerry when he needs me. And when time allows, I pursue my love of the stage and screen. Not that I ever get paid for that."

"What about Annie?" I asked, realizing Cy knew things about her life I couldn't, things I wanted to know.

"Let's see," Cy said, counting off the jobs on his fingers. "She works for Jerry, too, but you already knew that. She waits tables at a diner near Olvera Street. She makes deliveries for a bookie, reads movie scripts for an agent. And she works at Marty's."

"She's one of the girls who drinks ginger ale and pretends it's champagne?" I asked, taken aback.

"She's pretty dazzling at it," Cy said. "No businessman's wallet is safe when she is near."

"Oh."

Maybe I was a sheltered little priss after all, but I wasn't sure how much more I wanted to hear about it. Something in my face must have given away my thoughts, because Cy's smile stiffened, and I could tell he wanted to take back what he'd said.

That was when the telephone started to ring. I froze in place at the kitchen table, staring down the hall toward it.

After four rings, Cy asked, "Are you going to answer it?"

I let it ring twice more. If it was my mother, I didn't want to talk to her, not in the shape she'd be in.

The phone rang again.

If it was Conrad Donahue or Rex or the man with the blue polka-dot suspenders, I didn't want them to know I was here.

If it was my father or Jerry Shaffer, I didn't know what I'd say to them. And if it was the hospital calling with bad news, I didn't want to know.

"They'll hang up," I said.

Twelve rings. Then fifteen.

"Listen, my car is parked outside," Cy said. "If it's Conrad or Rex, we'll go out the back door, and I'll have you out of here in less than a minute."

I shook my head. There wasn't anybody I wanted to talk to badly enough to take the risk. Or at least that was what I'd thought until Cy asked, "What if it's Gabrielle?"

I scrambled for the phone, picked up the receiver, and held it to my ear.

"Hello?" I whispered.

In the background, I heard shouting, then a siren.

"Who is this?" I asked.

As soon as she opened her mouth and drew a breath, I knew who was calling. Cassie sounded tired, scared, and at least as shaky as I did, and the first thing she said to me was, "You were telling the truth."

CHAPTER 17

breathed a sigh of relief.

"Cassie, what's going on?"

"I'm at the hospital with Annie and your mother."

I sat down on the floor in the hallway, my back up against the wall, my legs stretched out in front of me.

"With my *mother*? What are you doing there? How did she—"

"I stayed up to make sure you came back," Cassie said. "But I fell asleep, so I didn't know if you'd made it home or not, and I was worried, so I realized that the only way to find out was to break into your house and see if you were there."

"You did what?"

"I climbed the palm tree and went in through your bedroom window, but I tripped, and the noise woke up your mom, and she came running in, and I was there and you weren't, and it was one in the morning."

"So you told her," I said.

Cy met my eyes and mouthed, "Who is it?" I motioned for him to wait, then grabbed a pen and paper from the hall table and started to write while Cassie explained.

"I'm sorry, Alice. I didn't know what else to do."

"It's okay, Cassie. It doesn't matter."

I held up what I'd written and showed it to Cy:

Cassie (my friend) at hosp. w/ Annie & Mom

"How is she?"

"Not so good, Alice. I think she's about to snap."

I was confused until I realized she wasn't talking about Annie, and that my sheltered friend with her teetotaling Midwestern parents was in no way prepared to deal with my mother.

"Keep her calm. Go through her purse and hide her pills, her flask, whatever she brought with her. Get her some coffee. See if you can get her to eat something, and I'll be there as soon as I can. What about Annie? How is she?"

"That's the other thing," Cassie said. "Your mom had Annie transferred out of County Hospital. We're at Cedars of Lebanon now. It's fancier or something? I don't know."

Ordinarily, I would have rolled my eyes at my mother's snobbishness—god forbid her daughter should lie in a coma at County Hospital alongside the riffraff—but when I heard the news, I felt like cheering. Conrad thought he knew where Annie was, but thanks to my mother, we were still one step ahead of him.

"What happened to you, Alice?" Cassie asked. "Why didn't you come back?"

"Conrad Donahue kidnapped me at the pay phone, and he and some of his goons took my father and me up to Griffith Park to . . ."

I trailed off, worried that Cassie would hang up on me if I started talking about movie stars again.

"It's okay, Alice," Cassie said. "I believe you."

I wondered if it was wise to tell Cassie anything else. I didn't want to worry her or put her in any more danger than I already had, but it wasn't fair to keep the truth from her, either. Whether she'd meant to be or not, she was in the middle of things now.

"Cassie, it *was* Conrad. He's the one who tried to kill Annie. He had my father tied up in the trunk of his car. I thought he was going to kill us."

I heard a hitch in Cassie's breath.

"How'd you get away?"

"I ran," I said. "I think my father got away, too, but I don't know where he is now."

"What should I tell your mother?"

"Tell her I'm on my way," I said. "And Cassie . . ."

"Yeah?"

"Thanks."

After I hung up with Cassie, Cy said, "Let me give you a ride to the hospital."

"Won't you be late for work?" I asked.

"I don't care."

We cleaned up the kitchen first, put away the frozen peas, and gathered up the iodine-soaked cotton and the bloody hand towel to throw out.

"Why were you carrying this around?" Cy asked, holding up

the old copy of the *Los Angeles Times* I'd picked up at the Red Car stop. It was spotted with blood, too.

I took the newspaper from him and folded it under my arm.

"I like to stay informed about the news of the world," I said with a shrug.

"Even when you're getting punched in the face?"

"Especially then."

I followed Cy out the back door, locking up behind us, and we cut through the neighbors' backyards until we came to the street where his car was parked. As we stepped out onto the sidewalk, I looked up and down the block for the Rolls-Royce, but there was only one car in sight. With its battered fender and flaking paint, I knew there wasn't a chance it belonged to Conrad Donahue.

As we walked toward it, I thought about my father and wondered where he was right now. Was he still making his way through the brush, down the steep gravel paths to safety—or had Conrad caught up with him?

It was a huge park, I told myself, and my father would be able to go places a car wouldn't. But it was so dark. Even if he got away, if he got lost or hurt, he'd be all alone out there. There was nothing I could do for him, I told myself, so it was better not to think about it. Only it wasn't that easy.

Cy held the car door open for me, but when I started to get in, he put a hand on my shoulder.

"Wait," he said.

I felt my body tense up. My thoughts had drifted a long way off from his kindness, off to a place where a hand on your shoulder meant you were about to get tossed into the backseat of a car.

"What?" I asked, jerking away from his touch.

His hand slipped from my shoulder, and he backed away, a hurt look on his face.

"You're one of those nice girls, Alice. Nice house, nice things," he said with a sad smile. "Only you're not nice."

When I pulled away from him, I hadn't meant anything by it, and he hadn't done anything wrong. But then he opened his mouth, and it was just like back at the restaurant. Once again, he stepped just a little too close, assumed just a little more than I liked.

"How would you know?" I asked, getting into the car and slamming the door behind me.

I sat there by myself for quite a while. Cy took his time walking around to the other side of the car, and when he finally got in, he stared straight ahead without saying a word.

I was about to get out of the car and find my own way to the hospital when he turned to me.

"I'm sorry," he said.

He put the car in gear, and we pulled out into the street. He didn't turn on the headlights until we'd pulled onto Fairfax.

"I didn't have any business talking to you like that."

I waited for the explanation, the "but" that would wipe out all the words before it. It never came.

"It's okay," I said. I thought about saying more, but decided to follow Cy's lead and leave it at that.

"What was it you wanted to tell me?" I asked a moment later. "Before we got in the car."

When we stopped at a red light, he turned to face me and said, "I wanted to tell you that your sister has friends. She borrows cars and goes on road trips. She throws herself birthday parties. She still sings when she feels like it."

"Why are you telling me that?"

"Because I don't want you to think her life is ugly," Cy said. "I saw your face when I told you she worked at Marty's. I just didn't want you to think that was all there was to it."

"I don't think that," I said, even though I knew he was right. I'd been horrified at the idea of my sister sitting in a bar and flirting with men for money. It *had* seemed ugly to me.

But it wasn't the whole story, and I'd missed the last four years of it. Besides, nothing about Annie could ever be ugly.

But that wasn't the only thing Cy was right about.

He barely knew me, we weren't friends, and it was none of his business, but he'd still landed on the truth of it: I wasn't nice. I never was. I'd pushed away the last friend I had, hidden the truth about Annie from my mother, even though I could see she was suffering. And when a boy who'd been nothing but kind to me touched my shoulder, I flinched away from him.

I decided to pack the last few minutes away, to move someplace a little brighter.

"Might I read to you a passage from scripture?" I asked, unfolding the newspaper and snapping the pages open. "Something from the gospel of Hedda Hopper?"

"Oh yes, please," Cy said.

The tension that had settled in between us melted as I read him stories from the gossip column about whether Elizabeth Taylor would have to dye her hair for her upcoming role in *Little Women*, whether a certain MGM leading lady was pregnant, and whether Mickey Rooney was ruining his career. Next, I put on a high, breathy voice and fluttered my eyelashes as I read aloud to Cy about the many challenges facing a particularly vapid newlywed starlet.

"'I just want to be a good wife to Bobby. I never have been the kind of girl who made many pot roasts, but, boy, I sure hope I can learn!'"

"Read another one," Cy said, laughing as we crossed Western.

But I didn't have it in me. My eyes had drifted back down the page to the picture of Conrad and my father and Gabrielle and the dress that Gabrielle was wearing.

"Cy, please stop the car," I said, grabbing the dashboard as I turned to him. "I need to get out here."

I'd seen that dress before, somewhere a party dress definitely didn't belong.

"Are you nuts? I'm not doing that."

"Please, Cy, it can't wait."

"I thought you needed to go to the hospital."

"The hospital's not far from here. I can walk."

"Alice, you're being very strange."

"Please trust me," I said. "I'll tell you all about it after you get off work. You can meet me at Cedars."

"And you'll be there?"

"I promise. Just please let me out of the car."

Cy pulled over on Sunset Boulevard, a puzzled look on his face.

"Are you sure about this, Alice?"

I nodded, practically leaping out of the car.

"Be careful," he called after me as I slammed the door shut.

"I will be," I said. "I'll see you soon, Cy."

As soon as he pulled away from the curb, I dashed across Sunset Boulevard, thinking about a yellow chiffon dress I'd seen dancing on a clothesline.

That was why Ruth didn't make sense.

CHAPTER 18

A few minutes later, I was sneaking through the overgrown courtyard at the Stratford Arms, which seemed even less hospitable in the gray hours before daybreak. As I approached Ruth's bungalow, I dropped to my knees and crawled through the grass. There were no lights on, but I circled the building, looking for signs of movement through the windows. The bedroom window was open, and I hoisted myself up on the sill and pushed aside the gauzy white curtains that fluttered in the breeze.

Ruth slept on her back, one arm tucked around her waist, the other raised up and cradled around her head like a ballet dancer's pose. I lowered my feet down to the floor without a sound. She let out a dainty snore as I crept past her bed, and I began to explore the rest of the bungalow.

It wasn't like Irma's place, where you could tell that once upon

184

a time there'd been carefully chosen possessions, lovingly arranged. Here, there had been no effort to make the place homey. The living room I'd already seen, but every room was the same way. Nothing in the bedroom but a bed. One glass, one bowl, one spoon in the kitchen cupboards. A toothbrush in the bathroom.

A woman with these possessions, a woman who ran a dirty-picture racket with Rex, who kept her drug stash on the pantry shelves, did not spend her Monday mornings washing yellow chiffon party dresses. Not for herself, anyway.

Finally, I went into the back bedroom, the only other room I hadn't seen. An empty bed. A slight indentation in the pillow where a head had rested, blanket and sheets pulled back.

Then I heard a creak on the floorboards and turned to find Ruth standing behind me, ghostly in a white nightgown that hung to the floor. No wonder she could get away with sleeping with her windows open. She'd probably been awake the second my fingers touched the windowsill.

"I wondered when you'd be coming back," she said.

Gabrielle had been here.

She had been here the day when I first came to the Stratford Arms, hiding in the back bedroom while Ruth and I drank Cokes in the living room. And she'd slipped out the window when Rex went out the back door, chasing after me.

"Sorry about that," Ruth said with a shrug.

If Gabrielle had fallen into Rex's hands, she was a dead girl. If I'd fallen into Rex's hands, well, Ruth had just met me, and we hadn't really hit it off. I understood. Sort of.

Irma and Millie's building wasn't far from the Stratford Arms;

Gabrielle had stayed there. She'd stayed at Annie's Main Street flophouse, and other places, too. Places Ruth didn't know anything about.

"She moves around, never more than one night in any place. But not for much longer," Ruth said. "She's running out of places to hide. We need to get her out of town."

It seemed like such a sensible thing to do that I wondered why they hadn't done it right away. And why Ruth seemed so disappointed at the prospect.

"Back to her parents?" I asked. Jerry had said she was a runaway. Maybe they had found a way to get her back to them.

"Annie told me she would rather we turned her over to Conrad." Ruth shook her head distractedly, then sighed. "What was she even doing there that night? She was supposed to be here."

I remembered what Jerry had told me about the way Annie could sense when to help a girl home to her parents and when the girl would be better off where she was.

"Who's she going to stay with? Millie?" I asked, cringing because I realized that this was the plan Ruth had in mind. Millie might have been safely out of town, but it was still no good. Her face had been plastered on the front page of too many movie tabloids. Even with a dye job and conservative clothes, she was bound to attract attention wherever she went. And I had my doubts that she would prove to resemble anything close to a fit guardian.

"Not forever, but for now, it's the safest place to send her. Conrad doesn't know where Millie is, Jerry doesn't know, you don't know."

Should my word fail to convince you, go to Irma's apartment at 6326 Lexington and lift up the floorboards under her bed.

Suddenly, I got a horrible, hollowed-out feeling in my chest, and the sour taste of bile rose in the back of my throat. I half sat, half fell onto the bed as I thought about Millie's letter. Conrad had read all of it, and the second he and his goons had finished dealing with my father, I knew exactly where they'd be going.

I believe what you find there will be of interest.

"What's wrong with you?" Ruth held her hand to my forehead, brushing back the damp strands of hair that stuck there.

"Is there any chance that Gabrielle is at Irma's apartment right now?" I said.

Her hand dropped from my forehead, and she lifted me up by my elbow. "Alice, I don't know. I lost track of her after she ran away from Rex."

I didn't know whether she was telling me the truth or not.

"If she's there, you have to get her out!" I shouted, breaking free of her grasp. "There's some kind of evidence under Irma's bed, and Conrad knows about it. He's probably headed there right now!"

Looking almost ill, Ruth shoved me aside and ran from the room. I followed her to the other bedroom, where I found her already out of her nightgown and tugging a dress over her head.

When she saw me standing in the doorway, she said, "Want to do something useful?"

I nodded.

"Start the car, the blue Lincoln out front. Wanda keeps the keys in the green bowl on her desk."

"I don't know how to drive," I said, feeling like a baby.

Ruth gave me a poisonous look as she reached behind her back to zip up the dress. "What *can* you do?"

Rather than stand there and be sneered at, I ran out the front door and up the sidewalk to the large bungalow that served as

Wanda's office. This time, I was careful of the screen door and closed it quietly behind me. The bowl was buried under a pile of newspapers and movie magazines, all clipped for Wanda's macabre scrapbook, but the keys were there, just like Ruth said they would be. I snatched them and ran down the sidewalk and out the Stratford Arms gates. The Lincoln was right where Ruth said it would be, too.

In fact, everything was right where Ruth said it would be, except Ruth. After five minutes had gone by, I took the key out of the ignition and went back to check on her.

She was long gone, out the back door, and I didn't know why I'd expected otherwise. I stepped outside and saw what I hadn't during my last visit. A hard-packed dirt lane ran behind the row of stuccoed buildings, all the way to the road. I could see the tire tracks, and even a city girl like me could tell they were fresh.

Why had my sister been working with this prickly, lying girl?

No, I thought, correcting myself. *Girl* wasn't the right word for Ruth. It wasn't the right word for any of them. Girls had someone to take care of them. Annie took care of herself. Girls cried when boys broke their hearts. Ruth didn't look like she'd cry even if one broke her hand. Girls fluttered about like canaries in a cage. Millie had packed up her entire life in an afternoon and gotten out of town. Their lives were hard—too hard for some of them—but they were free, too, and none of them seemed to be afraid of anything.

I didn't exactly like Ruth, but I admired her a little bit.

Feeling more useless than I'd ever felt before, I turned around and went back into the kitchen, sitting down at the table to collect my thoughts. I could go back to Millie and Irma's building, but why? If I'd just stayed out of things, none of this would have happened. Ruth knew it, too, and it was no wonder that she wanted me as far away from her as possible. I couldn't save anyone, couldn't help anyone, and I certainly couldn't stop people like Conrad and Rex from doing any twisted, wicked thing they liked.

So why did Millie give you the letter, then? Why did Annie send you that postcard? You didn't stumble onto those things by accident. They'd meant for you to have them. They knew what would need to be done, and probably in some way, they knew they wouldn't be around to do it themselves. You might not be the best girl for the job, but you're the only one they have.

I still didn't know what to do, but one thing was clear in my mind—I didn't want anyone else to get hurt.

Ruth didn't have a phone, but I knew that Wanda did. Back up the sidewalk I went, hoping that she wasn't an early riser. The sky was still gray, but streaked now with ribbons of pink and gold light.

I unearthed the telephone from Wanda's desk, picked up the receiver, and dialed the police. I knew Annie's friends seemed skittish about the police, but I didn't know where else to turn. And even dirty cops would respond to a burglary in progress. I gave the dispatch Millie and Irma's apartment address, and threw in Rex's description for good measure. When she asked my name, I hung up. And then, outside the gates of the Stratford Arms, I taught myself how to drive. I'll say this for it: it wasn't the hardest thing I'd done in the past twenty-four hours.

I flipped the ignition switch on, pushed the starter button, and tapped my foot on the accelerator, just like I'd seen my father do a hundred times. The only problem was, when I did it, nothing happened. I tried again, and each time, the engine wheezed and chugged but wouldn't start. I beat my hands against the steering wheel in frustration and wished I'd been paying more attention during my sixteen years of being driven around in cars. Suddenly, a little wisp of conversation drifted into my head. Cassie's father had been teaching her to drive this spring, even if he wouldn't let her leave the driveway. I remembered one night when I was sitting in my room with the window open and hearing his panicked, half-yelled instructions. "Just a little gas, then pull out the choke. That's enough! Stop! No! Well, now you've flooded the engine, Cassie."

With Mr. Jurgens's nasal Midwestern voice in my mind, I tried again. I pulled out the choke, and the engine wheezed again, but this time, it turned over and the car started. As the car idled, I applied myself to the task of getting the thing in gear, which was easy once I figured out the difference between the brake and the clutch. I put the car in the lowest gear, tapped my foot on the accelerator again, and the car jerked away from the curb.

I won't say I drove well, or that the ride was smooth, but I only stalled out three times. All the same, I was glad there weren't many other cars on the road, early as it was. I parked around the corner from Irma's and Millie's apartments, then navigated my way through a maze of alleys, backyards, and parking garages, approaching the building from the rear.

I wasn't the first to arrive. As I hunkered down in the mass of shrubs beneath the pepper trees, I saw Rex dash up the stairs. The man with the blue polka-dot suspenders stood at the foot of the stairs pretending to read a newspaper and looking about as natural as a smiling undertaker. It didn't help that the front of his shirt was spattered with a fine spray of blood. I wondered whose.

I scanned the street for the others. There was no sign of Conrad's Rolls-Royce. Then I heard shouting coming from a second-floor window. Both voices were ones I'd heard before.

"Hand it over!" Rex bellowed. "I know you have it."

"What, so you get all the credit? Get your hands off of me."

The moment I recognized Ruth's voice, my heart sunk. If she

was here, that meant I'd been right about Gabrielle's hiding place. Now Gabrielle was trapped up there with Rex, and if she tried to escape, the man in the blue polka-dot suspenders would be waiting at the foot of the stairs for her.

Or did it mean something else? The way Ruth and Rex were yelling, it didn't sound like they were fighting over a girl. I'd assumed she was worried about Gabrielle, but maybe it was the evidence under Irma's bed Ruth had really come running after.

Either way, it was trouble.

As they continued to shout at each other, a police car pulled up in front of the building and a pair of officers got out. One was skinny and freckle-faced with red hair. The other was sandy-haired and more solidly built, the beginnings of a gut spilling over his belt. They walked up to Conrad's man, who put down his newspaper and bid them a good morning. The police officer pointed up toward the second-floor apartment windows and asked the man in the blue polka-dot suspenders something I couldn't hear.

The man in the blue polka-dot suspenders whispered something to the two police officers, and I watched in disbelief as he reached into his pocket and pulled out a roll of cash. He peeled several bills off and handed a healthy pile of cash to each of the officers, then winked and laid a finger on the side of his nose. The sandy-haired cop returned the gesture, the thin one tipped his cap, and without another word between them, the officers turned to go back to their car.

No wonder Annie had worried about turning Gabrielle over to the cops.

Just as the officers were pocketing the money, though, I heard the creak of rusty metal coming from above. I craned my neck and peered through the branches of the pepper trees to see a petite figure in ill-fitting clothes climbing down the side of the building on the fire escape. A thick tangle of hair hid the side of her face, but I didn't need to see it to know that this was Gabrielle. Somehow, she'd gotten out of the apartment without being seen, but climbing down the side of the building, she was exposed. From where he stood, the man in the blue polka-dot suspenders wouldn't have been able to see her, but if he took even a few steps closer to my hiding place, she'd come into view. If he spotted Gabrielle, there wouldn't be anywhere for her to go, and there wouldn't be anything I could do about it.

I held my breath as the police officers walked to their car, hoping the man in the blue polka-dot suspenders would stay where he was, his eyes fixed on the officers, hoping nothing would give Gabrielle away.

Suddenly, there was a crash from the second-floor window. Ruth screamed and a gunshot rang out from inside the apartment building. The two police officers looked at each other, then ran back toward the apartment, guns unholstered. One circled around the man in the blue polka-dot suspenders while the other started toward the stairs.

Conrad's man whistled loudly, and I heard footsteps slapping down the steps. Rex emerged into the sunlight, pushing Ruth along in front of him.

"Search her, boss," Rex said to the man in the blue polka-dot suspenders. "She's got the goods."

Each of the officers drew their weapons and dropped to one knee, shoulders squared to line up their shots.

"Let go of the girl," said the bigger one with the sandy hair.

I burrowed in as best I could behind the row of stones. On my belly, I crawled through the bushes, hoping I could make it to the relative safety of the overgrown backyards where I could at least stand up and run if bullets started flying.

They exchanged a short glance, then Rex pushed Ruth to the side and gave the officers what might have once been a charming smile without putting down his gun. The man with the polka-dot suspenders smiled, too, and released his grip on the gun, letting it dangle off his thumb. With his free hand, he slowly reached into his pocket, pulled something from it, and tossed it so it landed in front of the two officers.

The older cop burst out laughing. The younger, redheaded cop looked confused until his partner picked it up and shoved it in front of his face. The man in the blue polka-dot suspenders had thrown down an LAPD badge, just like the ones they wore. The younger man's eyes grew wide, and he opened his mouth to stammer out an apology.

Rex shot him in the chest before he could get it out.

Before the other officer could register what had happened, the man in the polka-dot suspenders drew up his gun and fired a shot into his head.

For a moment, everything seemed to happen in slow motion—the bullets whizzing through the air, the men falling to the ground. But the blood pooled on the sidewalk so fast, more blood than I'd ever seen at once, more than I'd known could come out of a person. Just as fast, Rex grabbed Ruth and all three of them piled into a black car parked in front of the building and peeled off down the street.

I looked up at the fire escape, but there was no sign of Gabrielle.

I ran from my hiding place. One officer was already dead, his gray eyes motionless and wide open. His partner was still alive, though. He lay on his back, clutching at his chest and sucking for breath. I peeled off my sweater and pressed it to the wound.

"I'm sorry," I whispered.

My sweater was already soaked through and hadn't even slowed the bleeding, so when he lifted a hand from his side, I took it. It seemed to calm him somewhat, and the wet, heaving breaths grew easier and farther apart. I sat with him until his eyelids fluttered for the last time before falling shut for good.

My hands began to shake, and I couldn't make them stop. The shaking spread up my arms, into my shoulders, and down my legs. "I'm sorry, I'm sorry, I'm sorry," I said over and over as I rocked back and forth.

How long Jerry had been standing there, how much he had seen, I didn't know, but suddenly he was kneeling beside me, his arms wrapped around my shoulders so tightly that when I shook against them, it was like waves breaking on a rock. Gently, he unwrapped my fingers from around the dead man's hand.

"You're here," I said.

"Of course I'm here," he said, staring at the cuts and bruises on my face.

Jerry pulled me to my feet, but when he started to run toward the bushes, I froze in place.

"Come on, Alice," he said, tugging on my arm. "We have to go."

He was right. I knew that, but all I could do was look back over my shoulder at the bodies on the sidewalk and think about how the police officer's last breaths had sounded, the way his hand loosened its grip on mine as he died.

"Alice." Jerry's voice sounded like it was coming from the other side of a dream. "There'll be more police here any minute."

"Gabrielle," I said, looking up to the fire escape she'd climbed down just a minute before. "She was here, Jerry."

Tears filled my eyes, and I fought the urge to sit down on the pavement and sob. Gabrielle had come so close to falling into Conrad's hands, and I hadn't been able to help her. She was still out there on her own, and it wouldn't be long before they were on her trail again.

From the things Rex had been shouting, it sounded like Ruth had managed to collect whatever piece of evidence Millie had hidden in the lockbox under Irma's bed, but she was in a car with Conrad's cronies. It wouldn't be long before they forced it out of her hands.

And worst of all, two men were dead.

I couldn't move. I couldn't think straight. My head felt like it was full of tangled string, and every thread I picked up led to a giant knot in the space where my brain should be. There was one thread, though, that spooled out yard after yard after yard—*I'm sorry, I'm sorry, I'm sorry.*

They were both the right age to have been soldiers not so long ago. It seemed cruel to think that they'd escaped German and Japanese and Italian bullets, only to be brought down by American ones. And I'd as good as killed both of them.

"It's my fault the police were there," I said, my breath coming in gasps as I tried to hold back the scream I could feel rising in my throat. "I called them. I told them to come."

Jerry dragged me through the shrubs and around to the back of the apartment building so at least we were out of view.

"Alice, tell me about Gabrielle," he said patiently. "Is that the girl Annie was protecting? She was *here*?"

I stammered out what I'd seen. I told him about the fire escape, about Rex shouting for the man in the blue polka-dot suspenders to search Ruth before shoving her into their getaway car.

"It's not too late," Jerry said when I'd finished talking. "We can still find her, but we need to move fast. Can you do that, Alice?"

He looked at me with concern, and I nodded. Then he reached inside his coat pocket and drew out a Kodak Brownie camera.

"I found this under Irma's bed," he said, putting his arm around my shoulder. "Conrad doesn't have it, he doesn't have Gabrielle, and he's not going to. Now, let's go."

I stared at him, stunned by what he'd just shown me. I'd doubted Jerry, believed the things that Millie had told me, and yet, when I needed him most, there he was.

"How did you find me?" I asked. "How did you know I was here?"

"Not now," he said. "We don't have much time to look for her."

Together, we set off through a row of hedges. We cut through the backyards at breakneck speed, searching every garden, shrub, alley, and derelict shed on the block without success. As we neared the street Jerry slowed to a walk and peered up and down the sidewalk, looking for any signs of danger before we stepped out into the open. A few yards away, I saw his beat-up Plymouth.

"Act natural," he said.

We walked down the sidewalk at a leisurely pace, like we were two ordinary people out for an early morning stroll. However, our talk was anything but small.

"We should check bus stops," I said, thinking back to my escape from Griffith Park the night before. "Streetcar stations."

"Good idea," Jerry said.

We got in the Plymouth and drove, zigzagging through the streets of Hollywood, as far as Gabrielle could have run in the ten minutes or so since she'd climbed down the fire escape. First, we checked the main streets: Sunset, Vine, Santa Monica Boulevard.

When we didn't find her waiting for a bus or a streetcar, we took to the less-trafficked streets.

"I called Cy at Marty's an hour or so ago," Jerry said, steering the Plymouth down a sleepy residential street. "That's how I found you. He told me you jumped out of his car at the corner of Sunset and Western at four thirty in the morning for no reason. I could only think of two places you'd be going from there."

"Ruth's place or Millie and Irma's," I said.

"I went to both."

"So did I."

We could drive more slowly on these streets without attracting attention. I peered out the passenger-side window, under cars, behind fences, between houses, but there was no sign of Gabrielle anywhere. It was like she'd just disappeared.

After a few more minutes, Jerry turned to me and said, "We can't keep doing this much longer, Alice."

I wanted to argue with him. It felt wrong to give up the search when we were this close, but this time, I knew he was right. If Gabrielle had managed to catch a streetcar, she could have been two miles away. She could have been hiding in a backyard we'd missed. She could have been anywhere, and we were out of time.

Someone would have found the two bodies on the sidewalk. The police would be on their way. They'd find my sweater at the crime scene. They'd start combing the neighborhood for suspicious cars.

And if they found us, there would be no hiding my hands, the front of my shirt, the tips of my shoes, all smeared with a dead police officer's blood.

CHAPTER 19

"W here are we going?" I asked. We were heading south now, away from Hollywood.

"My office," Jerry said. "I'll feel better once we get you cleaned up and I have the film in this camera developed."

As we neared downtown, Jerry swerved into a narrow alley, dinging a trash can with his fender. Instead of slowing down, he pushed the gas pedal to the floor. Finally, we stopped near the back entrance of a seedy brownstone that might have once been someplace comparatively nice, maybe a state mental hospital or a women's prison. Jerry parked the car in the alley, and I followed him inside.

We took the stairs to the fourth floor. Jerry unlocked the door to an office at the top of the stairs, then handed me the keys to the washroom at the end of the hall.

"Come back to my office when you're finished," he said. "I'll be in the darkroom."

After locking myself in the washroom, I peeled off my shirt and ran it under the faucet, scrubbing soap into the fabric until the bloodstains faded to pink. Then I scrubbed my shoes, my hands, and my arms before getting dressed again.

As I studied my face and my sodden clothes in the washroom mirror, I thought about my father and wondered what kind of shape he was in at that moment. It was morning, seven or eight hours since he'd made his escape from the trunk of Conrad's car. Where had he run from there? Conrad's cronies had made their way out of the park in that time and gone over to Irma's apartment. Did that mean they'd found my father, or that they'd given up looking?

I closed my eyes and pictured him running out of the park toward Hollywood Boulevard, just like I had. I hoped that was how it'd happened. Even if I couldn't imagine what might have happened to him after that.

When I went back to Jerry's office, there was percolator coffee brewing on a hot plate, a clean mug drying on the edge of the sink for me.

And Cy, staring out the window that looked onto a fire escape and another seedy brownstone.

When I opened the office door, he jumped and nearly knocked over the percolator. Jerry's office was about the same size as one of my mother's closets, and Cy crossed it in two steps. For a moment, I thought he was going to hug me, but he seemed to think better of it when he saw my soaking-wet shirt. Instead, he took my hand and squeezed it.

"I was so worried, Alice."

"I'm here now." I squeezed his hand back. "And I'm fine."

"Why didn't you go to the hospital? After Jerry called me, I tried to get ahold of your friend Cassie there, and she said you never showed up. Then I went by your house, and after that, I just drove up and down Sunset Boulevard looking for you."

Behind what looked like a closet door, I heard a thump and a clatter, followed by swearing.

"Everything's okay. Don't come in," Jerry shouted once he'd recovered himself. "Light will ruin the film."

Cy continued. "When I couldn't think of anyplace else you might be, I came here. I thought maybe Jerry had found you."

I took the mug from the sink and poured myself coffee from the percolator. I needed it badly.

"How'd you get in?" I asked, taking a sip.

"Let myself in," Cy said, pulling a huge ring of keys from his pocket. There was probably one for every job he had, or had ever had.

"You're supposed to be at work right now, aren't you?"

"I went to Marty's for an hour or so before Jerry called, but I wasn't exactly in a toilet-scrubbing state of mind. Mostly I just paced around the bar worrying about you," he said. "Alice, I'm so sorry. I never should have let you get out of the car like that. I should have gone with you."

Looking at Cy's tired face and bloodshot eyes, I remembered I wasn't the only one who had been up all night. I handed him my mug of coffee.

"No, you shouldn't have," I said. I wouldn't have wished the things I'd seen that morning on anyone. "I'm glad you're here now, though."

Too tired to stand another minute, I took a seat on the window-sill. Cy sat down next to me, and we passed the mug of coffee back and forth, sipping quietly, until Jerry emerged from the darkroom. A heady brew of developing solutions wafted out.

Jerry unclipped the freshly developed negatives from the wire where they'd been drying, and brought them over to the window.

"Let's see what we have," he said, holding the negatives up to the light.

We all gathered in close and studied them, one image after another. None of us lasted more than a few seconds. Cy gasped. I covered my mouth with the back of my hand. Jerry looked away.

The pictures were dark and hard to make out, but then I guessed that whoever took them hadn't dared use a flash. In the first, Conrad Donahue punched my sister in the face. In the second, Rex swung a baseball bat at her. Her back arched from the force of the blow, her arms lifted out to the sides as if she was about to take flight. In the third, Conrad kicked Annie in the stomach while she lay huddled on the ground.

"Thank god we found these first," Jerry said, his voice hardly above a whisper.

"How did you get them?" Cy asked.

I wondered myself. Jerry had never seen Millie's *Open If I Am Dead or Missing* letter, so I wondered how he'd known to look under the floorboards.

"Annie told me about that hiding spot in Irma's apartment a long time ago. She just happened to mention it in conversation—she thought it was neat," Jerry said. "The way Millie was watching that apartment like a hawk—when she should have been getting out of town—made me think there was something up there she didn't want me getting my hands on."

Jerry continued. "Better me than Conrad, though. I think even Millie would agree with that."

"What about the pictures?" I asked. "Who took them?"

"My guess is Millie. If Annie didn't trust the meeting enough to bring Gabrielle, maybe she thought something was going to go bad. Maybe this was her insurance."

Stunned, I took the negatives from him and held them up to the light again.

"Why wouldn't she just call the police?"

"Annie was supposed to be *meeting* the police. I didn't know it was a setup," Jerry said quietly. "I never told anyone except the cop she was supposed to meet. But maybe there's really nobody left in the department we can trust anymore. I didn't even know Walter Hanrahan was dirty until I saw him shoot a man in cold blood this morning."

"Who's Walter Hanrahan?" I asked.

Jerry cleared his throat, and I remembered that I could narrow down the number of police officers who had shot a man in cold blood that morning to exactly one.

Hanrahan. So that was his name. I'd wanted to trust him last night in the hills, taken his polka-dot suspenders as some sign of genial goodwill. Of course I had. He was my friendly neighborhood police officer. Looking trustworthy was his business.

Jerry rapped his knuckles on the desk. "I say if we can't go to the police, we go to the papers. The pictures nail Conrad and Rex for what they did to Annie. It'll be safe for Gabrielle then. She won't have to hide anymore."

"She won't be safe. She'll be in more danger than ever if we turn over those pictures," Cy said, shaking his head. "Jerry, has it occurred to you that maybe the reason you haven't found Gabrielle by now is that she doesn't want to be found?"

Jerry looked baffled. "Don't you want justice for Irma and Annie?"

"I'd rather get Gabrielle out of town in one piece."

They continued to argue, but their voices became indistinct and turned to white noise in my ears. They were talking about a future where Gabrielle could come out of hiding or get out of town, but it didn't change the fact that we needed to find her first. She wasn't safe yet, and what Ruth had told me a few hours before was more true than ever—Gabrielle was running out of places to hide.

I wondered where Annie told her to go if things went bad. If Gabrielle was really desperate, where would she turn? Jerry? Cy? Me?

"I need someone to take me to the hospital," I said, interrupting Jerry and Cy's argument in midsentence.

It hit me all at once where Gabrielle had been headed when she climbed down the fire escape. If things got this bad, if she had nowhere else to turn, if everyone she knew to trust was gone, there was only one option.

Gabrielle would go to Annie.

"Are you okay?" Jerry asked.

Millie had been hiding Gabrielle, too, and she knew Annie was in the hospital. If the girl had asked, I was sure Millie would have told her where my sister was—maybe even what had happened to her.

"I-I think that's where she is."

It sounded so possible when it was only in my head. Once the words were out of my mouth, though, I didn't feel half so sure of them.

Jerry wasn't convinced, either.

"You need sleep, Alice. You're not making any sense," Jerry said. "Even if Gabrielle decided to go to the hospital, how would she know which one?"

"I'll take you," Cy interjected, but Jerry wasn't finished.

"And even if she did find her, what good would it do? Your sister isn't in any position to help her now."

Cy and I both turned on him, our eyes narrowed.

"Do you have any better ideas?" Cy asked.

"Are you saying we *shouldn't* look for her?" I asked.

Jerry threw up his hands.

"Look for her," he said. "By all means, look. You should. Maybe your luck will be better than mine."

"Do you want to go with us?" I asked.

Jerry shook his head. "I'm going to stay here and make prints of these negatives for the newspapers. I know you don't like it, Cy, but I still think it's the best chance we have."

Cy shifted his feet, a thoughtful look on his face as he considered his next words.

"No, I get it," he said. "If you go to the papers with dirt like this on Conrad Donahue, there's going to be blowback. Just make sure you're ready for it."

"I have to go," I told Jerry, feeling disloyal for leaving him here. "I have to look for her."

"I know you do," he said. "Just don't . . . I don't know . . . try not to get your hopes up."

"Give me one of those business cards for keeps," I said.

"What for?" he asked, but reached into his pocket and handed me one. It was bent at the corner and smudged with a thumbprint.

"So I can call you when I find her," I said.

Cy and I went down the steps and out the back door, squinting in the too-bright sun. Cy led me around the corner and down the alley, where we found his car stashed by the loading platform of a store that looked like it had gone out of business long ago.

"Are you sure you're up for this?" he asked, opening the door for me. "You look terrible."

"I know I do," I said. I didn't need Cy to tell me about it. I'd had two hours of sleep in as many days, my clothes were wet and stained, and I knew that wasn't even the worst of it.

After I climbed into the car, Cy went around to the driver's side and slid into the seat next to me.

"I'm sorry," Cy said. "I didn't mean anything by it. I mean, you do look terrible, but there are extenuating circumstances. I get the feeling that most of the time, you look very nice."

"Cy, it's not important," I said, oddly touched that he'd try to make me feel better about the state of my face at a time like this.

"Okay, better than very nice," he said, starting the car. "I could go as far as 'pretty.' 'Pretty' would not be an exaggeration."

I couldn't help smiling at that.

"Are you coming to the hospital with me?" I asked.

"I thought maybe we'd split up," he said. "Jerry had a point about Gabrielle not knowing which one to go to. If she got her information from Millie, she might have gone to County Hospital instead."

"Should we go there first?" I asked.

He pulled out of the alley and turned onto Wilshire Boulevard.

"I'll do it," he said. "You should get to Cedars anyway. You were supposed to be there hours ago."

"Okay," I said, already dreading what my mother would have to say when she saw me.

"I'll meet you at the hospital as soon as I can," he said. "Maybe by then Jerry will have his pictures to take to the newspapers, and one of us will have Gabrielle."

"I hope so," I said, and put my hand on his shoulder. The cotton shirt he wore had been washed so many times that the fabric was thin and soft as a petal.

We drove like that for a while, Cy's eyes fixed straight ahead, my hand resting on his shoulder, and with every block, I felt another muscle unclench. When we got to Vermont Avenue, he said at last, "I just want all of this to be over."

"It can be over," I said, so insistent that I squeezed his arm without meaning to. "You and Jerry and Millie and Gabrielle and me. We tell them everything we've seen, show them the pictures. How can they not believe that?"

He brushed my hand away. "The word of an ex-cop? People like Millie and me? You'd be amazed how much they won't believe us."

"What do you mean, an ex-cop?" I asked.

Cy pursed his lips and downshifted as he turned onto Vermont.

"I guess Jerry didn't tell you. Well, he was, and from what I hear, it wasn't the most amicable parting of ways."

"Is that why Millie doesn't trust him?"

"It has nothing to do with that. Alice, Jerry means well, but he's a screwup. Millie knew where Gabrielle was, and she still didn't tell him. She wouldn't have trusted Jerry Shaffer with a potted plant, much less a girl's life."

I didn't like thinking that way about Jerry, but Cy wasn't entirely wrong. It didn't matter to me that he used to be a cop—not everyone with a badge was dirty, not even in the LAPD. But he'd trusted the wrong person, and it had almost gotten Annie killed.

And then, this morning he'd shown up like a miracle, just at the moment I needed him the most. He'd swooped in and intercepted the camera before Conrad or his people could get to it. He was going to get the photographs to the newspapers, and make sure Conrad paid for what he'd done.

"Maybe Millie's wrong," I said.

"Maybe," Cy said with a shrug. He was quiet for a minute or two, then asked, "What do you hope happens when all of this is over? Perfect world and all that."

I looked out the window at the billboards and sandwich shops that lined Vermont Avenue. I couldn't imagine a time when this would ever feel like it was over.

"I want Annie to wake up," I said. "I want Gabrielle to be safe. I want Conrad and Rex and Walter Hanrahan to go to prison for the rest of their lives."

"I want Gabrielle to find a home. A real one," Cy said.

"I want to crack a Nihilist cipher on the front porch with Annie."

Cy laughed. "I want Millie to make a triumphant comeback in some smash hit, and maybe talk the director into finding a teensy part for her dear pal Cy."

"I want to sleep for a thousand years," I said.

"I want to know I'll see you again."

There was something else I'd been about to say, but Cy's words knocked me off center, and all I could think to ask was, "Why?"

Cy's smile deflated, and I realized how nasty and defensive I must have sounded. Only I wasn't trying to be cruel. What I was thinking about was his eyes, how warm and kind they were, and how I didn't know what they saw in me.

We had pulled up in front of the hospital now, and Cy put on the parking brake and turned to face me.

He took a deep breath and said, "I want to know what you're like when you're not having the worst week of your life. You're not like anyone I've ever met before, Alice. You're up against the most powerful movie star in Hollywood and the LAPD, and you're still talking like you're going to win."

"You think I'm naive."

"I think you're brave," he said.

He leaned in toward me, his head tilted to the side, and I saw where this was going.

That's not what I want, I thought. Not now.

Visions of the dead police officers, of Conrad kicking my sister in the ribs, and Rex hitting her with a baseball bat, still swam up before my eyes. It was all still so fresh, and I knew that if I kissed Cy now, that's what I'd be thinking about, that's what I'd remember whenever I thought about what it was like to feel his lips on mine.

I didn't want it to be that way between us, always tethered to violence and fear and the worst week of our lives.

Maybe he could tell what I was thinking, or maybe it was what he'd planned on doing all along, but before I could pull away, Cy touched my chin with his fingertips and kissed me gently on my good cheek.

"I want to know I'll see you again because I think you're smart," he said. "And determined."

As he leaned back in his seat and went on talking, I fought the urge to touch my face in the spot where he'd kissed it.

"And pretty."

"You said that one already," I said.

"And not nice."

"You said that already, too."

Then he plucked a beautiful handkerchief from his pants pocket and handed it to me.

"Take it," he said. "That cut is bleeding again."

I pressed the fabric under my eye and was surprised how good it felt. I'd expected a coarse pocket square made of cambric or cotton, but there was no mistaking this was pure silk. Something like that had to have been a gift, and now it was ruined.

"I'm sorry," I said, pulling the handkerchief away from my face as though I could undo the bloodstain.

Cy shooed me away. "It's nothing, Alice. Get that cut looked at, okay?"

"I will," I said.

"And say you'll think about it," he said. "Seeing me again."

I got out of the car, shutting the door behind me. As I walked toward the hospital, I looked back over my shoulder and smiled at him.

"I already have."

CHAPTER 20

Talking with Cy made me feel like I had some kind of electric current buzzing through my veins. It kept me alert, kept me upright. By the time his taillights disappeared around the corner, though, I could feel all of it drain away. I walked toward Cedars of Lebanon in a daze, the task before me suddenly too large to manage on my own. I couldn't search an entire hospital for Gabrielle. All I wanted was to pull a cot up next to Annie's bed and snuggle in next to her. I'd close my eyes and drift off and think about a future where all the things I wanted came true—everyone safe and well and happy and together. Everyone who deserved it, anyway.

But as soon as I opened the door and stepped into the hospital lobby, I knew I wasn't going to be getting any sleep.

A crowd of reporters and photographers huddled around the pay phones and paced cagily around the lobby, snapping photographs and shouting punchy, over-caffeinated questions at a stocky nurse, who shouted back and shooed them away from the desk. I waded into the crowd and tugged at the sleeve of the least agitated-looking of the reporters.

"What's going on?"

He was no taller than I was, but twice as wide, and his knees seemed to bend inward under his bulk. A light brown fringe of hair ringed his head, and he had craggy red skin, heavily veined. He wore an LA EVENING HERALD & EXPRESS press pass in his breast pocket.

"Conrad Donahue was admitted this morning. Statement says he 'shot himself' in the leg 'while he was cleaning his gun,'" he said, rolling his eyes. "I thought I might actually get to write a real story today."

"Conrad Donahue is *here*?" I asked. "What room is he in?"

Last night in Griffith Park, I'd seen my father go for Rex's gun, and as I ran away with my hands tied behind my back, I'd heard a gunshot. I'd been worried about whether my father was dead or alive—it had never occurred to me that the bullet might have struck someone else, that the fine spray of blood across the front of Hanrahan's shirt might belong to Conrad Donahue.

And now Donahue was here, in the same building as Annie and Cassie and my mother. My blood ran cold.

The reporter took my gape-mouthed surprise for that of a star-struck girl and chuckled. "Don't get any wild ideas. They're not letting anyone near him."

The nurse muscled the crush of reporters back, wielding her clipboard like a shield. It was a madhouse. What they needed right about now was for someone at Insignia Pictures to issue a press release. Give the reporters a nibble—a decent, if watery, quote—and they'd go away happy. Too bad Conrad hadn't thought of that before he locked up the head of publicity at Insignia Pictures in the trunk of his car.

"I'm not going to *do* anything," I said. "I'm here to see my sister."

"Well, then he's somewhere on the fourth floor, I think. That's where all the private rooms are."

I thanked the reporter and shoved my way through the sea of notepads and patched tweed sleeves until I reached the front desk.

"What room is Annie Gates in?" I asked the nurse at reception. "She would have come in last night with my mother and another girl."

The nurse studied her clipboard and gave me a room number on the third floor. Then I saw her expression turn skeptical as she asked, "Who's your friend?"

When I looked over my shoulder, I saw the *Herald* reporter standing two steps behind me, his press badge and notepad hidden away in a pocket, and the grave look of a hospital visitor dashed across his face.

"He's nobody," I said, then backtracked as the nurse's lips pursed in mistrust. "I mean, he's my uncle. We're here to see Annie."

Why not, I thought as she waved us through the door. Most of the reporters in that waiting room would have told me to get lost. Besides, I wasn't feeling particularly respectful of Conrad's privacy, and it couldn't hurt to have a reporter who owed me a favor.

"That was swell of you," he said, huffing a little as we wound our way up the stairwell. "You like movie stars?"

"Not particularly," I said.

"Me neither."

He paused on the landing, and I waited with him as he struggled to catch his breath. Then I had an idea.

"Did you hear about the police officers who got shot this morning?" I asked.

"Sure," he said.

"If you want to write a real news story, see if you can get someone to compare the slug in Conrad Donahue's leg to the ones they pulled out of those officers this morning. I bet anything you'll get a match."

He knitted his brow as my words sank in, then grinned nervously.

"Do you know what you're saying, kid? How can you know something like that?"

"Just do it," I said, ignoring his indulgent smirk. "You won't be sorry."

The smile faded as he pulled the notepad out of his jacket pocket.

"It's not every day I see a schoolgirl with a shiner like that," he said. "I'm going to guess you didn't get it in a car accident."

"Not even close," I said.

We parted ways at the top of the stairs, the reporter looking back over his shoulder at me, wary and puzzled. My fingers twitched with adrenaline at having told a stranger so much, so carelessly. They shook as I opened the door to Annie's floor and started down the hall.

It was too quiet, too dim. At the County Hospital the floor had buzzed with activity, so even in the middle of the night you never felt totally alone, but here, something felt wrong.

Cedars of Lebanon was shaped like a V, with rooms extending down each wing. I stood at the center of the V, snaking my neck around the corner to examine the area near Annie's room. The stairwell door glided shut, its latch catching on the jamb before closing with a soft click.

DEAD TO ME

A second later, there were two men coming down the hall, one of them wearing a police uniform, the other in blue polka-dot suspenders. I gasped and turned down the other wing, not quite walking, not quite running. I skated along the floor, moving so that the hard soles of my shoes did not clatter against the tile, and tried the first door I came to.

It opened into a dark room with the sharp chemical whiff of a hospital supply closet. I closed the door behind me and dropped to the floor. It was too dark to see, but sitting in what I judged to be the middle of the closet, I could feel a concrete floor that stretched about three feet in any direction before giving way to flimsy metal shelves lined with bottles, bedpans, gauze, and rags. I crawled toward the darkest, farthest corner of the closet, careful not to send anything crashing to the floor. My hand grazed a bottle, a metal grate, a pile of rags.

No, I thought. It was too solid and too warm to be a pile of rags. I squinted into the darkness, and the outlines of things slipped into focus. A mop of hair, sharp features, and big, round eyes, just like I'd seen in the picture in my father's safe, the picture from the *Los Angeles Times*.

"You," I said.

I didn't flinch away from the rag she waved in front of my face. It was a supply closet, after all, and it was just a rag.

As the rough fibers brushed against my lips and nose, though, I caught a whiff of something acrid and sweet. I knew something was wrong, but by then, it was already too late. My body slumped to the floor.

CHAPTER 21

When I opened my eyes, I heard a small raspy voice whispering in my ear, "Wake up, wake up, wake up."

"Gabrielle," I mumbled, still woozy from whatever she had doused on that rag.

I heard a rustle of skirts as she crawled around to the side of my body before taking my hand and helping me sit up.

"Thank god you're all right," she said. "I'm sorry I knocked you out. I didn't know it was you."

Rubbing at my aching temples, I accepted her apology.

"What happened to your face?" she asked, tossing a head full of ratty black curls so they fell in front of her eyes.

The only light in the room fell across the floor in three thin strips through vents near the bottom of the door, but it was enough to get a good look at her, now that I knew who I was looking at.

She had the same small face, the same pointed chin, the same dark eyes I'd seen in the pictures, now alert and staring with undisguised curiosity. She looked more like a bratty kid than a pinup girl, and I couldn't imagine how she'd come this far, gotten this lost, without someone taking her by the elbow and marching her straight home, possibly stopping to feed her a sandwich on the way.

I wanted to keep my face neutral—she must have been looking for a reason to run, a reason to decide I wasn't worth trusting. Unfortunately, my insides were feeling anything but neutral. Had she intended for me to find her here? Had she been followed? Now that I'd finally found her, what was I supposed to do next?

The cut under my eye had opened again, and the skin around it was raised and sticky. The other side of my face was less damaged, but lopsided from the swelling in my jaw. Even the lightest touch made me wince in pain.

"Conrad?" she asked.

"How did you guess?"

"Rex would have hit you somewhere it didn't show."

It sounded so wrong to hear those words coming out of her mouth. Maybe we were only two or three years apart, but it felt like more.

"Did you know he was here?" I asked.

"No," she said. "Annie told me, 'If something goes wrong, find me and I'll take care of you.' I got so lost. I didn't have anywhere else to go. So that's what I did."

"How long have you been hiding here?"

"Not long," she said. "I went to County Hospital first, but they wouldn't tell me where she was. I pretended to leave, then I hid around the corner from the nurses' station until I heard someone tell an orderly to clean the room where the girl who got moved to Cedars had been so they could put someone else in it.

"I wasn't sure it was her at first, but they kept talking. They were arguing about how she got all beat up like that, and why the girl and the detective who'd been visiting her didn't bother calling her mother. It was pretty clear who they were talking about then."

"So you came here," I said.

Gabrielle nodded. "I can't get close to her room, though. There's police everywhere."

"Conrad's looking for you. They all are," I said. "And Annie still hasn't woken up."

Gabrielle said, "But you're here now."

I rubbed my temples, wincing in pain.

"I don't see how that does us any good. I'm stuck in here just like you are."

Gabrielle was insistent. "Annie told me about you. She said you were smart, that if I didn't have anywhere else to go, I could go to you."

Really? I thought. Why would Annie tell Gabrielle a thing like that, steering her away from older, smarter people who might have helped her?

"Me?" I asked.

"I didn't know where else to turn," Gabrielle said, hugging her knees to her chest.

Well, that made two of us.

While I nursed my ether hangover, Gabrielle told me everything that had happened. Everything.

She'd only had a few seconds to hide before she heard the door open. It had been Ruth, and she'd run straight for the bedroom. A minute later, Rex came running after her. She knew they'd be looking for whatever Millie had hidden in the lockbox under Irma's bed, saw her chance, and bolted out the door and down the hall to the fire escape.

Millie had shown her the spot where the boards came up the first night Gabrielle stayed there. It was two nights after she met Irma, one month after the day she met Rex, and sixty-four days after the afternoon her mother threw all her clothes onto the front lawn and told her not to bother bringing them back inside.

"I lived at the YWCA until I ran out of money. After that, I stayed at a hotel and got a job doing dishes, but the whole place was infested with rats and cockroaches. I used to sleep with my shoe in my hand so I could whack them with it if they got too close."

When she saw the ad for the modeling agency, she'd answered it, and when the man on the phone asked when she could come in, she'd said now. The man on the phone met her at the agency, told her his name was Rex. He offered her a seat and a glass of lemonade with vodka in it, and told her she was cute enough to eat. Gabrielle let him take her picture.

"He was creepy, but he wasn't the worst one. He looked me in the eye when he talked and he didn't touch me except to shake my hand," she said.

The third night, Rex said she was pretty enough to be in the movies. Gabrielle had her doubts. She was gawky and skinny-legged, with unruly hair and feet so big she had to have her shoes specially made. But then he showed her the pictures he'd taken the day before, and they almost took her breath away. Rex had somehow caught all the flaws in her face and turned them into her best points. Her pointy chin looked striking, her too-big eyes were hypnotizing, even her messy hair fell around her face like one of the maidens in a Pre-Raphaelite painting.

"I showed some of these around," he'd said. "People liked your face, but they said you looked too young."

Since Gabrielle had been out on her own, she'd noticed that there was always a moment in conversations with people who wanted something from you. And up to that moment, you could walk away whenever you wanted without feeling as though you'd been rude or stuck-up or led someone on. And after that moment, it became almost impossible to walk away at all, no matter how badly you wanted to. After that moment, it was too late.

She'd had moments like that since being on her own. There had been a man at the bus stop who chatted with her about the weather and the movies. One day, he asked where she lived, and when she told him the name of a neighborhood, he asked for a street. And when she wouldn't say, he said it was only because he wanted to walk her home sometime, that he didn't mean any harm. That was the moment when she started waiting at a different bus stop.

The moment Rex said she looked too young was the moment she should have found another modeling ad to answer. But instead, she turned to him and said, "I can look older."

A couple of nights later, he gave her another drink, but this time there was something else in it that made her feel giddy and foggy at the same time. He gave her a wig and a makeup kit and a bag full of lacy bras and garters, and took her to have her picture taken again.

The next morning she woke up in one of the bungalows at Stratford Arms with a horrible headache, and Ruth was standing over her with a glass of seltzer water and an aspirin.

"She told me that no matter where I came from, I should go

back because it was better than this. I told her I wouldn't go back and she couldn't tell me what to do," Gabrielle said.

"What did Ruth say?" I asked.

"That I was right. She couldn't make me go back."

A few nights later, Rex came back. This time, he brought a pretty yellow chiffon dress for her to wear, put her in his car, and drove her to a party unlike any she'd been to before. It was just like the movies—there was music and champagne and handsome men lined up to talk to her, to freshen her drink, to ask her to dance. There was one man she liked right away. He had a nice smile and said she was the cutest girl in the whole room, but after a few minutes of talking to her, a strange look crossed his face.

"Sweetie, are you sure you're in the right place?"

I had no problem imagining it. The same thing had happened to me before at my parents' cocktail parties, and I was sure it had happened to Annie, too. A man would be talking to me, and then something would change as he realized the young woman he was flirting with was really a young girl. He'd cross to the other side of the room in a hurry muttering about jailbait, and for reasons I didn't completely understand, I'd wind up being the one who felt like I'd done something wrong.

"I should have said something," Gabrielle told me. "Instead, I just drank more champagne and told him I didn't know what he was talking about.

"At first, it hurt my feelings, but there were lots of other men who wanted to talk to me. There was more champagne. There was dancing, and then suddenly, Conrad Donahue was standing right there in front of me. Everybody else who was hanging around me went away, and pretty soon, it was just the two of us."

He'd pulled her onto his lap, and whispered funny things about the other people at the party into her ear. The man in the pinstripe suit was bald as a boiled egg under his hairpiece. And the sour-faced man who drank sidecar after sidecar still lived with his wife but hadn't spoken to her since Pearl Harbor.

He'd pointed to a man in light-blue suspenders standing in the corner, a fedora pulled down over his eyes at a rakish angle. "And that tough old screw? He's nothing but a dirty old cop."

"Why did you invite a cop to your party?" Gabrielle asked.

"Because he's *my* cop," Conrad said. "Like a pet. Watch."

He looked across the room and snapped his fingers, and the man came to attention. Lithe as an eel, he threaded himself between the bodies massed on the dance floor and around the bar, and before Gabrielle could say a thing, he was there. He didn't speak, but stood like he was waiting for orders.

"Get me a car," Conrad said to him. "We're leaving."

He chucked Gabrielle under the chin and smiled at her. "Don't look so sad, sweetheart. You're coming, too."

The police officer left and was just as suddenly replaced by two older girls, one at each of Conrad's elbows. One had blond hair and dramatically arched eyebrows. She whispered something in Conrad's ear, while the pale dark-haired one wrapped an arm around Gabrielle's shoulder as though they were school chums.

She wriggled out of the girl's grasp, but as she did, the girl leaned down and whispered in her ear.

"I'm Irma. Stay with us, and everything will be okay."

"Everything *is* okay," Gabrielle hissed back, but Irma acted like she hadn't heard. Instead, she threw her head back and let out a peal of laughter, as though Gabrielle had just said something uproariously funny.

"I'd had Conrad all to myself, and then these other girls

show up, acting like they own him. I'd seen the blond one some-where before, but it was hard to tell since she had her tongue in Conrad's ear."

Millie, I thought.

"They were trying to protect you from him," I told Gabrielle.

She shook her hair in front of her eyes and covered her face with her hands.

"I know that now," she whispered.

It was a long time before she spoke again.

More girls had trickled up to Conrad and had their picture taken with him, and Gabrielle had fallen back to the edges. Then a man with shiny black hair and a neatly trimmed mustache materialized in the middle of the group. He seemed more like a host or a waiter than a guest at the party, constantly bustling around and smoothing things over, but never staying in one place for very long.

"Is everything all right here, Conrad?" he asked, twisting his hands in front of him.

"Actually, Nicky, we were just leaving."

The man with the mustache extended his hand to Gabrielle and said, "I don't believe I've had the pleasure of meeting formally, but Rex has told me so much about you. He says you're a promis-ing new talent."

When Gabrielle said that, my body tensed. If what she was saying was true, then that was the moment the *Los Angeles Times* photographer had snapped, the one that had shown up on the same page as Hedda Hopper's column. Not only had she met my father, they'd had a conversation, and even then, he hadn't helped her. No, he'd tried to recruit her for his stable of party girls.

"Are you okay, Alice?" Gabrielle asked.

"I'm okay," I said, fighting the urge to be sick. "I think it's just the ether."

Gabrielle folded her knees up to her chest and continued her story.

Conrad had said, "Give him your number. Nicky's always looking for new faces. And he'll get you better work than Rex, I guarantee you that."

"I don't have anything to write on," Gabrielle said. The blond woman stared at her with open hostility.

Conrad reached a hand into his pocket and came out with a matchbook and a pen, and wrote down the number that Gabrielle gave him.

The man with the mustache put the matchbook in his pocket and said, "I hope we'll be seeing a lot more of each other."

Conrad put an arm around Gabrielle and the blond girl, and said, "Come on, ladies," and they all left. Irma too. He took them out the back door, and a moment later, his car pulled up.

The blond pushed her way forward to claim the front seat with Conrad. Gabrielle still couldn't shake the feeling that she'd seen her somewhere before. Those penciled-on eyebrows, those angular features.

"Hey," she said, placing her at last. "You're Camille Grabo."

The girl tossed her head and laughed. "I get that all the time."

Conrad took a step back and held her at arm's length, studying her face.

"Well, I'll be," he said. "It *is* Camille Grabo. I almost didn't recognize you."

As he spoke, the boyish smile faded from his lips and a snarl replaced it. "Sweetie, don't even think about getting in my car. The last thing I need is a swarm of *Tell-Tale!* reporters peeking over my fence."

Camille Grabo smiled and tried to purr something in Conrad's ear, but he shoved her away roughly.

"She was either really drunk, or Conrad pushed her really hard. She fell over backward into the trash cans. Conrad laughed about it, but Irma didn't. She looked worried."

Conrad leaned inside the car and whispered something to the cop, who threw on the parking brake and gave up his seat behind the wheel. Conrad took his place and called to Irma, patting the seat next to him.

"Hey, honey, we haven't had a chance to talk yet. Why don't you climb up here with me?"

As Irma got into the car, Gabrielle watched the cop help Camille Grabo to her feet and lead her back inside the club with her hair askew and the back of her dress stained with wet bar trash.

"Are you girls ready for the real party?" Conrad asked. Gabrielle wasn't sure what he'd meant, but Irma giggled, so she did, too. "Where to?"

"Your place?" Irma suggested.

"That's boring. I want to have some fun," he said, turning around and smiling at Gabrielle. "You look like you know how to have fun. Where do you want to go?"

Gabrielle thought about it for a moment, trying to imagine what Conrad's idea of fun might be.

"The beach?" she suggested timidly.

Conrad's smile brightened. "I like the way you think."

Gabrielle thought she saw something like worry flicker across

Irma's face, but she said nothing, and they were on their way. Conrad chatted constantly as he drove, regaling them with tales of directors he'd worked with, who was a genius, who was a stand-up guy, which actresses were swell dames, and which ones were too full of themselves. As he talked, he put his arm around Irma's shoulder and pulled her across the bench seat until they were hip to hip and she was nestled in the crook of his arm.

They drove up Highway 1, through Santa Monica and Malibu, leaving the city farther and farther behind until its lights were just a faint glow in the rearview mirror. Finally, Conrad pulled onto a narrow dirt road that wound through a forest of dense brush before emerging on a perfectly empty, perfectly gorgeous beach.

Gabrielle rolled down her window to take in the waves, the air that left a salty, sandy film on her skin, the night sky so dark you could almost make out the stars. She'd hardly ever been to the ocean before, and never at night. It was all she could do not to throw open the car door, kick off her shoes, and run right into the waves.

She hardly even cared that Conrad had his arms around Irma, or that she was whispering in his ear. They parted, and Gabrielle watched as Conrad peeled a few bills out of his wallet. He made as if to hand them to Irma, but pulled them away at the last minute. When she reached after them, he slapped the back of her hand.

"Not so fast," he said, reaching across her lap and plucking her purse from the car seat. He opened the clasp and made a big show of putting the bills inside, though not before he'd pawed through its contents.

"What have we here?" he said, pulling a small silver vial out of the purse. "Naughty, naughty."

Conrad unscrewed its lid and filled the tiny spoon that was attached to it with a rounded scoop of white powder. He snorted it up, then filled the spoon again and put it up his other nostril.

"I don't have that much left," Irma said, a note of panic in her voice.

Conrad ignored her, and scooped out another spoonful of powder, passing it across the backseat to Gabrielle. She shook her head and wrinkled up her nose in what she hoped was a cute, girlish expression. He scowled and shoved the spoon toward her face.

"Take it," he said.

Irma reached for his hand. "It's okay. She doesn't have to."

As she touched his wrist, Conrad's hand jerked back and the contents of the spoon drifted to the floorboards of the Rolls-Royce. Irma shrank back into the seat, and for a moment, Gabrielle was sure that he was going to hit her. But instead, he dropped his hand down and a slow smile spread across his face.

"For a second there, I forgot it was your dope."

He chuckled heartily at that, and Irma laughed, too, a short, choked laugh that sounded more like a cough. But then he tossed the vial to her and she snorted some of it, and soon everyone was all smiles again, the bad moment forgotten.

Then Conrad said that he wanted to take a walk on the beach, so the three of them went down to the water together. By that time, though, he was only paying attention to Irma. Gabrielle might as well not have even been there, so she split off from the pair and went the other way down the beach until she came to a rock that hung out over the ocean. She climbed up on top of it and dangled her feet out over the edge.

She found a handhold in the rock and gripped it just to be safe, but quickly enough she lost interest in being safe. The air was so fresh, the night so clear, the ocean so impossibly big, that it all almost made her forget how she'd gotten there.

She looked down the beach and saw Conrad's and Irma's figures like miniatures in the distance. But not so miniature that she couldn't tell what they were doing. Gabrielle looked away, blushing. After another minute or two, she got down from her rock and walked back to the car to wait for them. By the time she climbed into the backseat, she could see them wading into the water, their clothes in two small piles just beyond the reach of the waves.

From where Gabrielle sat, it looked like they were having fun. Irma squealed that the water was too cold. Conrad splashed her and waded in up to his waist. She followed after him, laughing and splashing him back. Then he picked her up by the waist and threw her over his shoulder like a bag of laundry. She screamed and kicked her legs and slapped at his back with her fists, and Conrad dunked her under the water, still holding her over his shoulder.

"They stayed under for a long time, and when they came back up again, Conrad was laughing. Irma wasn't, though," Gabrielle said.

Conrad had taken a deep breath before going under. Irma hadn't, and she emerged from the water struggling in Conrad's arms and gasping in heaving, panicked breaths, her hair matted across her eyes.

"Take it easy," Gabrielle heard him say. "I was just fooling around."

But Irma's survival instincts had kicked in as Conrad held her underwater, and she was all flailing limbs and adrenaline. One of her knees caught Conrad in the stomach, then her elbow flew out and caught him in the temple, and even from the distance of the car, Gabrielle could see the thoughtless, instinctive rage flare on his face, the way it had in the car when he'd spilled the spoonful of cocaine. Except this time, he didn't catch himself. This time, he didn't freeze in place and burst out laughing as though his terrifying anger was all one big joke.

Instead, he held her around the waist and pushed her face into the water, holding her down with one hand on the back of her head.

Gabrielle watched in horror as Irma's arms pinwheeled uselessly, then convulsed, then went limp. As he held her down, the rage gradually faded from Conrad's face, and a stony calm replaced it. He looked almost businesslike as he drowned her.

Gabrielle found she could neither move nor scream, that at that moment she could only think a single thought, over and over again: *This is the moment when I die. This is the moment when he kills me.*

Every other thought she had, like *Get out of the car and run* or *Hide in the rocks*, was overpowered by it. The moment to run was before she'd gotten in the car, before she'd gone to the party, before she'd let Rex take all those pictures, before she'd left home. That moment was long past.

But then she saw him walking toward the shore with Irma's body slung over his shoulder, and she did move. Irma's shoes and purse were still sitting on the front seat where she'd left them. Gabrielle threw them onto the floorboards in the backseat and flung herself on top of them as though they might wriggle away.

She'd missed her best chance to escape and knew it, felt powerless to do anything except stretch out across the floor of the car, her eyes squinched shut as if not being able to see would make her invisible, too. Maybe it would be dark enough. Maybe Conrad wouldn't look. Maybe he'd *think* that she ran away.

She heard light footsteps padding just outside the car, and the squeal of hinges as the trunk opened. There was a thud, and the rear of the car rocked, and then the trunk slammed shut and the footsteps padded away.

"He was getting their clothes," Gabrielle explained.

Soon she heard him return, heard the sound of pants being zipped up. He hummed to himself as he dressed. It couldn't have been more than fifteen minutes from the moment that Conrad drowned Irma to the moment he slid behind the wheel and drove away with her body in the trunk.

They drove for at least an hour, twisting along winding canyon roads. Gabrielle couldn't see the terrain, but she could feel it, every hill, every bump. Conrad turned on the radio and sang along with the songs in the broadcast. After a while he turned to a news station, and once he was bored with that, he started running lines.

"You bet your life I'll get your wagons to Oregon Territory, or my name isn't Clay Macomber!"

He must have said it fifty times, in different accents, with the emphasis on different words. Gabrielle thought she would scream. How had she never noticed before what a terrible actor he was?

"You betcher life I'll get yer wagons to Oregon Territory, or my name isn't Clay Macomber."

Of course, that was the least of his offenses. Between the bumps in the road and Conrad's insipid line readings, Gabrielle felt half crazy and scared out of her wits besides. The sharp little heels of Irma's shoes dug into her chest with each bump until finally she could bear it no more.

As slowly and carefully as she could, Gabrielle slid the purse and shoes out from under her and pushed them underneath the driver's seat. By the time she was done, she could almost hear her heart pounding at the insides of her rib cage.

Conrad drove on, careening around the hairpin turns at

dangerous speeds. He tried out a few more of his lines, then switched the radio back on and began to hum along.

And then he cleared his throat and said, "I haven't forgotten about you, you know."

That was the moment when Gabrielle should have given up, cried for the series of choices that had led her to this backseat on this night, prayed that it would all be over quickly.

But it wasn't.

"That was the moment when I made up my mind that I was going to live."

CHAPTER 22

Gabrielle was counting on my help because Annie had told her she could. Knowing that made me brave enough to let myself out of the supply closet. I held my breath as I inched down the hall and turned the doorknob to the stairwell, and didn't let it out until I was halfway down the stairs. My mind worked furiously, trying to make sense of everything that had happened, everything that Gabrielle had told me, the size of the lie and the number of wrongs that had to be righted. It was like a web that spread from Malibu to MacArthur Park, impenetrable and impossibly dense.

When I made it to the hospital lobby, there was a line five deep to use the pay phones, and my friend from the *Los Angeles Evening Herald* was standing in front of one of them. He leaned against the wall, barking his copy over the wire as he flipped through the pages in a wallet-sized notebook. All the other reporters in line behind him eavesdropped shamelessly.

"Nick Gates told police that he shot Donahue in a 'prank gone wrong.' However, Donahue denies Gates's version of the events, calling him 'a dear man, but quite confused.' He maintains that he accidentally shot himself in the leg while cleaning his gun."

I felt a surge of relief when I heard the reporter say my father's name. Somehow he had gotten a statement out of him, which meant that Conrad's driver had been right—my father made it out of the hills alive that night. The big question now was, where was he? And what on earth was he doing lying to reporters at a time like this?

"That's what he said, hand to God. I got more, too." He cupped his hand around the mouthpiece and turned his back. The other reporters nearly fell over themselves leaning forward to make out his whispering.

"I'll see if there's anything to it; have something for you tomorrow if there is," he said, and started to hang up.

When he'd finished, he turned around to face a line of reporters, tapping their toes and glaring as they waited. It must have been close to deadline for the afternoon editions of the papers, and every second the reporter from the *Herald* stayed on the line was a second less they'd have to file their stories.

So they were extra furious when I shoved my way to the front, took the phone from his hand, and said with a desperation that was only slightly faked, "Please can I use this line? It's an emergency!"

The reporter from the *Los Angeles Herald* ignored the audible grumbling from the men in line and handed me the phone. I was glad I'd helped him sneak up to see Conrad.

"Where did you find Nick Gates?" I asked, fishing through my skirt pocket for a nickel. When he told me, I was so surprised I dropped it.

I didn't know my father well, but over the years I had picked up a thing of two about his line of work. Most men in a predicament as bad as his would have emptied out a bank account, bought a train ticket, and stayed gone for about a decade. But my father wouldn't have been happy in Spokane or Chattanooga or even New York. He was a Hollywood man, through and through. And more than that, he was a publicity man, and even now, after everything that had happened, he was trying to find a way to control the story.

That was my guess about why he'd issued the false statement. The where was already confirmed.

My father, Nick Gates, director of publicity for Insignia Pictures, was in custody at the Hollywood Precinct of the Los Angeles Police Department after confessing to shooting Conrad Donahue in the leg.

I took the smudged business card Jerry had given me out of my pocket and dialed his number.

"Jerry," I said when he picked up the phone, "you need to get to Cedars of Lebanon in a hurry."

"Is that you, Alice?" he asked. "The prints are still drying."

"Bring them anyway," I said. "Bring every single one of them."

Then I told him about the reporters, about my father and the bullet in Conrad's leg. I told him about everything except Gabrielle. I'd meant to—that was why I asked for his card in the first place—but with so many people milling around, sniffing out whatever scraps of information they could, I decided the news could wait until we were face-to-face.

After I hung up, the newspaperman from the *Herald* stood there, his mouth hanging open like a door with a broken hinge. He'd listened to everything.

"Nick Gates is your father?" he asked.

I nodded, and he took me by the elbow and swept me off to a corner of the room. The other reporters descended upon the pay phone like it was made of rib eyes and dollar bills.

Away from prying eyes and ears, he asked, "So, kid, any chance you'd let me buy you a cup of coffee and help me understand why Conrad and your dad can't get their stories straight?"

I told the reporter that if he could sweeten the pot with some food, we had a deal. It would be a few minutes until Jerry arrived, and I hadn't had anything to eat since the bacon sandwich my mother had made me the night before.

Soon, we were sitting at the counter in the hospital cafeteria, a cup of coffee and a ham-and-cheese sandwich in front of each of us.

"Conrad isn't following the script," I said after I'd eaten half my sandwich in two bites and washed it down with a swig of coffee.

He fumbled for his notebook. "What do you mean 'following the script'?"

That was something else I knew about my father's job. The actors at Insignia Pictures thought he existed to herald them, to polish up their stars so they shone as brightly as possible. But I saw him when he got home, when he loosened his necktie and poured himself three fingers of scotch. It seemed to me that at least half of his job was cleaning up the messes they made, smoothing over the careless things they said.

I tried to explain to the *Herald* reporter what I meant.

"'Shot himself while cleaning his gun'? That's more or less code for 'botched suicide attempt.' The studio doesn't let a story like that get out, especially not about one of its big stars," I said, wolfing down the rest of my sandwich.

When I'd finished chewing, I said, "On the other hand, they don't care if people think Conrad Donahue and his friends get drunk and shoot off their guns. And if one of them occasionally gets hit in the leg, that kind of headline doesn't hurt movie ticket sales."

It was only a hunch, but it seemed like that was what my father was up to. What I didn't understand was why. It certainly wasn't for Conrad's sake. Was it for the studio? Himself?

"So you're saying Conrad tried to kill himself?"

"No, of course not."

"Then what happened?"

"I don't know," I said. "But my father does. You should go to the Hollywood Precinct and ask him again, only this time, tell him his wife and daughters are in the hospital about a hundred yards away from Conrad Donahue. I doubt he'll care, but he should probably know."

The reporter and I finished our coffees and went back out to the hospital lobby. He thanked me and started for the door, but before he could go, I tapped him on the shoulder.

"And you should talk to him, too," I said, pointing toward the reception desk.

When Jerry saw my waving arms, he made a beeline for the corner where I stood with the reporter.

"Jerry, this is..." I trailed off, realizing I'd never asked the name of this person to whom I'd entrusted so much.

"Amos Carey," he said. "*Los Angeles Evening Herald.*"

Jerry handed him copies of the prints that showed Conrad standing over my sister's prone body, Rex hitting her with the baseball bat.

"Make sure you show those to my father, too," I said.

CHAPTER 23

When I told Jerry that Gabrielle was hiding in a closet down the hall from Annie's room, he went pale and looked a little as though he might be sick. I tried to reassure him about her resourcefulness by telling him how she'd knocked me out with ether, but for some reason, it didn't seem to make him feel any better.

As for me, with Gabrielle found, pictures of Conrad guaranteed to make the front page of every newspaper in Los Angeles, and my father positioned to spill the beans on any amount of incriminating activity, I thought, why hide? Why not get Gabrielle out and march her down the hall right past the uniformed goons Conrad had stationed there? What could they do to us now?

Those thoughts all disappeared the moment I saw the man in the blue polka-dot suspenders—Walter Hanrahan—leaning against the door outside Annie's room, gun holstered at his belt. I took hold of Jerry's arm and tried not to think about sitting with my hands bound in the back of Conrad's car or those police officers lying dead on the sidewalk. Hanrahan smiled at me and tipped his hat as Jerry pulled me quickly through the door.

My mother sat next to the bed holding Annie's limp hand to her cheek. Her eyes were closed and her lips moved without sound. I didn't know if she was praying or whispering, but either way, I hated to interrupt.

"Mom?" I spoke in a gentle whisper so as not to startle her.

No sooner had she opened her eyes and seen my face than she got up and ran toward me. The tendons in her neck were stretched taut as bowstrings as she grabbed me by the arm and yanked me into a hug that crushed my bruised cheek against her chest.

"What happened?" she asked, shaking me furiously against her. "Who did this to you?"

My eyes darted nervously toward the door. I was terrified that any minute, I'd see Walter Hanrahan come through it, gun drawn.

I leaned in and whispered in her ear, "Conrad Donahue."

I didn't expect she'd believe me right away. I thought it would be like it had been with Cassie, and that she'd be furious at me for lying at a time like this.

She didn't look surprised at all, though.

Her face reminded me of a woman I'd seen years ago in a newsreel. It'd been during the war, and in the scheme of things, not a big story, just something sandwiched in between some cartoons and a bad Lassie movie. All three of the woman's sons had been killed in the war. One was a pilot who had been shot down over Germany, one had been blown to bits during the invasion of Sicily, and the third had died in a freak submarine accident in the

DEAD TO ME

Solomon Islands. When they interviewed her for the newsreel, she'd said all the right things—that her boys had gone off to war together and now they'd come home together, that they had served bravely and not died in vain—but her eyes had told a different story, and I was sure that there was a part of her that would have waved the white flag to Hitler himself if it meant one more day with her boys.

"No," my mother said, her voice quaking. "No, no, no."

She pulled away from me and went to the window that looked out over Hollywood. There was something dangerous about her as she stood there, crackling and quivering like an electrical line on a humid day. She pressed her palms against the glass, fingers splayed open.

"I'll kill him," she whispered, striking the window with the flat of her hand. "I'll kill him, and he'll never come near this family again."

She clenched her hands and began to pound on the glass with her fists.

And then Walter Hanrahan did come storming into the room, hand on his holster. I thought about how fast he'd pulled out his gun when he shot the police officer in the chest earlier that morning. The man hadn't even seen it coming.

I pulled my mother's hands down from the glass and wrapped my arms around her.

"Is everything all right in here?" Walter Hanrahan asked.

"It's fine," said Jerry.

"The lady seems upset."

"Her daughter almost died," Jerry said, gesturing toward Annie. "She *is* upset."

"Please leave us alone," my mother said.

"If you don't mind, I think I'll stay a moment," he said, giving Jerry a nasty look, "just to make sure everything is okay."

"I do mind," my mother said.

I could feel every muscle in her body coiled tight, ready to explode in Walter Hanrahan's direction the moment I let go of her.

"The LAPD is here to help, ma'am."

"Like hell you are!" she said. "I asked you to get out. Now, are you going to do it or not?"

That was when Cassie came in, bearing a stack of sandwiches wrapped in paper and two bottles of soda, and looking like a soldier who had seen combat. Without batting an eye, she put down the sandwiches, took my mother by the arm, and sat her down in a chair on the far side of Annie's bed.

I knew Cassie had a head for movie stars and Hollywood gossip and field hockey, but when it came to keeping people calm in a crisis, she was a miracle worker. My mother stopped screaming at Walter Hanrahan and followed her, meek as a lamb.

"What happened?" Cassie whispered in my ear as she guided me toward a chair next to my mother. "You were supposed to be here hours ago."

Then she looked around the room and saw Jerry Shaffer standing uselessly in the corner. She saw my mother clutch my hands and hold them in hers. She saw all three of us, our eyes fixed on Walter Hanrahan with some mixture of anger and terror.

Hanrahan had propped himself up against the wall, arms folded across his chest. He stood there watching us watch him, and smirking.

"What's he doing in the room?" Cassie asked my mother.

Without taking her eyes off Walter Hanrahan, my mother said,

"He tells me Annie is in danger and they have to post a guard around the clock."

Her voice betrayed nothing but scorn, but I could see the fear in her eyes as she squeezed my hands in hers again and again.

"He won't tell me why, though. Isn't that strange?"

I nodded as she spoke, then my eyes went wide, though it wasn't because of anything she said. It was the way she kept squeezing my hands.

A short squeeze, then a long one. Another short squeeze, then two long squeezes. Short, then long. Long, short, long. Short.

Short, long.

Short, long, long.

Short, long.

Long, short, long.

Short.

Again and again she did it. At first I didn't see the pattern, but then there it was, Morse code as clear and steady as a metronome.

AWAKE

AWAKE

AWAKE

Our eyes met, and my mother dropped my hands and pulled me into her arms, more gently this time.

"Please don't leave again, Alice. Please stay here with us," she said. "I need you with me."

As I hugged my mother, I wished I could pour all the things I wanted to say to her through my arms.

I'm so sorry for everything. Once this is over, things will be different. No more secrets, no more revenge. I'll stay with you as long as you want. I remember who taught Annie and me how to do the ciphers, who helped us learn Morse code during the war. I remember it wasn't all etiquette lessons and hors d'oeuvres trays. I remember there was cake baking and gin rummy and picture books, too, just the three of us. I know you tried to love us. But I can't stay. Not until this is done.

As I pulled away, I saw that her face was calm now. It had been so wild just a few minutes ago, when she was talking about killing Conrad.

He'll never come near this family again, she'd said. She wasn't just talking about me. Conrad had hurt all of us. He'd kidnapped my father, beaten my sister nearly to death.

But my mother didn't know about either one of those things, so what did she mean?

That was when I heard a girl's scream coming from down the hall, and there was only one girl it could have come from. I leaped up from the chair and darted around Annie's bed, past Hanrahan toward the door, with my mother calling after me, "Alice, don't—"

I didn't hear what she said next, because I was already halfway down the hall, just in time to see Rex crashing through the stairwell door. He pushed Gabrielle along in front of him, the muzzle of his gun jammed into her back.

Walter Hanrahan was right behind me. As he ran by, he checked me with his shoulder and sent me ricocheting toward the wall before he disappeared through the stairwell after Rex and Gabrielle.

I started after them, but then Jerry was there, clapping a hand down on my shoulder.

"Where do you think you're going?" he asked. "Get back in that room."

Under ordinary circumstances, I wouldn't have paid him the slightest heed, but back in that room was my sister. Awake. When Jerry ran down the hallway after Rex and Hanrahan, I didn't follow him. I went back to the room in time to see Annie's eyes, finally, blessedly open.

"Was that Gabrielle?" she asked.

I nodded.

"Don't let them take her."

Her voice was husky and choked-sounding, her words were slurred, but it was her. I would have jumped through a hoop of fire if she'd asked me to.

Before my mother could protest, I ran down the hall and took the stairs at the other end of the wing. Conrad was one floor up from my sister's room. That had to be where Rex was taking Gabrielle. Conrad had been after her for days now, and I knew from firsthand experience he liked seeing girls afraid. There was no way he'd miss the chance to let her know that she hadn't escaped from him after all.

The hallway was empty—Conrad's stardom must have earned him a private ward. But I knew better than to think he was alone or unguarded. I stayed where I was, looking out through the tiny window in the stairwell door. There was no sign of Jerry, and I wondered if I'd been wrong and Rex and Hanrahan had taken Gabrielle down the stairs rather than up them. They couldn't have lost him running up a single flight of stairs. But then, after a moment or two, Hanrahan emerged from one of the rooms empty-handed.

He and Rex had delivered Gabrielle straight to Conrad.

I wondered how many people were left in the room, and how many of them were armed. Conrad had a gunshot wound in his leg—if he was in there by himself. Would I be able to get Gabrielle out of there on my own? I had to get closer.

After Hanrahan reached the end of the wing and turned the

corner, I unbuckled my shoes and crept down the hallway, carrying them by the straps, my back pressed against the wall. I inched closer until I came to the room next to Conrad's, and slipped inside, hiding myself behind the door and pressing my ear to the wall. The voices were muffled, but I could still make out almost everything.

"I remember you being older."

That was Conrad, I was sure of it. It was the same voice he'd used on me in the hills, big enough to scare you into a corner, jovial enough to deny he'd meant anything by it.

"You look like a kid, but that doesn't mean anything. I truly could not care less."

"I was never going to say anything, I promise." Gabrielle's raspy little voice had an unpleasant wheedling sound in it that I didn't like. A begging sound.

"So then why were you chumming around with the Gates girl?"

Conrad wasn't alone. It was another man's voice I heard then—Rex, by the sound of it.

"I was scared. I didn't have anyplace to go. Please, just let me go home, and I swear I'll never tell anyone."

"Tell anyone what? Anyway, it's much too late for anything like that. There's only one way to make this go away now." His voice was gentle, honeyed, like he was trying to calm a crying infant. "I'm sorry, really I am. I just don't see any other way."

So placid, so sincere, as though he genuinely did feel bad about what had to be done, but really, wasn't it a small sacrifice? Gabrielle began to cry quietly, and then there was another voice in the room with them.

When I realized who it belonged to, I squeezed the doorknob

until my knuckles turned white and my fingers ached. I knew that if I didn't hold on to something, I'd run into the next room and wrap my hands around her neck instead.

"Pull yourself together," Ruth said. "It's not like we're going to kill you."

"You're not?" Gabrielle whimpered.

"Not if you're a smart girl. Not if you can learn how to sing the words we tell you to."

How could she?

How could she pretend she wanted to help my sister protect Gabrielle, then turn around and double-cross us all? That meant Ruth had been the one who'd set Annie up that night in the park. She must have led Conrad and Rex right to her. I gripped the doorknob with all my strength and bit down on the inside of my cheek to keep from screaming.

"She's right," Conrad said. "Ruth and I have been talking it over, and she's got me thinking there might be another way to sort this whole thing out. So, what I'd like now is for you to go with my friends here. I'd like you to go to the police and tell them what you *really* saw. How Nick Gates forced you to pose for those pictures, how he took you and Irma out into the woods after that party and made you do horrible things. And that somehow, things got out of hand."

Ruth chimed in. "And that you went to Annie because she told you that she'd help you, but instead she kept you under lock and key. That she only wanted to protect her dear daddy from what you knew."

"And that when I brought the police to the apartment to rescue you, Nick Gates gunned them down in broad daylight," Conrad said. "He shot me in the leg and would have finished me off if I hadn't managed to escape."

"Is that a story you think you can tell?" Ruth asked.

At first, there was no answer, then a choked sob, and then Gabrielle said, "Yes."

CHAPTER 24

In the end, none of it would matter. Not the pictures, not the newspapers, not Millie's letter, two dead cops, or the word of a girl who'd seen the whole thing happen. Maybe Conrad couldn't make those pictures of him and Annie go away, but he and Ruth could make them look like something else. I could already hear him telling the newspapers: *I didn't want to do it, but I had no choice. Annie Gates was holding that poor little girl prisoner.*

And my father deserved to be punished for what he'd done, but not like this. Not while murderers like Conrad and Rex and Hanrahan went free and everything else stayed the same. The parties, the pictures, the girls, and the horrible things that happened to them—none of that would change.

I'd found Gabrielle, but it hadn't even mattered. It would have been better if I'd never even looked.

I tried to tell myself that she was young and scared, that it wasn't fair to blame her for this.

I tried to tell myself that. But it didn't sit well.

Gabrielle wasn't too young and scared to run away from home, to live on her own, to slip through Rex's fingers time and time again. She didn't give up when she was trapped in Conrad's car in the middle of nowhere, Irma's body locked in the trunk.

No, she'd made up her mind that she was going to live.

Deciding had been the easy part. She lay on her stomach across the floorboards of the Rolls-Royce, feeling half sick as Conrad chuckled to himself in the front seat.

"I haven't forgotten about you, you know."

Gabrielle didn't know where they were. At first she'd tried to keep track of each turn, but the roads were so hilly and winding that she quickly lost track of which direction they were going in. It didn't matter now, though. She could just get up from the floor and see for herself. Gabrielle sat down on the long leather seat next to the passenger-side door.

"It was very thoughtful of you to stay here," Conrad said. "Not very smart, but very thoughtful."

There was no sense in answering, so Gabrielle didn't. Instead, she looked around for landmarks and road signs. All she could tell was that it was one of the many low, scrubby mountain ranges around the city, perpetually brown and burned-looking. She couldn't tell them apart, especially not in the dark.

Conrad had noticed her looking out the window and said, "I wouldn't start getting any ideas now."

"If I thought about what I was going to do next, I knew I'd

never go through with it," Gabrielle told me as we sat huddled together in the janitor's closet. "It was so dark I could only see right in front of us. I didn't know whether there was a shoulder on the side of the road or a cliff."

Don't think, Gabrielle had told herself, and when Conrad downshifted to climb a hill, she threw open the rear suicide door. She'd heard that gangsters liked cars with doors like these for exactly this reason. It was easier to throw a body out of a moving car when the wind was holding the door open for you, not blowing it shut. Conrad slammed on the brakes just as Gabrielle tumbled out of the car and the Rolls fishtailed, then spun out as its rear wheels slid from pavement to the gravel shoulder.

"I landed in a patch of scrub near the side of the road. My shoes had blown off my feet, but other than that, I was okay. I got up and started running."

Behind her, she heard Conrad put the car in gear and the sound of tires spinning in gravel until finally the engine roared, the car popped free, and the tires squealed as their rubber caught hold of the paved road again. Gabrielle looked back over her shoulder and saw he was gaining on her.

Conrad swerved into the wrong lane and edged alongside her, pushing her onto the shoulder where the gravel bit into her feet, and she realized what he was doing. No more than twenty yards ahead, the shoulder ended abruptly in a sheer cliff.

She turned on her heel and bolted back up the hill. As she ran, she caught a glimpse of Conrad's face and saw that he was laughing his head off.

It was difficult for him, however, to turn the long, heavy Rolls-Royce around on a narrow mountain pass, and for a moment Gabrielle thought that she might crest the hill and get far enough ahead to lose him. Maybe there'd be a town up ahead or a wooded spot where she could hide. But in a matter of seconds, she was caught in the headlights again. It didn't matter. She kept running. Her legs ached and her lungs felt like they were on fire, but she kept running toward whatever hopeful thing lay on the other side of the mountain.

There was no town and no place to get off the road and hide, but what Gabrielle saw when she came to the crest of the hill was no less lovely. No more than a quarter mile away, a little truck was climbing the hill from the other direction. She darted across the road and tucked herself behind a rock outcropping. A lousy hiding place, but it only had to fool Conrad long enough for him to drive past her. If he turned the Rolls-Royce around again, it might attract the driver's attention. With his famous face and a body in his trunk, Gabrielle had to hope that he'd avoid taking chances like that.

For a moment, Gabrielle wondered whether she should flag down the driver of the truck, but decided against it. There were few good reasons to be out on a road like this at four in the morning, and fewer honest ones. What if the person behind the wheel had intentions every bit as bad as Conrad's? And even if the driver was a farmer, carting something as innocuous as milk or produce to market, Gabrielle wasn't sure she knew how to explain what had happened to her. There was no lie, no cover story that would account for the presence of a fourteen-year-old girl barefoot in a party dress on a narrow mountain pass at four in the morning. No story that didn't raise more questions than it answered, or end with her being delivered to the nearest county sheriff.

Sometimes, when she was low on bus fare, she'd hitched rides from women or the occasional man, if he was especially elderly or kindly looking. They all asked a lot of questions and usually dropped her off with some sort of scolding or lecture about there being all sorts of perverts out there in the world, and did her parents know where she was?

She wouldn't risk taking the ride. She'd walk, at least until it got light. She'd gotten away, and if she saw Conrad's headlights coming up the road now, she'd have time to hide before he saw her. Another thought had buoyed her spirits.

"It was almost morning, and Conrad still had Irma's body in his trunk. He could get rid of her, or he could get rid of me, but he didn't have time to do both," she told me.

She'd stuck to the shoulders, in the trees and brush when she could, and in her bare feet, Gabrielle began walking toward Los Angeles.

Whatever Gabrielle decided to say when Rex and Ruth took her to the police, I knew I had to forgive her. This wasn't about being young and scared. It was about making up your mind that you were going to live. If Gabrielle told lies about Annie and my father, it was only because she had no other choice to save herself. It wasn't right, it wasn't fair, but nothing about any of this was.

I huddled against the wall in the room next door to Conrad's, fingers still clutched around the doorknob, when I heard the squeal and thunk of the hallway door closing behind Rex, Ruth, and Gabrielle. And I realized that Conrad was alone in there now. Alone, with a gunshot wound, in a hospital bed.

As I put my shoes back on, I turned over the things my mother had said the night before and the things she said a few minutes ago. I'd been trying so hard not to think about them, and I didn't want to let them come together now.

I wouldn't have said she made the whole thing up.

He'll never come near this family again.

I wouldn't have cared how it made the studio look.

Finding out the truth is like solving a puzzle. You snap the last piece into place, crack the last letter in the code, and you feel a surge of gratification at finally unlocking some secret unknown.

That's not what this felt like.

At last, I knew why Annie left. I understood why she'd risked everything to protect Gabrielle, why she'd dared to involve the police.

Knowing didn't make me feel better. It didn't give me any relief or satisfaction. All it gave me was another awful thing to carry around in my heart.

Only this wasn't about me. It was about justice for Irma and Gabrielle, but it was about something else, too.

It was about a father who betrayed his older daughter, a mother who wrapped her up in evening gowns and sent her out to sing for a room full of wolves.

And one night four years ago, Conrad Donahue had been one of them.

I wondered whether he'd started off trying to charm her, or whether he'd cornered her in a dressing room; whether the other men at the party had known what had happened or not; whether my father's first impulse had been to save his daughter, or his movie star. When my mother said she'd kill Conrad Donahue, she meant it. Now I felt the same way.

I looked around the room for something that I could use as a weapon, but there was nothing sharper or heavier than a bedpan. I wondered if I'd be able to do it with my bare hands, strangle him or hold a pillow down over his face until he was dead.

At that moment, I felt like I probably could.

I wasn't thinking straight—every sensible thought in my head was consumed by white-hot rage as I crawled out from behind the door and into the hallway, rehearsing in my mind how I'd do it. I'd climb up on the bed and pin his arms down with my knees, and I'd smother him. I thought about the story Gabrielle had told me, how he'd drowned Irma for less than no reason; I thought about what he'd done to Annie. There wasn't a doubt in my mind that the world would be a better place without Conrad Donahue in it.

I didn't think about whether I was physically strong enough or whether I'd be able to go through with it. I didn't think about what I'd do after it was over. All I could think was that Conrad Donahue was going to get away with everything unless I did this.

The problem was, every time I steeled myself to leap out of my sprinter's stance and run into Conrad's room, the faces of people I knew, people who cared about me, began to swim up before my eyes. I could see Cy telling me he wanted to see me again, my mother asking me to promise I'd be careful. I could hear Cassie's voice saying, *Don't make me sorry I helped you, Alice*, and Jerry asking, *Do you think Annie would want you mixed up in any of this?*

I was in no shape to listen to reason or conscience or Jerry Shaffer, and I certainly wasn't listening for Ruth. The shoes she wore were flat with rubber soles, ugly, sensible, and quiet. But not silent. I should have heard her doubling back down the hall, would have heard her had I not been crawling on my hands and knees down a hospital hallway, revenge seething in my brain.

With a single swift motion, she lifted me up by the elbow with one hand and covered my mouth with the other, then marched me down the hallway. Only when we were through the door did she let me speak.

"Where's Gabrielle?" I asked, gasping for breath.

"She's in the car with Rex." My face must have indicated what an insane idea I thought this was because Ruth waved me off and said, "He's not going to lay a finger on her."

Then I remembered. Of course he wouldn't—not now. Conrad had just sent the three of them off to the police station so Gabrielle could tell everyone about the terrible things Annie and my father had done to her.

I wrenched my arm out of Ruth's grip.

"You set Annie up," I said. "I won't lie for you. You can't make me say anything."

A strange look crossed Ruth's face as she caught hold of my arm again and bent my wrist between my shoulder blades.

"If you're smart," she said, "you won't say another word."

I struggled to get loose, but Ruth was stronger than she looked. She shoved me in the direction of the stairs.

"Where are you taking me?" I asked.

Ruth didn't answer, and I realized it didn't matter. She must have known I'd overheard everything. There was no way she'd let me out of her sight until she'd delivered Gabrielle to the police. And after that, there was no telling what she, Rex, and Conrad had in mind for me.

As we wound our way down the stairs toward the hospital lobby, I found one tiny hope to hold on to. Ruth didn't know Gabrielle had trusted me with her story—the real version—and now we were about to share a ride to police headquarters. Maybe seeing me would prick her conscience and remind her of what my sister had done for her. Maybe she'd at least think twice about going along with Conrad and Ruth's plan.

Down in the hospital lobby, it was bedlam. Reporters and

photographers fought their way into the hallways and stairwells while lines of unblinking LAPD officers forced them back, night-sticks at the ready. A few who tried to reach for a door handle or who were shoved from behind into the police barricade got a taste of those. No chance we were getting out this way.

Ruth steered me behind the line of officers, then down another hallway to the hospital's rear entrance, where the ambulances were dispatched and the truly dire cases were admitted. Conrad's Rolls-Royce was idling there, Rex behind the wheel and Gabrielle sitting next to him in the front seat.

"Get in," Ruth said. She shoved me into the backseat, then crawled in next to me.

"Gabrielle," I said, but she wouldn't look at me. She wouldn't even turn around.

The tires squealed as Rex threw the car in reverse and peeled out of the lot. But not before I saw two things.

First, the ambulance bay door flew open and Jerry appeared, panting, arms pumping as he vaulted down the flight of steps and hit the pavement without breaking his stride. His hat was missing, and blood streamed down the side of his swollen face. I turned around and watched through the back window as he chased the Rolls-Royce across the parking lot, looking like he might collapse at any moment.

As I wondered what had happened to his face, I saw Walter Hanrahan stroll out from between two parked ambulances and tip his hat to Jerry before getting into his police cruiser.

I pressed my hand to the glass as the last wisps of hope I'd held on to melted away.

It was over. Just like that.

CHAPTER 25

A s I stretched my cramped, prickling legs out in front of me, one of my feet bumped a broom that was propped up against the wall of the supply closet. Both Gabrielle and I scrambled to catch it before it hit the floor and the noise gave away our hiding place.

"How long did it take you to walk back?" I whispered, leaning the broom in a safer corner of the closet.

"The whole day. It was almost dark when I got back to the Stratford Arms," said Gabrielle. "I went straight to Ruth's. She didn't ask me where I'd been, not at first. She fed me spaghetti and made me drink about fifty glasses of water, and then I went to bed."

"What happened the next morning?"

"She asked a lot of questions then. What happened at the party? Did somebody hurt me? I wouldn't tell her anything. Then she got mad and said she knew I was a runaway from the moment Rex set me up in the bungalows.

DEAD TO ME

She said she knew I was underage, and that she should have turned me over to Juvenile Welfare when she'd had the chance.

"Then she fed me another plate of spaghetti and said that she was going to take me to stay with her friend Annie. She told me Annie was smart and knew how to keep a secret. And if I was smart, I'd do what she told me."

Ruth pointed out a spot across the street from the police station, and Rex parked the car. The Rolls-Royce had already turned enough heads that there was no sense trying to sneak in the back door now. When we got out of the car, Rex took Gabrielle roughly by the arm and began to drag her toward the station.

"For heaven's sake, Rex, lay off," Ruth said. He glared at her, but let go of Gabrielle. Ruth stepped between them and patted the girl on the shoulder. "Just do what we talked about, and this will be over before you know it."

Gabrielle flinched from her touch, and I saw a look of worry cross Ruth's face, like she'd realized for the first time that maybe Gabrielle wouldn't go along with Conrad's plan.

The four of us got into an empty elevator, and Ruth punched the button for the third floor, checking her plum lipstick in the chrome paneling. As the door closed behind us, I saw a flash of movement out of the corner of my eye, a flash of metal, and I thought, Uh-oh.

Ruth knocked Gabrielle to the ground and threw herself between Rex and the girl.

"Did you see that?" Rex asked. "She tried to take my gun!"

"Put that down," Ruth said, putting a hand on Rex's forearm. "We're in a police station. You can't just go waving your gun around every time a little girl looks at you funny."

Ruth punched a button, and the elevator screeched to a stop between floors.

Then she looked down at Gabrielle, cowering in the corner of the elevator, and said, "The next time you want to take somebody's gun away, do it like this."

By the time we reached our floor and the elevator doors opened, Ruth had snapped a pair of handcuffs around Rex's wrists and disarmed him. She marched him down the hall and threw him into the first interrogation room she came to. We passed a blue-uniformed LAPD officer in the hall. I felt sure he'd stop us and ask what the meaning of this was, but he only nodded in our direction and said, "Detective Forrester."

Ruth nodded back and continued down the hall. Gabrielle and I followed behind, about as surprised as Rex had looked the moment Ruth handcuffed him.

It was a lot to take in at once. I had never been able to make sense of Ruth. She didn't seem like a pinup girl, a party girl, a junkie, Rex's partner in crime, or Annie's friend, but I wouldn't have guessed she was a cop, either.

As they walked down the hall, Ruth made sure that every cop she passed knew that one of the men who shot Officers Greeley and Carver that morning was ready to be questioned.

"Go on in and take first crack at him if you want to," she sneered.

When Ruth stopped in front of an office door, Gabrielle looked up at her, her big eyes filled with worry.

"What are you going to do to me?" she asked.

"I'm going to open this door, and you're going to go into that room," Ruth said. "And you can tell them whatever you want to.

You can even tell them what really happened. But whatever you say here, you can't unsay. You can't change your mind later if you don't like the way that things turn out. So think hard about how you want to play this, because this is your one chance."

Gabrielle said she understood.

"You," she said, turning to me. "Wait here a minute."

They disappeared behind the opaque glass, and I sat in the hallway feeling like I'd just been used as the rope in a game of tug-o-war. Had this been Ruth's plan from the beginning?

Before I had a chance to consider that, she stepped out into the hallway, cocked her head to the side, and asked, "What were you doing outside of Conrad's room anyway?"

"I was going to smother him with a pillow," I said.

Ruth smirked, then frowned. "I almost wish I hadn't been in such a hurry to find you. Come on."

I didn't know where she was taking me, but when she snapped her fingers, I got to my feet and followed her down the hallway. She stopped in front of another office door and gave me a hard look. "Are you ready to make your statement?"

It had never occurred to me that I would be asked to talk to the police, too. *Whatever you say here, you can't unsay.* The words Ruth had spoken to Gabrielle hadn't meant much to me a few minutes ago. Now I realized how serious they were.

"What am I supposed to tell them?" I asked.

"Be careful," Ruth said. "Stick to the truth, but only the version of it that's easiest to verify. And hope that's enough."

As pep talks went, it wasn't much of one. She opened the door, and I found myself in a room with white flaking walls and a hulking wooden desk that took up nearly its entire width. On one side of the desk sat a policewoman wearing a small round hat that looked like a breakfast Danish sitting on top of her head.

"I'm supposed to be on break," the woman said. When she spoke, the tight gray curls at her temples shook like a pair of tiny fists.

"I'm sorry, Detective Cobb. This shouldn't take long," Ruth said, then closed the door behind her before the policewoman could protest further.

"Sit down," she said, sighing heavily. "State your name, age, and home address."

I looked the policewoman in the eye and saw nothing. Not a single clue as to whether she was kind or cruel or inclined to believe a word I said. But I didn't care. For years, I'd been lied to about the biggest, most important thing in my life. And at that moment, the idea of being careful, of telling a watered-down version of the truth, felt uglier to me than a lie.

I knew I wouldn't want to unsay any of it. I wanted it all out and open and said.

Detective Cobb didn't interrupt me much while I told my story, which was fortunate because every time she opened her mouth, I felt like screaming.

"You realize that's the police department's job," she said, when I explained how I'd planned to track down my sister's attacker. And instead of going to the Stratford Arms myself, why hadn't I just asked my parents about the postcard?

When I told her about being kidnapped from the pay phone by Rex, Conrad, and Walter Hanrahan, she asked, "What were you doing out by yourself at that hour?"

"Making a phone call," I said through clenched teeth.

When I reached the end, she looked at me with her blank, bored face and said, "This is all very difficult to believe, Miss Gates."

"It's true."

"I didn't say it wasn't true. Only that it was difficult to believe."

"Oh."

"If there's nothing else, you're free to go."

"Are you going to do anything?" I asked. "What happens now?"

"Don't worry, Miss Gates. This is in our hands now."

I left the room feeling like I'd just spent a week in bed with the flu, weak and emptied out and desperate for company. There was no sign of Ruth or Gabrielle in the hallway, so I found a bench and lay down on it, curling my knees up to my chest. I only meant to rest my eyes for a moment, but when I opened them again, the light in the hallway had changed and Jerry was there, shaking me by the shoulder.

"Hey there, Alice," he said.

I pressed my hand to my cheek and felt the grain of the wood slats imprinted there. My hair stuck out in chicken wings on one side and my shoulder ached from sleeping on the hard bench, but I smiled anyway. I think Jerry was glad to see me, too.

The blood that streaked his face as he chased the Rolls-Royce through the hospital parking lot had been wiped away, but he had a lump the size of a golf ball on his forehead and the beginnings of a black eye.

"What happened to you?" I asked groggily.

Jerry looked over his shoulder, then leaned in and whispered, "When I went after Gabrielle, I found Hanrahan waiting for me in the stairwell. He gave me a whack with his billy club and pushed me down the steps."

I sat up so fast my head spun.

"Are you all right?" I asked.

Jerry shrugged and waved me off. "I've had worse. What about you? People have been trying to wake you up all afternoon."

It had been nice to pass an hour or so when all my cares and worries were the size of a bench in a police station hallway, but now I was awake and back in the world—and I remembered the news I had to share with Jerry.

"Jerry, I was wrong about Ruth. She wasn't working with Rex—"

"She's an undercover cop," Jerry said, finishing my thought.

"You knew?"

"Ruth and I have known each other for a long time," Jerry said. "We used to be on the vice squad together."

So what Cy had told me was true. I wondered if he'd known about Ruth, too.

"Why didn't you tell me?" I asked.

"When Ruth sent Gabrielle off to Annie the first time, she didn't know about Conrad and Irma. All she knew was she had a scared underage girl on her hands, and all she wanted to do was bundle her off someplace far away from Rex and the Stratford Arms in a hurry.

"The kind of cop I was, things were more straightforward, at least in theory. You arrested the bad guys and brought them in. But if you're undercover like Ruth, it's different. Certain things you let slide, sometimes because they're small potatoes and not worth your trouble, and sometimes because you can help a girl more by turning her over to someone like Annie than you can sending her downtown.

"Once Annie found out what had happened to Gabrielle, what Conrad had done to Irma, keeping her safe wasn't enough. Annie wanted to go to the police, but she didn't know who to trust. Ruth was suspicious, too. It wasn't how your sister usually worked, and Ruth thought maybe it was a setup. She was worried it would blow her cover, too, seeing how she and Gabrielle already knew each other.

"I talked them into trusting each other. I promised Ruth we wouldn't blow her cover. I told Annie that if Ruth had gone bad, then the whole LAPD had. In the end, your sister agreed to meet with her, and, well, you know the rest."

"Ruth didn't show up," I said.

Jerry nodded. "It's been a long time since I was LAPD, and vice squad has a way of changing people. When I saw it was starting to change me, I got out. I was beginning to think it had changed Ruth, too. That I'd made a terrible mistake in trusting her."

Now I understood why Millie hated Jerry so much—she blamed him. And no wonder he hadn't been in a hurry to tell me about Ruth. What difference did it make if she was a cop or not if she was as crooked and dangerous as the rest of them?

"When did you know you hadn't made a mistake?"

"When I found you here," Jerry said. "She figured out a way to get you girls out of there, away from Conrad. And when I found out she'd turned Rex in, I knew she'd decided to blow her cover. That's not a decision she'd make lightly, Alice. Once the word gets out, she'll be a marked woman."

I remembered the bag of dope I found while I was hiding in Ruth's pantry at the Stratford Arms. I couldn't see Ruth using it herself, but it occurred to me that she might sell it if she ever needed to disappear. As big as it was, I bet she could disappear for a long time on that money. Maybe Ruth had intended to bring Gabrielle in to the police all along—she just needed more time to get her house in order in case the worst happened.

She wouldn't have gone to all that trouble if she was secretly working for Conrad, and she certainly wouldn't have brought Gabrielle here.

"That means Ruth wasn't the one who'd set Annie up," I said.

"No, it doesn't look that way," Jerry said. "There's something else that happened while you were sleeping, Alice."

He took off his hat and set it down next to him on the bench.

"The county sheriff's department found Irma's body. It was a couple of hours ago, not far from where Gabrielle said Conrad had taken her. The strange thing is, someone called in an anonymous tip this morning that led them right to her. The body wasn't anywhere a person was likely to stumble across it. You couldn't see her from the road. Even with what Gabrielle had told them, it might have taken days to find her, maybe longer. That phone call was a lucky thing. A strange, lucky thing."

Not luck, I thought.

I might not have been able to figure Ruth out, but I'd thought long and hard about Millie. If she had intended to run, she would have done it before the night I met her. And she didn't strike me as the running-away type anyhow. She hadn't become a recluse after her disgrace, hiding out in Chicago or living in obscurity in Palm Springs. She'd rented a one-bedroom in Hollywood where anyone could see her. The night Millie had pulled me inside Irma's apartment, I'd assumed that she was removing all trace of herself to avoid being implicated in so sordid a thing as Irma's life. It had never occurred to me that she might be saving the scraps and mementos of their friendship. It never occurred to me how dangerous it would have been for her to stay put, waiting until she'd found the girl and heard the words from Gabrielle's own mouth about how Irma had died and where Conrad had taken her.

Not until later. And not until later did I realize that a person who would do that would never leave her best friend's body to rot in a shallow mountain grave. A person like that would look.

The call to the sheriff's department was anonymous, but I knew who had placed it immediately. No matter how they tried, Conrad and his dirty cops couldn't control everything. Annie wasn't the only person out there who cared about justice. I wasn't, either.

"What they need now is evidence," Jerry said. "Something beyond Gabrielle's word that puts the three of them at the beach that night."

"Beyond her word?" I asked. Really, it was more like yelling than asking. "Didn't about fifty people see them leave that party together? Would *their* word be good enough? Does someone famous have to give a statement before they do something?"

Jerry caught one of my angrily flailing hands in his and said, "Hard evidence, Alice. Something beyond words and who saw what. They believe Gabrielle. But they know Conrad will have lawyers. Good ones. It's for Gabrielle's own good—and yours and Annie's, too—that they do this the right way."

"Have they found anything yet?" I asked.

"No, not yet, but it's early. They'll find something. And then there are those pictures from the park...."

For a moment, Jerry went somewhere else. I don't know where it was, but from the look on his face, I guessed it was a dark, windowless, guilty place, and I doubt it was his first time visiting there.

"Those aren't nothing," I said gently, and Jerry came back to himself.

"No, they aren't. Those alone should put Conrad away for a long while."

But there was a hitch in his face when he said it, a smile with more confidence than he really had. There was something he wasn't telling me.

"How long?" I asked.

Jerry sighed. "The prosecutor will try for attempted murder, but Conrad's lawyers will bargain them down to simple assault. He'll plead guilty, but spin a completely false and terrible story about your sister in the process. Maybe he'll say she tried to rob him in the park. Maybe he'll come up with something worse. The judge will sentence him to three to five years, and then we won't hear a peep out of him for about a year. His behavior in prison will be excellent, and his lawyers will begin clearing their throats to point that out. People will remember the things he said about Annie, not the crimes he committed. They'll decide she probably deserved it somehow. They'll remember that scene in that one movie where he kisses Lucille Ball and falls off the horse and how funny that was. They'll forgive him. And they'll let him out to do it all over again."

When Jerry finished talking, he looked like a punching bag that had all its stuffing ripped out. I probably did, too. We sat there for a minute, a couple of flopped-over and useless human beings. I wanted to curl up in a ball and cry. I wanted to crawl underneath the bench in the police station hallway and hide there more or less forever.

And then, suddenly, I didn't. Maybe Gabrielle's word wasn't good enough, but I knew something that would be.

Dragging Jerry behind me, I leaped up from the bench and ran pell-mell down the hall, down the stairwell, out the central station front door, and down the street to the spot where Rex had parked Conrad's Rolls-Royce.

"What's this all about?" Jerry asked, huffing to catch his breath.

"It's under the seat," I said.

"What is?"

"Hard evidence."

I told him about Irma's purse and shoes, how they'd jabbed into Gabrielle as she hid on the floorboards of the car and how she'd stuffed them underneath the seat. Conrad was careful about not being seen, careful about where he hid the body, careful to dump Irma's clothing in a place it wouldn't be found. But he wouldn't have looked for her purse and shoes in the car. I bet anything he'd forgotten all about them.

Jerry's eyes grew to the size of saucers as he handed me a pocketful of change and a stack of reporters' business cards.

"Go," he said. "Tell Ruth. But before you do that, call Amos Carey. Call as many reporters as you can. Call the *Times*, the *Examiner*, the *Herald*. I want someone outside the LAPD getting pictures of this."

I went back inside and stood in line with the drunks, streetwalkers, and juvenile delinquents to use the pay phone. After I'd made my calls, I found Ruth drinking a cup of coffee. When I told her what was in Conrad's car, she said, "Get back out there right now, and don't let anyone touch that car until I get there."

Soon, everyone began to arrive. The reporters and photographers descended upon the Rolls-Royce first, like a flock of tweedy crows. A half-dozen beat cops pressed them back, and a gasp passed my lips when I saw they were clearing a pathway for Walter Hanrahan. Gone were the high-waisted pants, the gangster's fedora, and the blue polka-dot suspenders, exchanged for a police captain's uniform. He was followed by two white-haired policemen and Ruth, wearing the same little breakfast Danish hat and boiled-wool jacket as the woman who'd taken my statement. Hanrahan's face was a cipher: flat, ordinary, and official-looking. I tried to crack it, to figure out what combination of rage, astonishment, fear, and cunning lay beneath the surface as he approached the car, as his gloved hand disappeared beneath the seat and came out again.

A gasp went up from the crowd and the light in the street went blindingly white as the photographers' flashbulbs exploded in unison.

I saw the picture in the papers the next day. Hanrahan is holding Irma's purse in one hand, her shoes in the other, smiling so triumphantly you'd think he solved the crime himself.

Ruth stands by his side, and even though her face is smaller than a dime, it's the face of a woman who knows too much, knows she's in danger, knows the life she built for herself is over.

I wondered whether she thought it was worth it.

CHAPTER 26

"What about Gabrielle?" I asked as we wove through the gathering crowd. "We can't just leave her back there."

Jerry doubled his pace, and I had to trot along to keep up with him. I thought he must not have heard me, so I asked again.

The Plymouth coupe was parked near the *Los Angeles Times* building, and the big clock on the side told me it was later than I'd originally guessed. It had been hours and hours since Ruth had dropped Gabrielle and me off with the police matrons. How long had I been asleep? Two hours? Maybe three? Gabrielle should have been sitting on that bench with Jerry when I woke up.

I put myself between Jerry and the Plymouth and stuck him in the chest with my forefinger.

"Where is she?"

He didn't seem surprised that I'd figured out something was wrong, only sad that he'd have to be the one to break the news.

"Alice, they wouldn't turn Gabrielle over to me. She's been transferred to the Juvenile Hall while they look for her parents. And if they can't turn them up, they've petitioned to make her a ward of the court so they can hold her there until Conrad's trial."

Jerry opened the car door for me. I got in, gripping the dashboard as the information sunk in. The Plymouth gave a feeble cough and a sputter before agreeing to start, and Jerry pulled away from the curb, out of downtown.

Neither of us spoke until I asked, "What about after Conrad's trial?"

"I don't know what happens to her after that."

It was all I could do to keep from flinging myself into Jerry and beating him with my fists. This was what he and Annie did, what they were supposed to be good at—telling the girls who should go home from the ones who shouldn't. Gabrielle had said almost nothing about where she came from, nothing about the circumstances that had driven her away, and even I knew which kind of girl she was. Jerry should have known it, too.

"You shouldn't have let them take her," I said. "You should have stopped it."

"I tried," he said.

"You didn't try hard enough."

Jerry clenched the steering wheel until his knuckles turned white.

"Alice, you have no idea how sorry I am," he said.

I knew he was sorry. I knew he cared what happened to Gabrielle, that what had happened was an accident, an oversight. He'd taken his eyes off her for a minute, and she was gone. And yet, the whole thing was so sloppy and careless. If Annie had been there in his place, there was no doubt in my mind that Gabrielle would be sitting in the car with us.

Instead, she was locked away in a cell where no one knew her and no one would be looking out for her. It would be easy for Hanrahan to get to her, and they'd have a powerful bargaining chip to hold over her: *Say what we want you to say, or else we start looking for your parents.* When Conrad threatened her, Gabrielle had agreed to turn on Annie. Who knew what kinds of things she might agree to say if one of Hanrahan's goons came to visit her in Juvenile Hall?

Jerry turned onto Vermont, and I realized that in a few minutes, I would see my sister, alive and awake. After all this time, I was finally going to get the thing I wanted most in the world. It should have made me the happiest girl in the world. It should have at least cheered me up.

But all I could do was worry about Gabrielle.

The police outside Annie's room were gone, all of them either dispatched to hold off the reporters in the lobby or downtown with Ruth and Walter Hanrahan.

When Jerry and I got there, Cassie was drawing back the curtains so everyone could watch the smoggy Los Angeles sunset, and Annie was sitting up in bed, sipping from a cup that our mother held to her lips. One of her eyes was swollen shut, but the other was wide and clear, and it crinkled at the corner when she saw me.

The smile disappeared when she saw that Jerry and I were alone.

"Where is she?" she asked. "Tell me she's with you—tell me she's all right."

Even through broken teeth and a wad of cotton packing, it was the beautiful, musical voice I remembered. She peered over our shoulders as though Gabrielle might be hiding behind us or dawdling in the hallway. Jerry bit his lip and almost imperceptibly shook his head. Annie's face sagged, gray and emptied out. I could almost feel the frustration radiating off her, the impotent rage that she'd gotten hurt, and that the people she'd left behind to take care of things in her absence had completely and utterly failed her. Maybe Jerry was right when he'd said that I didn't know my sister anymore, but I knew what she was thinking at that moment.

"You let them take her," she said finally.

"I'm sorry," I said, knowing the words weren't enough. I could barely look at her.

"Alice, it's not your fault," Jerry said.

"I know it's not her fault," Annie said icily. "Of course it's not her fault."

Jerry flinched, and angry as I was with him, I couldn't help but feel a little bit of pity.

"Annie, she's alive. And you are, too," Jerry said. "And Alice is here."

I hung back behind Jerry, like a shy child being introduced to a roomful of strangers. My mother was the one who finally broke the ice, patting a spot on the bed and saying, "Alice, come here. Let me see my girls together."

I went, feeling grateful for her permission to approach.

"My two brave little girls," she said, and her eyes filled up with tears as she took our hands.

"Mother, please don't," Annie said, recoiling from her touch. "Not now."

Cassie hadn't spoken since Jerry and I arrived, and as what should have been our happy family reunion dissolved into bickering and blame, she'd retreated to a corner. Still, when Annie snapped at our mother, Cassie stepped forward and sat down in the chair next to her, good as her word. Watching the way my mother sat there, nervously touching her face, playing with her jewelry, and looking very much in need of a drink, I was glad she'd had Cassie there to look out for her.

Meanwhile, Annie had turned her wrath back on Jerry. "What were you thinking, dragging Alice into this?"

Jerry opened his mouth to explain, then thought better of it and sat with a hangdog expression on his face.

"You lose Gabrielle, you put Alice in all kinds of danger. What was she doing anywhere near Conrad? If I'd been there, it would all be over by now. Gabrielle would be safe; Alice would have been spared all of this."

Spared. I would have been spared.

Spared knowing that any of it had ever happened, what my sister did and how much she risked and how brave she was. I'd be exactly where I'd been for the past four years—nowhere near her life. And apparently, that was what she would have preferred.

"You have no idea how lucky you are to be alive, Alice," she said. "How did you even get involved in this?"

I bristled. What did she mean, how did I get involved?

"You had a picture of me in your shoe. What did you think I'd do when the hospital called?"

Annie shook her head, one hand pressed tight to her mouth.

"Oh, Alice, that's not what I meant to happen at all."

It struck me all at once and harder than any fist. It was so obvious, I couldn't believe I hadn't realized it before. When Annie had gone to the park that night, she'd known she was in danger. It'd probably occurred to her that the whole thing could be a setup, and if that had been the case . . .

She hadn't put that phone number in her shoe because she'd expected to end up in a coma. She'd expected to save Gabrielle or die trying.

Either way, she had never intended to see me again.

If Annie had known me at all, maybe what I did wouldn't have surprised her. But of course she didn't. She knew a twelve-year-old kid who loved puzzles and followed her big sister around like a devoted puppy. And yet, how could she not know me? How could she expect to find me just the way she'd left me?

"I'm sorry, Alice. I'm so sorry," she said.

Sorry you stayed away, I wondered, *or sorry you came back?*

Fortunately, I didn't have to dwell long on that question, because at that moment, my new friend Amos Carey from the *Los Angeles Herald* burst into the room.

"I've been looking everywhere for you," he said to me, before turning around and registering the battered girl and the silence that hung in the air heavy as summer smog and twice as combustible. "Sorry if I'm interrupting something."

"Not at all," Cassie said. I think we were all grateful for an interruption right about then.

"I just got back from downtown. The evening editions are out, and Conrad's picture is on the cover of every one. The police are going to arrest him any minute now. I thought you all might want to be there to see it."

CHAPTER 27

Over the years, I'd thought a lot about what it would be like to talk to my sister again. In my imagination, I would go to visit her in a cute stucco cottage in the Valley. We would make lemonade from lemons that grew in her yard and have a merry conversation that sparkled like sunshine on glass, and at the end of it, she'd invite me to come live with her. I knew it was a fantasy, but I'd never guessed it would be quite so far from the reality.

The room emptied out. Cassie went with Amos Carey when he left to take up his post outside Conrad's room. My mother excused herself to call our family's attorney. Amos had filled her ear with the kinds of stories my father was telling down at the Hollywood precinct, and by the time he was done, her face had turned chalk white.

"He's trying to do the right thing," she said, apologizing on behalf of her unhinged spouse. "If only he'd thought to try that a few years sooner."

I didn't see Jerry leave. One minute he was there, wordlessly absorbing Annie's anger and disappointment, and then he wasn't.

And then, it was just Annie and me. I was still sitting on the corner of her bed. I didn't feel like I belonged there, but I couldn't bear to leave, either.

"Conrad didn't...hurt you, did he?" she asked.

I gestured to my face. "You mean besides this?"

Annie frowned. "You know exactly what I mean."

Of course I knew. I looked away, ashamed at having been flippant about something so awful.

"No," I said.

Annie fell back against her pillow and let out a long sigh, as though asking had sapped the rest of her energy.

"I know about Conrad, what he did to you...." I said, still unable to meet her eyes.

Annie cut me off with a wave of her hand. "I wish you didn't. It was a long time ago, and I don't want to talk about it."

"I'm sorry," I said.

"Damn it, Alice, none of this is your fault. Stop apologizing."

I flinched at her words and clapped my hand over my mouth to keep from apologizing yet again. For a while, we sat, me staring at my hands, her out the window.

Finally, she said, "I'm sorry. It's just that I never wanted you to know. Some people, once they find out, that's the only thing about me they can see. Some just want the details. They want to know all about how it happened. And then my favorites are the ones who want to know what I did to deserve it."

"But it wasn't your fault," I said.

"That thought helps far less than you'd think," she said.

"It's not the only thing about you I see," I said.

Annie smiled. "That helps a little bit more."

She closed her eyes, and for a minute or two, I thought she'd fallen asleep. But then she opened them again and murmured, "How was Gabrielle? Was she okay?"

"I don't know," I said. "I didn't see her after she talked to the police."

"You mean after they took her."

"I was asleep."

She touched my hand and said, "I know it's not your fault, Alice."

Since she'd woken up, she'd asked about Gabrielle three times, and she and I hadn't even said hello. Maybe she sensed what I was thinking because she cocked her head to the side and studied my face for almost a full minute.

"It's strange," she said. "You're all grown up now. Just like I remember you, only..."

I wondered what word she was searching for. There were so many ways I wasn't the girl she knew four years ago. Four years ago, I ran everywhere I went because I was always excited to get there. I had been known to wear jumpers and shirts with puffy cap sleeves, often at the same time. I smiled more then.

"Older," she said at last.

"Older?" I repeated, certain it would have been something more. Or at least something else.

"Well, you are. You're old."

"You're older," I shot back like I was twelve again. "You're an *adult*."

"I'm not even twenty yet. I'm a baby."

She gave me a little grin and tapped the end of my nose with her fingertip, a gesture I would have found annoying coming from anyone else.

"So, the way I hear it, my clever little sis figured everything out. Found the girl. Found enough evidence to put Conrad and Rex away for a long time. Is that about right?"

"It was Jerry," I said. "Until he showed up at County Hospital to see you, I didn't know what to do."

"But he wouldn't have gotten anywhere without you," she said.

I should have felt proud, but instead, I thought I might cry. I knew I wasn't clever. Annie had to know it, too. She knew what had happened. I'd bungled so much, made so many bad decisions.

"I missed you, you know," Annie said. "I thought about you all the time."

I smiled, but a small, poisonous thought bloomed in my head. I could have crushed it, but instead, I gave it room to spread its roots. And when I should have said, *I missed you, too*, instead I said: "You promised you'd write to me."

"I did, didn't I?"

Her voice sounded distant, distracted, and I couldn't tell what she was thinking. I couldn't tell whether she was sorry, or annoyed that I'd even bring it up after all this time.

"I meant to," she said.

"Then why didn't you?" I asked. I hated the way the words sounded in my ears—petty, bitter, and accusing. "I didn't know if I'd ever see you again. You were just gone. You left me."

Annie let out a long sigh and turned her face away from mine.

"This was never about you, Alice."

She said it as kindly as you could say something like that. I could tell she tried to make her voice gentle, but her words still cut me because I knew they were true. Terrible things had happened, and because of them, my big sister disappeared. That she could have been more careful with my heart and her promises was the least important thing about it.

"And I really did think about writing to you," Annie said, staring out the hospital window, "but something always stopped me. Then so much time had passed. I didn't know if you hated me, or whether you even cared if I wrote to you at all. It was easier to think that you'd moved on with your life."

"But I didn't," I said, the tears finally starting to flow down my cheeks. "I was always waiting for you."

As she watched me cry, Annie drew in a jagged breath and held it. She started to look away, but then caught herself and lifted her head so her stricken eyes met mine. Though it must have hurt her to do it, she put her arms around me and pulled me close to her.

"Then that makes me impossibly sad."

Just then, Jerry came back in, two reporters trailing behind him. I wiped my eyes as Annie let go of me.

"I'm sure you don't want to be bothered right now, but these *gentlemen* wouldn't stop following me."

The so-called gentlemen in question didn't give us a chance to answer.

"So, girls, you claim that Conrad Donahue did this to you?" one of them asked. He wore a *Los Angeles Times* badge and a brown jacket that was speckled like a chicken egg.

"Yes, he did," Annie said, and I nodded in accord.

"Let's get a picture," said the other man. "You two squeeze in together there."

He took me by the shoulders and squared them up, folded

my hands into Annie's, and posed us there together, the devoted, damaged sisters.

"Can you try to look a little bit more . . . pitiful?" the photographer asked.

When Annie looked at me, I knew what she was thinking. We were the Gates sisters, crusading angels of the Allied forces. No one was going to pity us when they saw our picture in the *Los Angeles Times*. We put on our glamorous, elusive, uncrackable faces, but in the picture that ran in the paper, the one that I will never, ever cut out and glue into a scrapbook, we don't look pitiful or brave.

We look impossibly sad.

CHAPTER 28

Right behind the reporters came Cy.

He hugged me and gave me a peck on the cheek, but it was clear who he was really, finally here to see.

Annie clapped her hands over her mouth when he came through the door, and Cy threw his arms open wide and ran to her. He'd brought flowers. He hugged her gently and kissed her on her good cheek, and together they rehashed every terrible thing that had happened over the past week like it was a funny story.

"It took me forever to get up here," he said. "Once they found out we were friends, all the reporters wanted to get a picture of me for their stories. Do you think the casting people at Paramount read the crime section?"

"I'm sure you'll look devastatingly handsome," Annie said. "And you'll be called in for screen tests at every studio in town, but you'll just say, 'Oh, I fight crime. Motion pictures are so *beneath me.*'"

As they laughed together, I sat off to the side, eavesdropping and feeling jealous. Why could she talk like that with someone like Cy but not with me? Why couldn't it be easy between us like it was with them?

Down the hallway came the sounds of a parade, shouts and cheers and a phalanx of heavy footsteps. Cy and I stuck our heads out to investigate and saw the police officers and reporters winding up the stairwell to Conrad's floor.

"It's showtime," said Cy, rubbing his hands together. "Do you want to come, Annie? I'm sure I could find a wheelchair for you."

"I think I'll pass," Annie said.

"Alice?"

I understood why Annie might not want to be there, but I wouldn't have missed it for the world. As we walked down the hall, I wished that everyone could have been there. Millie. Gabrielle. Ruth. And, of course, Irma. Conrad Donahue and the girls who brought him to justice.

No, not girls.

When Cy saw the reporters standing up ahead, he threw back his shoulders and lifted his chin. Another small, spiteful thought entered my mind. *You never came to see Annie once until the reporters showed up.*

I chastised myself for the thought. Cy wasn't a high school sophomore on summer break. He had to work to support himself, and he'd come to see Annie as soon as he could. The reporters and the pictures had nothing to do with it.

Then I remembered something Ruth had said the night before at the Stratford Arms.

"What was she even doing there that night? She was supposed to be here."

At the time, I'd thought she was talking about Gabrielle, but she was talking about Annie. Annie, who was never supposed to have been in the park at all. Ruth hadn't betrayed my sister. She and Jerry had been waiting at the Stratford Arms for her to show up with Gabrielle.

Someone else told Annie to go to MacArthur Park.

Someone else sent her into Conrad and Rex's ambush.

And there was only one person it could have been.

Amos Carey made sure Cy, Cassie, and me had an excellent view of Conrad's hospital bed when they lifted him up and put the cuffs on him. One officer told us to step away, that there was nothing to see here.

"Are you kidding me?" Cassie asked, standing on her toes to get a better look.

Cy tried to put his arm around my shoulder as we watched, but I pushed it away and elbowed my way through the crowd of onlookers until I was standing next to the *Herald* reporter.

When I thanked Amos for saving us a spot, he said, "The least I can do. Thanks to you, I may never have to interview another insipid movie star again. Real news from here on out, baby."

"That's great, Mr. Carey," I said. "Are you interested in one more tip?"

I pulled him back from the others and whispered it in his ear. To him, it was just another story, but the words tasted like poison as they rolled off my tongue. If I'd had the slightest doubt, I would have swallowed them down. I would have told myself to forget about them. But when I said them aloud, I knew they were the truth.

"You're gold, Alice," he said as we joined the others at the front of the crowd.

I didn't feel like gold. I felt like I'd been gutted.

As I took my place between Cassie and Cy, I closed my eyes and remembered what I used to tell myself after Annie left home.

You are Philip Marlowe. You are Sam Spade. You are ice, you are stone, and nothing can touch you.

In an hour or a day, I would let myself feel this. I would hurt, I would be angry, and I wouldn't do it alone. But until then, I needed those words. I needed to believe they were true. If I didn't, I knew I'd never be able to say what I had to say next.

Conrad Donahue did not go quietly. He called the policemen names and swore he'd have their badges as they read off the long list of charges: murder, attempted murder, kidnapping, assault. He demanded the names of their commanding officers. He demanded his lawyer, the head of Insignia Pictures, and Nicky Gates. He demanded they leave him in peace, that he was in a great deal of pain and needed his rest. Didn't they know who he was?

In the end, someone brought up a wheelchair and they wheeled him out, still raving about the indignities that he'd suffered and how he'd make them all pay.

After it was over and the last of the reporters had trickled away, Cy squeezed my hand and said, "Would you care to accompany me downstairs to the hospital cafeteria for a slice of very mediocre pie? My treat."

I thought about the way he'd held me in my kitchen for as long as I'd needed him to, how he'd said I was pretty and brave. How he'd made me believe that when all this was over, there might be something between us, something sweet and good that had nothing to do with the worst week of my life.

But there was never going to be an us.

I unwrapped Cy's fingers from mine and turned to face him.

It was a handsome face, the kind that looked nicer the longer you looked at it.

"What do you say, Alice?" he asked, grinning like he believed the pack of lies he'd told me and Jerry and everyone.

"I don't think you're going to like the way your picture comes out in the newspaper tomorrow morning," I said.

"What are you talking about?"

Had he actually thought he could make it up to Annie by helping me? Was that his way of atoning for what he'd done?

I leaned in close, pointing my finger so it stuck him in the clavicle.

"I'm talking about how you should leave. Now. Because in a few hours, Annie, Jerry, and everybody else is going to know exactly what you did."

It wasn't Ruth or Jerry or Millie who'd betrayed my sister. It was Cy.

Before the night he kidnapped me, Conrad had thought Annie was dead. And then, as we idled in front of County Hospital, he'd said: *"A little birdie told me that Annie Gates is here."*

And earlier that same night, standing in the kitchen at Musso & Frank, I'd let it slip to Cy that Annie was still alive. I'd even been angry at Jerry for keeping the truth from him.

By itself, that might have been a coincidence, but as I sat in Annie's room, watching her and Cy compare notes, another question had tugged at me.

How had Rex found Gabrielle in the supply closet here at Cedars of Lebanon? I'd wondered. It didn't make sense. She was too smart to do anything that would give away her hiding place, and nothing she'd done would have led Rex to believe she was anywhere near the hospital. There was no reason for him to go searching for

Gabrielle at Cedars of Lebanon. Unless, after insisting we split up, Cy had scoured every corner of County Hospital and found nothing. Unless he'd called Rex when he was done to tell him where I was looking.

All along the way, he'd been feeding Conrad and his cronies little bits of information, assuring them he was loyal, that he'd never rat them out for what he knew.

Annie was never supposed to be in MacArthur Park the night she was attacked. She was supposed to bring Gabrielle to Ruth, but then at the last minute, plans got changed. Someone told Annie to bring Gabrielle to the park instead, someone she trusted. And there was only one person who could have made that call, only one person who could have told Conrad where Annie would be.

Millie hadn't taken the pictures of Annie being beaten. It had been Cy who'd hidden in the bushes and watched the whole thing, snapping photographs he never intended to develop unless whatever deal he'd made with Conrad fell through—in case he needed to blackmail him. It was smart of Cy to play both sides of it like that, to turn the camera over to Millie for safekeeping, to distance himself from the evidence, knowing he could always go to Irma's apartment and get it back if Conrad didn't cooperate. No matter which way things turned out, he should have gotten every little thing he wanted.

I remembered what the doctor at County Hospital had told me the morning I first arrived and saw my sister in that hospital bed. No one had called for help until later. Cy had left my sister for dead, left her body for the maintenance man to find like a piece of trash on the dock.

Cassie and I walked back to Annie's room together. Maybe I should have been dancing in the streets or cheering from the rooftop, but

I guess I wasn't really in a cheering kind of mood. Cassie seemed to feel the same way. Still reeling from the double shock of seeing one of her film idols up close, then seeing him hauled away in handcuffs, she shuffled down the hall in silence. I wondered how I was going to explain why Cy wasn't with us, but when we got there, I realized it didn't matter what I said. At that moment, nobody was going to care what had happened to Cy.

Because, somehow, Gabrielle was there.

Jerry and my mother stood side by side at the foot of Annie's bed, watching as Annie and Gabrielle wept and clung to each other like shipwreck victims in a lifeboat.

When she saw the look on my face, Cassie took me by the arm and dragged me out of the room. She led, and I floated along behind her down the hall, through the door, and into the stairwell. I didn't know how Gabrielle had gotten there, and I didn't care. All I could think was that it shouldn't have been Gabrielle crying in Annie's arms. It should have been me.

I was the one who needed my sister now.

I sat down on the steps, tears knotted in my throat. Why did everyone else get to see *that* Annie?

Cassie took a seat on the step next to me, her arms wrapped around her knobby athlete's knees. It was hard to tell where her tan ended and her bruises began.

She'd known that I needed to get out of that room in a hurry, and she knew the reason.

"It's probably easier for her with Gabrielle," she said.

I took a deep breath and tried to swallow the knot of tears. It stuck there, and when I spoke, my words came out in a high-pitched, whiny whisper.

"Why?" I asked. "She's known her a week. I'm her sister."

"She didn't leave Gabrielle behind. She didn't run away from her. She didn't let her down."

"Then why doesn't she say she's sorry if she feels that way?"

"Maybe she doesn't know it yet."

"Cassie, what if she doesn't love me anymore?"

Before I could get the sentence out, the knot in my throat loosened and filled my mouth with sobs. I buried my head in my lap and cried until the hem of my skirt was damp, while Cassie put her arm around my shoulders.

"She still loves you, Alice."

"What if she leaves? What if I lose her again?"

"Things go back to the way they were before," she said. "Or they don't."

It was such a cold thing to say, so unlike Cassie. But she looked me in the eye when she said it, and her arm stayed wrapped around my shoulders.

"What do you mean?" I asked.

"I mean, it's up to you what happens. I hope she stays, Alice. I really do. But if she doesn't, it can't be like it was before. It doesn't have anything to do with whether we're still friends or not. But if you want to sit alone in the dark waiting for her again, we won't be."

I hiccuped and wiped my eyes on my sleeve. Cassie wouldn't look at me while she talked, but it sounded like something she'd practiced saying before.

There weren't many people who would cover for me, break into my house to make sure I was okay, guard my sister from thugs, and babysit my mother the way Cassie had. Especially not after the way I'd treated her.

But she hadn't dropped everything for me, either. Cassie had a life, a whole group of friends and things she did that had nothing to do with me. She wasn't some pathetic sap, sitting around wait-ing for me to need her.

"You're such a good friend," I said, breaking into fresh sobs.

Cassie pulled her arm off my shoulder and gave me a shove. It wasn't very hard, but I hadn't expected it and nearly slid off the step.

"Yeah, so what?" she asked with a smirk—the smirk of a girl who would probably make fur coats out of kelp and do bad movie star impersonations at the beach whether she was twelve or twenty or forty.

"Cassie, can you forgive me?"

I wouldn't have asked if it wasn't important.

CHAPTER 29

I t's amazing the things my mother can do when she's sober. She can give fifty showgirls chignons that won't shake loose during the big song-and-dance number. She can arrange for the transfer of her comatose daughter to the most prestigious hospital in Los Angeles in the dead of night. She can actually be a halfway-decent parent.

And she can get a ward of Juvenile Hall released into her custody. I don't know what she said, what kind of stories she told, to make them turn Gabrielle over to her. All I know is no one ever showed up to try to take her away from us.

Gabrielle told the truth about everything—in the police station and in court—and she never tried to unsay any of it. Not even later, when certain parties made it known in the form of threatening letters and rocks through our windows that it might be safer, happier, and more profitable for her if she did.

I still don't know where she comes from. We were walking

home from school one afternoon and passed a shabby little carnival that had been set up in the neighborhood. She said that she used to be able to see the Dragon Bamboo Slide at the Venice Pier from her bedroom window. But another time, she said she was from El Monte, and another time, she said South Gate.

Some secrets are too big to bury, some things can't be hidden, but a girl is just about the right size.

My mother says that Gabrielle staying with us is temporary, but it's been months now with no sign of things changing. I think my mother likes having two girls around the house again, especially one who is coltish and sings and smiles a thousand-watt smile when she is happy. But Gabrielle is not Annie, and I hope that my mother is grateful for this, because I know that I am. Gabrielle is pliant and easygoing, where Annie insisted on her own way. Gabrielle is airy and affectionate, but she's also fragile in a way that Annie never was. She goes quiet sometimes, and it looks as if a light has gone out inside her. My mother and I are still trying to figure out what works best when this happens. Sometimes talking helps. Sometimes it really doesn't.

It's just the three of us now. After my father was relieved of his duties at Insignia Pictures, he was relieved of them at home as well. My mother sent him packing, and to his credit, he didn't try to fight her. Unburdening his soul at the Hollywood Precinct about the things he'd done seemed to have left him a changed man.

At least for a few weeks.

Once it became clear that he'd actually face trial for his crimes, his guilty conscience began to have second thoughts. He'd worked Hollywood magic so many times before for his troubled stars; now he began to conjure a little for himself. Nervous executives from Insignia Pictures materialized and began greasing palms, and just like that, the pandering charges were dropped; nobody ever remembered my father going anywhere near Rex's dirty-picture ring, and all that was left was one charge of contributing to the delinquency of a minor. He got a couple years of probation for that.

After that, his stock in Hollywood was reduced, but not ruined, and to a certain kind of movie studio, my father's notoriety was something of a selling point. Last I heard, he'd gone to work at Corinthian Films, where he does steady business pushing movies about women on chain gangs and the black-market baby trade.

He gets a lot of mileage out of being the man who shot Conrad Donahue in the leg.

Good for him, I guess.

Amos Carey—who now writes for the crime beat—matched up the bullets in Conrad's leg and in one of the dead police officers, and wrote all about it in the *Herald*. Rex was sunk. Both bullets had been fired from his gun, and my father had an airtight alibi—he was already in police custody when the officers were killed.

Rex had no choice but to confess. I was sure he'd point the finger at Hanrahan when he did it, but I hadn't counted on Rex's loyalty. He came out of the interrogation room at police headquarters with his nose broken, his eyes swollen shut, swearing up and down that he'd killed both officers himself.

The prosecutors were happy enough with that story. If anyone found it strange that the bullets pulled out of those police officers came from two different guns, that the second gun was never found, that no one ever breathed a word about sending Rex to the gas chamber at San Quentin for what he'd done, I suppose they kept those thoughts to themselves.

If you cover up a dirty cop's crime, he can make prison a little bit easier for you. It's in his interest to.

DEAD to ME

Jerry told me, "Alice, you make sure Hanrahan never finds out you were anywhere near Irma and Millie's apartment that morning. Don't get any crazy ideas."

He doesn't know that I told that part of the story to the policewoman that day at the station. The only thing is, nobody ever brought it up again. It was as if Detective Cobb had thrown that page away, the one part of my story she decided was simply too difficult to believe after all.

My mother invited Annie to come home again. She said it like it would be easy, but I knew better, and so did Annie. After four years out on her own, she didn't want to go back to school, keep a curfew, or live under someone else's roof. She did move home for a month after she got out of the hospital. It was nice to have her back, but nothing like I'd imagined. She slept more than half the day and spent hours stretching, learning how to walk without a limp, practicing the words that sometimes slurred off her tongue now if she wasn't careful. She and I worked on those things instead of ciphers.

But once she had healed, her face beautiful as it had ever been, the limp almost imperceptible, she surprised us with the announcement that she'd found a job and a little house in North Hollywood.

This time she didn't disappear, though I don't see her as often as I'd like to. Sometimes she invites me out to her house, which does have a lemon tree in the backyard, and I suppose our conversation is sparkling enough. On good days, I sit down at the upright piano in her parlor and accompany her as she sings. We don't sing show tunes anymore, though. Now Billie Holiday and Ella Fitzgerald are our favorites. On less good days, she nags me about what I'm going to do with myself when I finish school and reminds me that I can't keep working for Jerry forever. Annie's gotten out of the private-detective business herself. Now she works at a music shop and gives voice lessons on the side. Sometimes I wonder how she can be happy living such an ordinary life, but for now she says it's enough.

She comes over for dinner at our place sometimes. Whenever Millie's in town, she comes over, too, bringing with her stories about all the gangsters and movie stars she's met performing her act at the Flamingo. In Las Vegas, being Camille Grabo actually works in her favor. She's not a laughingstock; she's a star. She says Las Vegas is going to be bigger than Hollywood ever was. My mother, Cassie, Gabrielle, and I sit with our mouths open, hanging on every word of her stories, but Annie just shakes her head and tells Millie to be careful, for god's sake.

After everything was over, I was amazed how quickly everyone went back to treating me like a high school sophomore without a driver's license or any opinions worth inquiring after. Jerry was the one exception. I guess because he never knew me when that was all I was. He doesn't let me do anything that's actually dangerous at the office—mostly I develop film and answer the phone—but it's still interesting.

In the weeks following Conrad's arrest, it seemed as if everyone wanted to hire Jerry to find their stolen silver, lost cats, and faithless spouses, but most of them really only wanted stories to take back to their friends about the detective who helped bring Conrad Donahue down. Jerry never takes those people on as clients.

But there are others, too, people who come because they heard about Annie and Gabrielle. They never mention the case, but we always know when that's what brought them. They talk about lost children, lost brothers and sisters, army buddies and sweethearts. They're people who had given up on ever finding answers, but they all walk into Jerry's office with the same tentative hope in their eyes. More often than not, he lives up to it.

Annie never talks about Cy, who hasn't dared show his face in town since that day in the hospital, the same day the last of Conrad's worthless promises blew up in his face.

It wasn't for money that he'd done it—that came out later.

He'd done it for a part.

The movie was called *The Wrong Angel*, and there was a nice role in it, a kid who takes a bullet to save the leading lady just before the hero—played by Conrad, of course—bursts through the door and finishes off the villain. All Cy had to do to get it was tell Annie that the plan had changed and she was supposed to go to MacArthur Park that night.

Conrad promised he wouldn't hurt my sister, after he'd promised the part. He only wanted to talk to her, he said, but she would never agree to a meeting.

Maybe he was very convincing.

I know it's no good thinking about it like that. I'll never know how Conrad persuaded Cy to betray Annie, or how easily he betrayed her.

Ruth disappeared like Cy did. Jerry says she turned in her police badge the same day they arrested Conrad. Cassie, Gabrielle, and I went to her bungalow at the Stratford Arms after everything had happened and found it abandoned. The brown couch was still there, the unhemmed serge curtains. But there was no sign of Ruth.

At first, we wondered whether she'd been killed and left in the hills somewhere like Irma. Even in jail, I had no doubt that Rex and Conrad could arrange for something like that to happen. And so could Hanrahan, for that matter.

But one day I was waiting for a bus at the corner of Wilshire and Western when Ruth pulled up next to me in Wanda's big blue Lincoln and asked if I needed a ride home. I didn't, but curiosity got the better of me and I got into the car with her anyway. As she drove down Wilshire, she asked after Gabrielle and Jerry and Annie, as though they were old school friends with whom she'd fallen out of touch. I caught her up as cheerfully as I could, and with as few specific details.

Without taking her eyes off the road, Ruth said, "I'm leaving town. Hanrahan came out of it okay, but he knows it was a close shave, and the way he sees it, I'm the one holding the razor. It's not safe for me here anymore."

"What about my family?" I asked. While I didn't want Ruth to come to any harm, my priorities were elsewhere. "Are we safe?"

"Hanrahan's watching you—don't forget that for a minute. If you're thinking about making trouble for him, remember he could certainly make trouble for you."

I noticed that Ruth wasn't driving in the direction of our old house, but she wasn't driving toward the new one in East Hollywood, either. We couldn't afford to live in our old neighborhood on my mother's hairdresser salary, and we were too notorious for it anyway. Now my mother, Gabrielle, and I crammed into a two-bedroom rented cottage off Melrose. While Annie stayed with us, my mother slept on the couch.

It isn't much, but unlike our old house, it feels like a family lives there.

Ruth wove through the side streets south of Wilshire almost as if her turns were determined by the flip of a coin.

"So, are you?" Ruth asked.

"Am I what?"

"Thinking about making any trouble. Is there anything else you know that you haven't told yet?"

She still had her cop's instincts. She knew perfectly well there was, but getting me to tell it was another story. I thought about the phone call I'd placed from Wanda's office, the shots I'd seen Rex and Walter Hanrahan fire in front of Irma and Millie's apartment, the blood on the sidewalk.

"No," I lied. "There isn't anything else."

"Well, then I guess you don't have anything to worry about, do you?" Ruth said. "Anyhow, I'm glad I ran into you because I never got the chance to tell you I was sorry about Annie. For not being there to help her that night, I mean."

I nodded.

"You'll tell Annie I said that, won't you?"

I said that I would, and wondered why it mattered now.

"It's not the kind of thing you want to leave unsaid. Whether it does any good or not."

Ruth came through for Gabrielle in the end, but she'd sacrificed something of herself along the way. There must have been so many things she'd seen and turned a blind eye to, so many people she hadn't gone out of her way to help for fear that it would blow her cover. A person couldn't spend that much time around the likes of Rex and Hanrahan, covering up their small sins in the hopes of finding something bigger, without being somehow damaged by it.

I thought about the things I hadn't told Ruth and how dangerous that information could be in the wrong hands. When I put my hand to my forehead, it came away damp with sweat, and suddenly, I wanted very badly to be out of the car.

"Can you let me out here?" I asked.

"We're nowhere near your house," Ruth said.

"No," I replied. "We're not."

She gave me a strange look but pulled over to the curb. She straightened the kerchief around her head and gave me a little wave as I got out of the car. "See you around, Alice."

I waved back and watched as she drove away. It was west and it was into the sunset, but it wasn't like that.

ACKNOWLEDGMENTS

The first thank-yous go to Maddie Raffel, who discovered this story at the soda counter at Schwab's Pharmacy and got it a screen test, and to Laura Schreiber, who made it a star.

I'm also tremendously grateful to Josh Getzler and Danielle Burby for advice, encouragement, brilliant ideas, and talking me through the tough spots.

Thank you to Rachel Kitzmann, without whom this book never would have been started, and to Gwen Sharp, without whom it never would have been finished.

To my friends at the Los Angeles Public Library, thank you for all of your kindness and smarts, especially to thoughtful readers and genius fact-checkers Glen Creason, David Kelly, Christina Rice, and Jim Sherman.

Thank you to Cecil Castellucci, Kim Cooper, Kelly Loy Gilbert, Stacey Lee, Nicole Maggi, and Marc Weitz for being my encouragers, guides, inspirations, and friends.

I would never have become a writer were it not for the teachers who helped me to believe that I was one. Thank you to Christine Martuccio Mowrey, Julie MacRae, Kay Pollock, and John Warner for lighting that spark in me.

Thank you to my parents, John and Karla McCoy, for teaching me to love stories, for showing me the value of hard work, and for always encouraging me to follow my dreams. And thank you to my sister, Amy Browne, for always believing in me. If I could have picked any family in the world, I would have picked you.

Thank you to Brady Potts for a message written in code and hidden inside a necklace that I wear close to my heart. Thank you for understanding what makes me tick, and for all the times you put me before you so I could write this book.

And finally, thank you to Shelby, for keeping me company while I did.